EMBATTLED RETURN

JM MADDEN

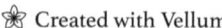 Created with Vellum

This one is for Grandma Marshall- you are a blessing.
Bad Moms, thank you for keeping me sane!

FOREWORD

For all the John and Shannon lovers. John, especially. Thank you for loving the fuck out of him. Lol!

Lost and Found Discussion Group- thank you all for being amazing and giving me incredible ideas for naming the Columbus group! I would have named you all off individually, but, honestly, FB deleted my post. Sigh...

Sandie, thank you for being my backup and the impetus in the discussion group. I appreciate you more than you know! Actually, I believe the whole group appreciates you!

Love you all!

Jen

PROLOGUE

Dear Shannon, My Brilliant Fucking Wife...

HEY, babe. I love you. I know you're going to come into the hotel room dragging ass after being in classes all day, but I wanted to let you know that everyone is okay and breathing. As soon as I finish this email I'm heading to bed myself. I promised you I would let you know what went on today.

You know, when I offered to watch the kids while you went to this damn conference, I had no idea what the hell I was agreeing to. Yes, they're my kids, but I had no idea what holy fucking terrors they'd begun to morph into! My God, woman, what the hell did we doom the world to by bringing these future despots to life?

This computer system or whatever the hell it is you're learning had better be fucking worth it!

Your parents are on their way to Arizona now. They were an incredible help and want you to call them when you get a minute.

I went to pick up the kids from preschool at four-thirty, just like you said, and I will never do it again. Chad or Zeke can go get them for me, or Duncan, since he sent you to the damn conference. The two girls that work there (is it Candice and Nene?) need to be sainted or something. As soon as I got out of the truck and started rolling into the building, women swarmed me. Have they never seen a man in a wheelchair before? One woman with brown hair in the tightest fucking ponytail I've ever seen insisted she open the door for me. Whatever. I've had people do that before so I let it roll. But then she followed me! Asking me if I needed help finding my own kids. I finally had to tell her to fuck off. You should have seen the outraged look on her face. I thought I was done with her, but the look changed into something truly terrifying.

"Oh, you naughty boy," she said, smiling this evil-ass smile. Then she tried to give me her damn business card!

Do all men get hit on this way or was I just special?

To make matters worse Flynn was in there picking up Raven. You know for a fact he's going to tell all the guys at work about the harpy that tried to pick me up.

The women that work there (they really need a raise or a bonus or something, babe, seriously) fought off the rest of the women trailing along behind me and found my kids. I put the harnesses on them, told Flynn to leave and made those kids chase Raven out of the building, pulling my ass all the way like sled dogs. I think I might have run over one woman's foot, but if she hadn't been so close it wouldn't have been an issue.

We got to the truck and mounted up, thanks to Flynn, again. Since we were both there at the same time do you think he'd mind picking our kids up while he's getting his own? Then I wouldn't have to run the pity gauntlet.

Anyway, Wyatt said he was hungry so I pulled through

Micky D's and got them each a kids meal. Yes, I KNOW you told me not to, but they were crying and shit! I forgot the bag of snacks you packed. I had to do something! They chowed down and we took off. But within about three minutes Wyatt said he didn't feel good. Approximately twenty-three seconds later he was spewing not-so-happy nuggets all over the back of my seat. As I sit here now I still get occasional whiffs of vomit, and my mouth waters. It was like that time I ran through Carmella's dog shit when she was a puppy and I got it into the tread of my wheels. It took forever to get it all out! Remember? And I gagged constantly. Same now, ugh...So, I'm glad they were dressed warm because we came home with the windows down on the truck. They loved catching the snowflakes in the back seat and eating them. When we got home I left the windows open while I took the boys inside. I didn't figure the extra moisture on the vomit could hurt... Thinking I would save time I stripped their little asses down and we all three rolled into the big shower. On the one hand I'm patting myself on the back for getting them clean and ready for bed early. On the other hand I'm worried that they have a new game. I'm sorry, babe. I really am. Don't let them shoot you with the shower hose. I told them no but then they were giggling like crazy and it was so damn cute. I hope I wasn't this bad when I was a kid. Maybe that's why my mother gave me up. *insert cynical laughter*

So, I wrangled the little monsters out of the shower but I might have swung Caden too hard. He yakked in the shower. Or maybe he was laughing too hard. I left it running with cold water in the hopes that it will magically go down the drain with no assistance... I'll check before I head to bed. Happy Meals, the meal that keeps on giving.

By the time we all three got dressed (just FYI, I have the biggest peepee ever!, according to both boys!) it's heading toward

6. Because they yakked I didn't think they'd be hungry, but we sat on the couch and watched Paw Patrol for a while. It's pretty cute, by the way. I don't mind them rotting their brains on that. Within about half an hour they were demanding food again, so we headed into the kitchen. Thank you for getting the family sized box of Honey Nut Cheerios. By the time we'd all three eaten a bowl of cereal and I had cleaned up what they'd spilled, and Carmella cleaned up the ones from the floor, we're down to about a quarter of a box. Her farts now smell awesome though!

Babe, I have to apologize. You are an absolute Wonder Woman. I thought I did a lot around the house, but I have to tell you, after wrangling these cats for just 4 hours, I'm whipped. Your parents helped out a lot and now that it's just me, I really notice the lack of you guys. And I understand why you do all the little prep work things you do. It does make it easier when you have everything ready. I still have to do a load of happy meal laundry, get them to bed AND clean the truck! Now, as I'm typing this on my iPad, they're watching dirt bike crashes on YouTube and I've actually had a chance to take a breath. They're giggling their asses off and I hope they just fall asleep here on the couch with me. I'll roll them to bed when I get the chance.

Please have fun and enjoy yourself, but know that we miss you. (My big peepee misses you too!) come home soon! Please!

NIGHT BABE.

JOHN

P.S. DON'T BITCH at me about the water bill next month.

~

Dear John,

Ok, *I might have giggled when I wrote that. Remember that old sitcom? I can hear the song in my head.*

Maybe I should cut back. I might have drunk just a smidge too much wine int he airport. The woman next to me started to sing too, though! Hey, that was fun! lol

I hate to tell you this babe, but I'm not going anywhere. Or coming anywhere. *damn* The world has ground to a halt in Toronto. The board says my plane is on the ground, but no one is getting permission to leave right now. There's this funky, icy spring snowstorm leaving a layer of ice on everything. The Torontians, Torontites? um, Delta people say this happens every once in a while and that I need to chill. Or warm up with a drink. So that's what I've been doing. Killing time and drinking. They have really good complimentary wine in the lounge.

As much as I want to see the boys, I think you're gonna be on the daddy hook for just a while longer. Yeah, the day care is an estrogen-laden man trap, and they have enough hits on their lures to keep things interesting. You wouldn't believe how many babies there are from hookups. The gossip! My gosh... I hope I'm never that interesting! I'm sure they saw you as sex on wheels, just like I do. Even your brilliant, shining, people-pleaser person-ality could be seen as a challenge. Sorry, babe. Flynn manages to wade through it so you should be able two too! To too.

Mickey D's is a definitely no-no! You'll get no sympathy from me about your truck. I told you not to take them there. Yes, they beg for it and yes, I know how damn cute they are. I gave birth to the little despots (good word by the way!) and I know how cunning they can be. When did you become so gullible you listen to 2 year-old tyrants? They must have really flattered your ego with the peepee compliment, although I do agree! lol

You know, I know we don't have sex as much since we've had the kids, but man, I'm craving you BAD! It's only been a week, which we've done before, but I think it's the fact that I CAN'T have you that makes me want you so bad. Does that make sense? Oh god, maybe I'm turning into one of those desperate women at the day-care!

But, wait, I get sex... that doesn't apply.

We really need to get some of this yellow fish wine. Yellow Fin? Yellow Tail? No, that wasn't it. It's really good and it goes down too easy. And I'm indulging because I really don't have anywhere to go. I guess I could go to a hotel but that feels like admitting I won't get home to you tonight. I'm going to stay here until I absolutely have to leave! Prosie. Promise. Not to freak you out or anything but the boys have a doctor's apartment, appointment tomorrow. 9:30. I think. Let me check my phone. Yup! 930.

Speaking of phone, I'm tryong to converse, by battery. Not sure but I think I might have left cord at the hotel. May have. Which is it? Anywhere, I'm at 18% and dying. I"l see if someone has a cord I can use. There's a guy down the row from me that has every coord imaginable, it looks like, and he keeps smiling at me. You'd probably like him. Maybe I"l ask him for power.

Shut, John. Shit. They just announced that all flights are cancelled until further notice. They have that deicer stuff but apparently it keeps refreezing and the snow keeps coming down. The wine lady up here says that it happens a good bit. I guess I get to hang out for a while longer. It's been the longest week ever, babe...

You know, I've been thinking. I think I want another baby. What do you think? I'm gonna go see what that wine is because I think the girls would love it. I know I dooo. Maybe is just hitting me so hard cuz I never get a chance tp drink.

I love you babe. Stay strong. And hard. Lol

SHANNON

PS I WON'T COMALPN about the water bill. probly.

Holy fuck. The woman was drunk and about to ask a man she didn't know for juice.

John read over the email again, wondering what the heck he was going to do about tomorrow? The Columbus team was coming to the office tomorrow, and they were hashing out some personnel issues before they signed the final contract. How the hell was he supposed to get the kids to the doctor at 930 when the meeting was at 900?

For the first time in a long time he felt inadequate, and it pissed him off. It was not Shannon's job to raise his kids. It should be both of their responsibility, and he realized how much he had taken her natural mothering for granted. Shannon had been born to have children, and she made it all look so effortless. She was such a natural mother.

But, another one? He didn't know about that. At least not right now.

As he thought about the past two years, he realized he hadn't been responsible for his own children for more than a few hours alone in that entire time. And in that two years this was the first time Shannon had really gone out alone. There had been a girls' trip with some of the other wives last year, but his in-laws had been here to help out with the twins that weekend. Just like they had been this week. Literally, they had only left today for Arizona because they knew Shannon was flying home tonight.

John started to feel a little offended. Did she not think he could take care of them? No, she wouldn't be like that. He knew for a fact she saw him as more of a man than anyone else in his life.

Caden conked out first. Very carefully, John hoisted him against his shoulder, trying to squeeze him between his upper arm and chin and still manipulate the wheels of the chair. This was the only time he ever wished for an electric chair. Normally he was okay with wheeling himself around. His lightweight racing chair was maneuverable and faster than any electric chair. Well, it wasn't faster than his tracked unit out in the garage, but that wasn't a normal vehicle anyway. But times like these were fleeting. The boys were growing like crazy, and he knew he wouldn't be able to do this much longer.

When he rolled into the room, he saw it was already made up for bed. Thanks, Mom, he thought, wishing he could give Shannon's mother one last hug. She was so amazing. He couldn't ask for any better in-laws.

Caden snuffled in his sleep as John placed him on the mattress and he went still. Should he change the boy's pull-up? Nah, he'd just let him sleep. He'd deal with it if he woke in the night.

Pulling the light blanket up to Caden's chin, John began to pull back. Then Wyatt was there, climbing into the bed with his brother. Smiling at the boys, and their connection to each other, John tucked them in, then drew back.

They had two toddler beds in the room, not that it did any good. From a young age one or the other of the boys would escape their cribs and climb into the other's. Usually it was Wyatt climbing into Caden's, because Wyatt was a little bigger and stronger and it was easier for him to get out. Every morning Shannon found them cuddled together, and sometimes she found them cuddled together with Gray Cat. It was damn cute and more than once John wished he'd had that kind of comfort when he was a kid in the orphanage. He'd had a brother but it hadn't done him any good at that time.

Now, though, he considered Aiden one of his best friends as well as his brother. The relationship had developed into more than he ever could have dreamed.

A lot had happened that he never could have imagined for himself. It had been a little more than ten years since he'd been injured, and he could still remember sitting in his chair on the balcony at Walter Reed, wondering if he was high enough up to die if he made it over the railing. He hadn't been in a good head space then, even with Duncan and Chad's friendship, and if he could have figured out a way to off himself he probably would have.

And if he had, he never would have seen his beautiful sons. Reaching out, he ran his hand over Wyatt's soft hair. It was as dark as his own, but Caden's was beginning to lighten, more like Shannon's chocolate brown.

And Shannon. If he'd offed himself he never would have felt the love of such an amazing woman. Every day with her was a blessing, and he didn't say that lightly. He wasn't wild about churches or religion for personal reasons, but he could recognize the fact that miracles happened. Shannon was his miracle and salvation, on so many levels.

Worry edged in and he wanted to talk to her. Wheeling out of the boys' bedroom he headed toward their bedroom. Parking in front of the window, he drew out his phone and pressed the appropriate buttons. ICE-Shannon. He knew he was under her own In Case Of Emergency listing.

The phone on her end rang several times before dropping to voicemail. Maybe she had her tablet out and was trying to conserve her phone battery. Swiping through the screens he found the messenger app and PM'd her. No response, and there was no little checkmark that she'd seen the message. Fuck...

He was left to stew in his own juices as he sent her a message to call him. Then, with no other options for procrastination, he rummaged beneath the kitchen sink to find supplies to clean out his vomit-reeking truck.

∾

HEY, Babe,

I'M SETTLED in my hotel and my wine buzz has worn off. Lol! Assuming they get the ice under control I'm booked on the morning flight home. I won't make it in time for the boys' appointment, so you'll still have to do that. Sorry. You know where the office is, right? Dr. Patterson. Oh, and be warned. I think they're getting the HepA shot. Sorry. :-)

I'M GOING to head to bed. I'm stressed out from worrying. I placed a wake-up call with the front desk so that I won't miss my shut-

tle. *I'm not sure where my phone cord is. I either left it at the hotel or threw it in my checked bag. Either way, I'll get a new one in the morning and charge as much as possible before I get on the plane.*

I LOVE YOU DEARLY, John. Stay strong! Lol

SHANNON

As soon as she walked into the airport, Shannon Palmer headed for a lit gift shop. Her poor phone was completely dead now and if she wanted to talk to her husband she needed to get a cord. The shop had one, though it was almost three times the amount she would have paid anywhere else. Sigh. Serves her right for not keeping track of her own cord.

There were no more hiccups as she checked in at the counter and parked in the waiting area near an outlet. It took her a while to get the damned tamper-proof package open, but she eventually got her cell phone plugged in. She let it sit for almost half a minute before she turned it on to check her messages. John had sent her several pics of the boys, and her heart clutched at seeing them. They were so damn cute, even if she did say so herself. Their hair was so dark and thick...their eyes lit with trouble.

The flight went off without a hitch. No more ice, apparently. She had a two-hour layover in Chicago, then a three-hour flight to Denver, and her testosterone laced house. As the kids neared the terrible twos, she could tell Wyatt was going to be just like his dad. Strong and direct, he was a bruiser, and she'd already had to talk to the ladies at the day care because they were concerned he was playing too roughly.

It was because their dad got down on the floor and wrestled with them like they were teenagers, but she didn't tell the daycare workers that.

Caden was her mastermind cuddler. Yes, he could scrap with Wyatt when he needed to, but Shannon knew for a fact that Caden was the one that planned the trouble they got into.

They were both too stinking cute. She needed to see their adorable little faces.

As she walked through the airport toward her next gate, her attention was caught by a tall man on arm crutches struggling along in the same direction, hugging the opposite wall. Shannon wasn't sure exactly why he drew her attention, but she slowed her steps to keep pace with him. She thought, looking at his dark hair under the ball cap, that he must be military, though he wasn't wearing a uniform, just jeans and a gray wool coat, it looked like. No uniform didn't mean anything, though. If tensions spiked in the Middle East, military stateside were ordered to wear civilian clothing when traveling.

The man was having issues, though he tried to hide it, and her heart ached for him. Why hadn't someone gotten him a wheelchair to use to get through the huge airport? O'Hare was a bitch on a good day, let alone dealing with injuries like this guy appeared to have. The man dragged a brand-new looking, soft-sided black suitcase, not one with the handy roller wheels. This was a standard Base Xchange special, no frills. If he wasn't careful, it was going to overbalance him.

As if fate had heard her thoughts, the suitcase caught on the heel of his boot, and he almost went down. The man stopped and backed up to the wall, bracing himself against it, his head down, the bill shadowing his face. Even from across the massive aisle way, Shannon could see the trembling in his body as he tried to gather his strength. She didn't understand why he didn't have help. The airport was usually pretty good about making sure people got from one place to another, but the guest had to ask for the help. And men were prone not to ask.

She sighed, thinking about John. The man could be stuck in the mud with his hair on fire and he wouldn't ask for help. It just wasn't in him. Even before the injury that stuck him in the chair she doubted he'd have ever asked for help. Every once in a while he let her open a door for him, but not much more.

Shannon was drawing closer and she didn't want to pass him up, so she paused long enough to stand in line at a kiosk and get a five-dollar bottle of water. She wasn't sure what made it so expensive, because it looked like any other Dasani bottle. Living in an airport apparently made it special.

By the time she paid for the water, the man –soldier— had started off again. An older gentleman walked alongside him for a moment, but the man snapped angrily and jerked his chin, motioning him away.

Ah, yes, the defensive hero. She couldn't even count the times she'd seen it at Lost and Found. If he was military she doubted he would want any kind of help, especially from a woman, but maybe she could spin it in the opposite direction. She watched the man for a moment longer just to make sure there would be no family or girlfriend rushing up to help him, then she made her move. Stretching out her short legs, she pulled alongside him. Before he could say anything, she whispered, "Do you mind if I walk with you? Please? I have a guy following me, I think, and I don't want to look like I'm alone."

That seemed to steal the fire from his normal response. He glanced at her, then gave a quick glance behind. The great thing about airports was that it always felt like someone was following you, so he didn't say anything, just continued to struggle along. "Whatever, lady."

Well, that was part of the battle, Shannon thought. She tried to get a look at him, but he kept his face turned away. She glanced behind them like she was still worried about her 'follower', then faced front. "Thank you so much. The guy was on my plane and he would not shut up. If my husband was here he would tell him to fuck off, but I can't be that rude."

The young man's jaw clenched, and she realized it might have sounded like a rebuke to him. Ugh.

"But then," she continued, "he's a Marine. Before we had our twins, 'fuck' used to be his go-to word for everything," she snorted. "Now it's fudge. He's slipped a few times around Christmas and Caden picked it up, but he's kind of forgotten it now. Thank goodness."

"Twins, huh?" the man asked, glancing at her for a moment.

Shannon fought not to react to the man's face, though her heart was breaking. No wonder he was hugging the wall as he made his way slowly down the concourse. If she had learned anything working at Lost and Found, it was what healing burn scars looked like. "Yup," she said, slowing as they neared a corner in the concourse. "They're twenty-two months, now. And growing like crazy. What gate are you headed to?"

"E24," he said, pausing to straighten his back for a moment and look up at the gate display. Shannon realized he was much taller than she'd thought, at least a couple inches over six feet.

Shannon dug for her ticket. "That sounds familiar. Yup, that's where I'm going, too. Denver?"

The young man glanced down at her again, giving her a little more eye contact. "Yes, Denver."

Shannon made sure not to react to his injuries. The guy was younger than she'd expected- could he even be more than nineteen or twenty?- had heartbreaking dark blue-green eyes that were so pretty, so thickly lashed, they made the rest of his face look that much more ruined. She wanted to reach out and draw his big, damaged frame into a hug but that would negate all of the headway she'd made with him. She gave him steady eye contact and a gentle smile, then glanced back up at the board. "It doesn't load for another hour. Want to grab a coffee?"

She motioned to the faux diner across the way. There was tiredness etched into his face, and she knew he was tempted. "Come on," she urged. "My feet are hurting."

She held out a foot, clad in a very pretty heeled boot, giving her a few precious inches of height. The shoes were actually quite comfortable, but he didn't need to know that.

"Fine," he sighed, and planted his crutches to wade through the traffic.

Shannon made sure to try to block some of the travelers from running into them, but there was a lot of traffic. A few people gave her dirty looks, but she didn't care. The man arrived at the hostess stand first and asked for a table.

The young woman's eyes widened at the sight of the soldier, and she fumbled with the whiteboard on her stand. Then she looked at him again. Shannon cleared her throat sharply, drawing her attention, and gave a sharp nod of her head, trying to get the woman to focus on finding them a table. Flustered, the girl grabbed two menus and turned toward the seating area.

"I've got your bag," Shannon told the man, seeing that he was going to have to maneuver to even get his crutches through the obstacle course of chairs. He gave her a reluctant, almost glaring look, before relinquishing his hold on the case. "I'm not going to steal it," she told him, grinning, trying desperately to lighten the weight around him.

Without responding he turned away from her and followed the hostess to a table in the far corner. There was a short fence around the seating area, then the flow of traffic on the other, and Shannon knew he wouldn't relax there. "Miss," she called. "Can we get that one back there?"

It was against the wall and there was a convenient power outlet right beside it. The hostess gave the man a significant look and nodded. "Yes, ma'am," she said, leading them over. She placed the menus at opposite chairs and faded away. Adjusting his chair, the young man backed into it and lowered himself down. It was obviously painful and Shannon looked away, settling into her own chair.

The man was glaring at her, and she wasn't sure why. "We can move back to the front if you want, but my phone is almost dead and I need to plug it in."

Suiting actions to words she dug her new charger from the side pocket of her laptop bag and handed him one end. "Can you plug that in?"

The man blinked and she could tell she'd kind of stolen his building thunder. He thought she'd wanted the back corner because she didn't want to be seen with him or something. She stuck out her hand. "Shannon Palmer."

He took her hand, still scowling. "Logan Vance."

"Nice to meet you, Logan," she grinned, looking at his full face calmly. Yes, his injuries were bad, but not as bad as some they'd hired at LNF. It looked like he'd been in an IED blast or something, which would also explain the damage to his legs. "So, what branch are you in? I'm guessing Army."

Logan stared at her for a long moment before he gave her a nod. "That obvious, huh?"

She shrugged lightly. "I work with veterans."

He got an odd look on his face. "Yeah, I guess I'm that now. I'm medically retired from the Army. And I'm a veteran," he sighed, a world of experience in the sound.

"How old are you, if you don't mind my asking?"

"Twenty-three. Almost done with my six-year contract."

"IED?"

He gave her a single, tight nod, watching her curiously. Shannon could see the wariness in his eyes, until he remembered to look away. The skin on the right side of his face had the rough, melted look of burns, but they didn't seem to have been incredibly deep, like some of Zeke's scars. Some of his hairline had been affected but she could see thick dark curly hair behind his ear. It had been at least a few months since he'd had a fade or a crew cut.

"Your scars don't bother me," she told him softly.

"Whatever, lady." His square jaw tightened, but he didn't look up at her, and she thought he might have been fighting emotion. She picked up her phone and scanned through her notifications as she waited for him to get a hold of himself again.

A waitress stopped at the table a few minutes later and took their drink order, and he seemed fine, even glancing up at the girl for a moment.

"So, is Denver your home?" Shannon asked him.

Logan looked up at her and made a motion with his lips.

"Not exactly. My family was from there years ago, but we moved away. I wanted to see it again before..." He stopped and cleared his throat. "Well, I just wanted to see it again. The place where I was born. And I have some other business out there."

Shannon stared at him, something niggling in her brain. She hadn't liked that phrase, *before*. Before what, exactly?

Working where she did, she'd seen more than her share of PTSD and veterans struggling to find their balance after they'd been released from the military. In her opinion, they got kicked out, often with very little aftercare or reintegration training to civilian life, and it pissed her off. Even before she'd become involved with John, veteran's issues had affected her strongly. Duncan did his best to make sure his employees got the best counseling available, but he could only offer it. He couldn't physically walk them into it, and he'd met resistance a few times. For the most part, though, everyone went, even years after they'd had their original injury.

Even John went occasionally, though he called it a bitch session rather than counseling. His counselor, a woman named Maddowitz, didn't seem to mind, as long as he showed up occasionally.

Had this young man, his eyes aching with masked pain, gotten any kind of guidance? Had his family even cared?

You won't learn anything without asking questions, she told herself firmly. "Do you have any family left out here?"

He shook his head. "I don't think so. My direct family is all back east, in Virginia, though we don't talk much. I get the impression we moved because of something that happened. There were some things we weren't supposed to talk about at the dinner table."

"Yeah, I get it," Shannon said thoughtfully. "You know,

my husband is part owner in a detective agency. If you'd like we could check and see if you have any outlaws floating around."

"No, thank you, ma'am," he said stiffly, looking out over the moving tide of passengers, anger tightening his frame. "I'll figure it out."

"I wasn't offering you charity, Logan," she said softly. "I was offering a fellow military veteran aid. That's all."

He blinked, but the anger stayed. Shannon didn't know how to break through that hard shell. She wasn't really surprised though. Wounded men were like spiny little hedgehogs. Even the slightest whiff of charity offended them and set their spikes on end.

The waitress returned with their drinks and Shannon asked Logan if he wanted food. He said no, but when the waitress returned with the loaded potato skins and the tray of artichoke dip and pita chips she had ordered, he did help himself to a few things.

"So, have you seen your stalker in the past half hour?" he asked, voice gruff.

Shannon, grinning, wiped her mouth with her napkin. She appreciated that he was playing along. "Nope. I think he's gone. Thank you very much for being my chivalrous escort."

At her words, humor lightened Logan's world-weary gaze. "No problem, ma'am. I'm here to serve."

They walked to the gate together when it was time for their flight and even though he got some stares, he took advantage of the veteran priority loading. He jerked his head at her to follow along with him since she had his bag and no one said a word. They found his seat and he settled in. Shannon took his crutches and handed them off to one of the flight attendants, who put them into a long, vertical closet just for those types of things. Her seat was in 'first class', though with these little commuter flights there was no seat difference. Once the seats were filled and the plane was in the air, she moved back to sit across the aisle from him.

"So, how long are you going to be in Colorado?"

Logan shrugged, gazing out the window. "As long as I need to be. I also have to look up a friend's family. After that I'll be done."

Shannon frowned, again not liking the wording, or the implication. John needed to meet this guy. He would know what to do.

LOGAN DIDN'T KNOW what to think about the woman sitting across from him. The stalker thing had been a ruse, obviously, but for some reason he didn't mind. Actually, he appreciated the companionship, though he wouldn't tell her that.

The woman had to be in her thirties, with thick, wavy dark hair and pretty hazel eyes. Maybe it was because she kind of reminded him of Jana, short and curvy and with a pretty smile.

His breath caught as he thought about his sister, and he forced the pain into a corner of his mind. Now wasn't the time.

Shannon said she was married with kids, so he didn't get the vibe that she was hitting on the poor, wounded soldier, like all the other women on the flight into O'Hare. God, what a mess that had been.

Why was this woman helping him out, though? What was in it for her? Did she just want the companionship? He couldn't help but feel a little appreciative for her tagging along.

Hopefully, they'd get to Denver and go their separate ways. Then, after he found Miller's family, he would be free to do what he wanted with his life.

3

John glanced at Chad, sitting beside him in the truck. "Thanks for going with me, buddy."

Grinning, Chad gave him a nod, his blue eyes bright in the Denver morning. "No problem! I love going to the doctor," he said, rolling his eyes and grinning at the boys in the back seat. They giggled, Wyatt smacking his hands on the car seat. "I've had to take Mercy before. It may not be fun. Especially if they have to get a S-H-O-T."

John nodded, appreciating that his buddy hadn't actually said the word. He'd made that mistake earlier when he'd called Chad to see if he was available and the kids had both started crying. At their age he didn't think it was possible to correlate the word with pain, but that's exactly what they seemed to do.

Chad had been free. Kind of. Duncan wanted everyone at the Columbus branch meeting, so he'd reschedule the meeting for later in the afternoon. Once John got the kids taken care of and he dropped them off, it was only an hour before Shannon's flight got in, then the meeting an hour later.

It was one of those days that just needed to work correctly in order to get everything done.

"It's usually Shannon that does this and I'm not going to lie, I'm worried about it," he said, glancing at his friend. "I don't want to see my kids hurt."

Chad nodded. "I can imagine."

John glanced at him thoughtfully. "When are you guys going to settle down long enough to have your own kids? I know Mercy is a phenomenal kid, but weren't you planning on expanding the Lowell empire?"

Chad grimaced, his head shaking back and forth, the off-white cowboy hat brushing the ceiling. "Oh, if you had any idea how much my mom and dad have been nagging us, you wouldn't even joke about it. That's all we hear. Every single call. And I know it's just how they are, but Lora is stressing about it. We both are." He gave John a long look. "We've actually been trying, a lot, and nothing is happening."

"No sex or no pregnancy?"

Chad snorted, rubbing a hand over his bristled chin. "We've finally got the sex part down, thank you very much. Pregnancy isn't happening."

"Have you been to see the doc?"

"No," Chad admitted. "Lora thinks it has to be stress, but I think it's more than that. And I think it might be me that's faulty."

John frowned at him. "Why do you think that?"

"I don't know," he murmured, rubbing his palms down his jeans-clad thighs. "Maybe it's some side effect of one of my injuries or something."

"I seriously doubt you being burned has anything to do with your swimmers hitting the finish line," John said, smirking.

Chad laughed a little. "Knowing my luck, it is, though."

"The only way you can know for sure is if you go to a spank bank and have them test a sample."

"Would my regular doctor do that?"

John shrugged. "Not sure. I think it would be more of a fertility doc's forté."

"You might be right," Chad murmured, looking out the window.

What was it with babies on the brain? First Shannon dropping the hot potato that she wanted another, and now Chad confessing they were having issues. He felt for his buddy, he really did, and now wasn't the time to bring up what Shannon wanted.

The boys did great in the doctor's office. They did indeed have to get a Hepatitis shot. Wyatt went first for the weighing and measuring, and he was a bruiser. Well above where he needed to be for his age. The doctor, a kind older woman, teased the boy and he was laughing and giggling as the nurse slipped in to give him the shot. Then his face clouded over and he squalled, immediately reaching for John. It had only been a tiny little needle, so it couldn't have hurt that bad, but John felt his own eyes grow moist in shared hurt.

"Bite, Daddy, bite."

"Oh, buddy," John said, cuddling the tender-hearted little ball-buster.

Caden was concerned that something was wrong with his brother, so he didn't even flinch when the needle slipped through his skin. He just reached for his brother when it was over. Chad handed him over to John and he cuddled both boys on his lap. "You guys okay? Mommy is going to be so proud that you did this like little men. Good job!"

The nurse handed over two tiny little bags of fruit snacks

and the tears magically evaporated. Rather than let them go, John allowed Chad to push his chair out into the waiting room. He set the boys on the floor and took care of the bill, then guided them out of the doctor's office and back to the truck. That hadn't been too bad, he supposed, but it definitely wouldn't have been as easy if Chad hadn't been there.

Shannon normally brought the boys to the doctor herself, then told him about the visit later. He knew she didn't want to bother him or interrupt his work, but this was a two-man job. Next time they had an appointment he would go with her.

They dropped the boys off at daycare, Chad volunteering to wade through the swirl of estrogen. John had told him about the previous day's fiasco, and he'd laughed like a crazy man, but when he came out of the brightly painted building his eyes were wide.

"See what I mean?" John said brusquely.

Chad blinked and looked back at the building. "Let's get out of here. Do those women not work? Or do they just hang around there, waiting for some hint of blood? It was like they'd never seen a man before."

John laughed, he couldn't help it. Chad hadn't been especially sympathetic when he'd told him about the earlier incident. "You're just so handsome...Do you want to go to the airport with me to pick up Shannon?"

"Yeah, I can go with you," Chad agreed, "since Duncan shifted that meeting."

So, they both headed out to the Denver Airport. They got there about a half hour before her plane landed, but it gave them time to find seats at the baggage carousel. John glanced at the watch on his wrist, estimating times for her to walk out and find them. The woman had only been gone a week but it felt like so much longer. Anticipation hummed through him at the thought of seeing her beautiful, shining face.

Then his phone buzzed with a text. *On my way out with a friend. Don't scare him.*

What the fuck was she talking about?

The crowd in front of them surged with offloading passengers and the alarm rang, announcing that the baggage carousel would be starting. Where the fuck was his wife?

SHANNON SMILED AT LOGAN. "It's so much easier to just let them pass. They're in a hurry to get somewhere, so just let them."

They retrieved his crutches and bag, and she slung her own bag up over her shoulder. He scowled as she maneuvered up the ramp ahead of him, but there was no way he could get himself and the bag up the ramp. He had to accept her aid. At the top she waited for him, taking the few seconds to check her messages.

He reached out to take the bag and rather than fighting, she let him take it. At least she would be nearby if he stumbled or fell. The baggage claim wasn't very far away, either.

Her heart began to pound as they navigated the flow of traffic heading to retrieve their bags. It had been a long, stressful week, and she was more than ready to see her grumpy husband. Then she looked over against the wall, and he was there, looking incredibly handsome and strong in his leather jacket and black T-shirt. His shoulders were more broad than the wheelchair, but tapered to a strong, lean waist. There was a scowl on his dark bearded face, but as soon as he saw her his expression lightened and a sexy smile curved his lips. She motioned for Logan to follow her, then jogged across the tile to kiss her husband.

Grinning, he pulled her down into his lap, his mouth settling over hers. Shannon felt the tension from the week ease out of her as she sank into John's strength, and his hungry kiss. The thrill that she felt from his touch was as energizing today as it had been when they'd first gotten together, and she cherished that.

"I missed you," she breathed against his neck, hugging him tight.

He drew back enough to look into her eyes. "I don't like business trips."

She laughed and slipped off his lap, moving to hug the man standing beside them. "Hi, Chad. You let him drag you along, huh?"

Chad laughed, his blue eyes twinkling. He tipped his cream-colored hat back on his head. "He's just so cute, Shannon, with those big dark eyes. He needed a battle buddy today taking the kids to the doctor, so I volunteered."

"Fuck you, asshole," John growled, swinging around. "You were just bored. I could have done it."

Chad laughed and made a face. "Maybe."

"John," she admonished. "Language."

Scowling, he looked at Chad. "Fudge you, asshole."

Shannon shook her head, laughing at the banter. The two of them always had each other's backs, so she shouldn't have been surprised to see them together. She glanced over her shoulder. Logan had hung back, moving his bad side to the wall, but he watched the men, seeming a little shocked. She held out a hand and tried to remember if she had told him her husband was disabled. No, she didn't think she had. She barely even thought about John being bound to a wheelchair anymore. It was just part of him.

Chad had more visible issues, but he didn't try to hide them anymore. The tendons in his damaged left hand had contracted to the point of almost making a fist, and though they'd faded, the scars on the side of his neck were still visible.

"Logan Vance, this is my husband John Palmer and our good friend Chad Lowell, two of the partners from the Lost and Found Investigative Service."

John reached out a gloved hand. "Were you hitting on my wife, Mr. Vance? Do I need to kick your ass?"

Logan blinked, obviously aggravated. "No, sir. Your wife was just being kind and helping me out with my bag. I didn't hit on her, I swear."

"John," Shannon breathed. "Stop. You're embarrassing the guy."

Logan's face had flushed, the scars going pale against the floridness of the rest of his skin. John continued to glower, even as he shook Logan's hand. "Welcome to Colorado, then."

Chad stretched out a hand as well. "Chad Lowell. You have family out here, Mr. Vance?"

Logan shook his head. "Not anymore, I don't think. There's a chance, I suppose. My father's family was from here, but he said all the family was gone by the time he moved east. I just want to see our old house and the neighborhood where we lived."

Shannon looked at John, widening her eyes, trying to convey that there was more to the story. Her brilliant husband seemed to understand. "Do you know where it is? We can do a quick search at the office."

Logan's face shifted into a frown. "No, thank you. I've taken up enough of your time."

John shrugged, negligently. "You haven't taken up any of

my time. Why don't you come with us to the office? A few keystrokes and I should be able to tell you all you need to know about your family. I'll be helping a fellow veteran out."

Logan looked at his feet, then around the milling people of the airport. Shannon had a feeling he didn't want to try to make his way through the mass alone. He would do it if he had to, but she could see the struggle in his face.

"Have you rented a car yet?" she asked him.

He shook his head. "I planned on seeing what kind of shuttles were running."

"Then consider us your shuttle, for now," she laughed. "You can get a taxi when you leave the office, if you want."

His eyes slid over John's chair before, with a sigh, he nodded. "Okay. Let me grab my other bag."

They walked over and retrieved their bags, the last ones on the belt. Chad took them both, motioning for Shannon and Logan to follow John through the throng. As usual, her husband plowed through people like he was in a race, glaring at those that took too long to move. A wheeled baggage cart drifted over, rubbing the wheels of his chair. The woman pushing the cart was talking to her companion and didn't even see it happen.

"Hey, Oblivious," John snapped. "Watch what the fuck you're doing."

The woman's attention jerked around, and she corrected her cart. "I am so sorry," she gasped, her face going pale.

Shannon followed along in her husband's wake, keeping pace with Logan on his crutches. She leaned over conspiratorially. "John suffers from a particular form of wheelchair rage. He has no problem giving people a piece of his mind. Usually with the F-word involved."

Logan smirked, the first humorous response she'd seen from him. "I think we can all appreciate the F word."

She snorted. "Yeah, I know. Believe me, I've heard the arguments."

The blue and white handicapped placard hung from the rearview mirror and she gave John an appreciative look. He didn't dig it out of the glovebox very often. Normally he parked out in no man's land in parking lots, leaving himself *just* enough room for the driver's side lift to work. A couple of times the practice had backfired when someone had parked beside him, not leaving him enough room to maneuver or get in the vehicle.

As she watched Logan struggle on his crutches, she was very glad that John had forsaken his vanity for the day and parked closer to the elevators.

Logan watched as John rolled onto the platform and snapped himself in, then locked his wheels. "I've never seen anything like that," he murmured.

She smiled. "It is pretty cool. You ought to see the all-terrain chair he got for Christmas."

Logan's eyes widened a little, and he looked like he was going to ask her more, but she waved him to the truck. "Chad will put your bags in the back and you'll have to work it out with Chad who rides shotgun."

"Logan can have it," Chad said, slamming the tailgate. "I'll ride in back with Shannon."

"I don't need the front," Logan protested, scowling.

"You'll appreciate the room to stretch your legs. Go ahead," Chad said, swinging up into the back.

With no other option, Logan climbed into the front passenger side seat, settling his crutches beside him. He wrapped the seatbelt around himself and snapped in, and John reversed out of the space, hands working the controls on the wheel perfectly. They were quiet until they were in the bright Colorado sunshine and heading toward the Denver skyscrapers in the distance.

"So, where are you from, Logan?" John asked him.

"Virginia, now. My dad moved away from Denver about twenty years ago."

"He was a child when he left," Shannon said, leaning forward to rest her hand on John's hard shoulder. "So I was giving him some highlights on the flight out."

John flashed the man a grin. "If you can imagine doing it, it's probably here."

Logan smiled slightly. "That's what Shannon said. I don't know how much of anything I'll be doing."

John shrugged. "Well, we'll figure out some family details and you can decide. What branch of the service were you in?"

"Army," Logan said, sliding a look sideways. "Almost six years."

John scowled, and sighed heavily. "Well, Army's better than nothing, I suppose."

Then he winked, and Logan barked out a laugh. Shannon had heard it before. John had an ability to find veterans anywhere and if they weren't Marines, they tended to be teased unmercifully. They usually took it with good grace, though.

"Army wasn't my first choice either. I had planned to go to college first." Logan admitted, "but my dad had been in the Army and he... well..."

"You had something to prove. Where were you stationed?"

Logan stared at him for a moment, as if John had said something that maybe needed to be corrected, but he let it go. "Fort Benning. Intelligence services."

John nodded once. "Been there many times. Beautiful area."

"It is. I won't miss the heat, though."

"I don't know," Chad murmured. "You should hang out in Texas for a minute."

Logan laughed a little, shaking his head. "Nope. I've been there. Felt like I ate a plateful of dust by the time I got where I was going. And I've never had a worse sunburn..."

Chad laughed. "Yeah, she'll get you. Although, I think Afghanistan was worse in a way. Or maybe it just seemed that way at the time."

"Afghanistan was worse than any place else on earth," Logan said slowly, turning to look out the window.

The three of them shared a glance and Shannon was a little surprised Logan had been there. He was younger, so she would have expected him to be more familiar with Iraq. But, what did she know? If he'd been in Intelligence it was hard to tell what he'd done or where he'd been. The look on his face, though, and the tone of his voice told her there was more to the story, but the mood in the truck had changed. She needed to lighten it up.

"So tell me about my boys. How did they do?" John gave her a serious look in the rearview mirror and her heart dropped. "What?"

"I never knew what you had to deal with when you took them in on your own. I'll go with you next time, and every time you think you need me."

Shannon blinked, taken aback. Then tears filled her eyes. "Thank you, John. I love you."

"I love you too, babe. They did get a shot, and that about broke me. Wyatt cried, little badass that he is. Caden seemed more concerned that Wyatt was crying than why and he never even flinched."

Yes, those were her boys. And her amazing husband had stepped up and been there for them. Though she hadn't planned the trip or the emergency spring snowstorm, maybe it had been good for him to see what she dealt with every day.

"Everything else was good, though?" she persisted.

"Yes, Mama, everything is good. Wyatt is off the charts for his age and Caden is building. She didn't see anything to be concerned about."

"Good," she sighed. That really eased her mind. She loved her boys and it was hard not being there for them when they needed her.

They moved on to other subjects as they drove to the office, but Shannon didn't mind. As she took in the Denver skyline and the silhouette of the mountains to the west, she was just happy to be home. There was still snow on the ground right now, but the days were getting longer. Eventually flowers would start adding color to the rocky landscape.

The men fell into military chatter about bases and forts they'd each been to, and she watched Logan surreptitiously. His mood and the way he moved had been very...insulated, dark when she'd first seen him. Or maybe it was his aura that had been dark. She couldn't explain it. Now though, he seemed a little... lighter? Maybe? At the airport she'd gotten the impression that he wanted nothing to do with the people around him, like they couldn't understand what he was going through so he wouldn't bother trying to connect with them. But maybe he could connect with John and Chad, and the others at LNF.

That snow storm in Toronto made a little more sense now. She was supposed to be at O'Hare today to connect with Logan. Leaning back against the seat, she smiled, her gaze, as always, drawn back to her husband.

4

J ohn glanced in the rearview mirror again, Shannon's knowing smile a damn siren song to him. She looked stunning, as always, and he couldn't wait to get her alone. If he could just lay in bed with her for a few minutes...

That was their precious time, in the depths of the night after the kids had finally crashed or in the haze of morning before they got up to wreak havoc. The two of them didn't even need to make love. Just laying there in the bed looking into her eyes filled his heart with more emotion than he'd ever felt with any other human being. It was more than he ever wanted to admit. When his mother left him as a child, he had had to learn the hard way to rely only on himself, no one else. Shannon was the only person that had broken through that barrier. And he was so glad he had finally let her.

It was her choice to go to work today, because that was the kind of person she was. She knew the big Columbus planning meeting had been scheduled for today and had wanted to sit in and take notes, though the entire thing would be recorded for dictation later. She liked to be in the middle of the planning and more often than not, Duncan pulled her in anyway, just for her insight in logistics. As the primary office manager, Shannon managed resources for almost twenty-five men and women, which included their health insurance, payroll, and five million other things he was sure he had no idea of. She found the men apartments, chased down problems and was basically indispensable.

Luckily, they'd recently hired Shannon an assistant, Marigold Lee. Though she'd settled in well, the girl had only been there a few weeks. John was sure that Shannon wanted to check on her progress and make sure everything had gone smoothly in her absence.

John sighed as he thought about Marigold. What a mess that had been. Every time he rolled into the office, she threw him the death stare.

When the name had come up in one of the partner morning meetings several weeks ago, John hadn't been able to keep in an incredulous laugh. Who the fuck would name their kid that? It still made him shake his head. When he'd said as much to Shannon, she'd made an abrupt motion and snapped his name. It was only then that he'd realized that the unfortunately named young woman was standing out in the hallway, within earshot of Duncan's office. Even Chad had given him a withering look.

When Shannon had gone to bring her into the office, she'd returned alone.

"Damn it, John, I liked that girl," Shannon had cried. "You need to just shut your mouth and keep your opinion to yourself, especially at the office. Grow the fuck up!"

John had reeled back, not used to being on the receiving end of Shannon's anger. Instinctively, his own anger had risen, but he'd tamped down the impulse to snap back.

Shannon didn't get angry often and this time, he *had* been in the wrong. "You're right," he admitted. "I shouldn't have done that. I'll go find her."

By the time he'd gotten to the first floor and out the door into the parking lot, he'd seen Marigold Lee climbing into an older model dark blue Volkswagen Beetle. At least, he thought it was her, since she was the only one in the lot. Knowing there was no way he could chase her down and maneuver the chair through all the cars, he'd gone to the lot exit and parked himself there.

The lot had been repaved last year and repainted, angling the parking slots and creating a delineated flow. Now there was only one exit. If Marigold Lee wanted to leave, she had to go through him.

For a minute, he didn't think the woman was going to stop, and he was going to be a VW hood ornament, but she hit the brakes, making the tires bark. John caught a glimpse of her face and his gut twinged. He'd expected tears, and it looked like she had cried a bit, but anger was there now. She slammed the car into park and jumped out of the driver's seat, stomping around to him.

"Let me tell you what, asshole. My dad named me Marigold. He was a Marine just like you, and was killed at the beginning of the war in Afghanistan. I was told this group helped veterans and I wanted to be a part of it, but I can see you're just a bitter asshole. I never should have come here."

Fuck.

"I'm sorry," he growled, seeing the hurt on her young, mobile face. "I am an asshole, you've got that part correct, but my wife really likes you so I'm asking you to wait. You have the job if you want it."

She stared at him, arms crossed over her chest, and John

realized how very young she was, probably no more than twenty-two or twenty-three. She must have been really little when her dad had been killed. Dark, straight hair hung past her shoulders, and she wore a nice business outfit with smart, trendy black squarish glasses. It was obvious she'd dressed to come in today.

"I shouldn't have said that," he admitted. "It just took me by surprise and I opened my mouth before my brain could stop it. Come on back in."

She shook her head. "Are you this much of an asshole to everyone that comes in?"

In spite of himself he flashed her a grin. "I kind of am, actually."

The woman snorted and looked down at her feet, like she was trying to hide her own humor. Dark hair blew around her face, obscuring her expression, and for a moment John thought she looked a little familiar to him, but the impression faded away.

"Come on," he wheedled, "Shannon really liked you. She's only been interviewing assistants for five hundred years, it seems like, because she's protective of the group. If she brought you to the partner meeting you're pretty much a shoe-in for the job. Our approval is merely a formality. She really needs the help."

Marigold looked out over the cold parking lot, thinking. John didn't blame her for taking her time. Their group was a lot to take on.

In the end, though, Marigold Lee did return, and she'd morphed into one of the best workers John had ever seen. Shannon had been tentative about overloading her, but Marigold had taken everything in stride. Having Marigold on premises was the only reason Shannon had felt comfortable enough to leave for the week-long conference.

Marigold still gave John the cold shoulder, which was fine. He'd been a dick to her, so he would take her anger as long as it made Shannon's job easier. And he hadn't noticed her struggling with anything since Shannon had been gone.

They pulled into the Anderson building lot, where the LNF offices were located. Parking in his designated spot, he glanced at the man beside him. "Let's go see what we can figure out about your family. Just leave your luggage here for now. No one will mess with it."

John activated the lift and rolled off the pad, locking the truck as soon as the lift re-secured and the rest of them were out. Then he followed Shannon into the building and elevator, rolling to the back to give Logan room to maneuver his crutches. Chad stepped into the space left, and they were off.

"No problems while I was gone? Marigold did okay?" Shannon whispered to him, resting her hand on his shoulder.

He shook his head. "Fine, I believe. I think she might have asked Duncan about a couple of things but that was all."

When the doors opened, they were met with chaos. There were several men milling in the reception area. Logan got off the elevator and immediately stepped to the side to allow the rest of them to exit, looking a little spooked. He tugged his ball cap low over his eyes.

"Give me just a minute," John murmured to him.

John went to Parker Quinn, the current center of attention. He'd been in Columbus for the past year and it was obvious the men had missed him. Zeke had a thick arm over the man's shoulders, like he'd just drawn him in to a big hug. And Flynn was trying to show Parker something on his phone, his service dog Maya sitting patiently at his feet.

There was a grunt John didn't recognize standing to Parker's right. Size wise, he was on par with Zeke, and the guy didn't mind looking intimidating, wearing a sweatshirt with the arms ripped off and a black cap shading his eyes. John had a feeling the guy didn't miss much from beneath that hat.

Brian Calvert was sitting in one of the reception chairs, laptop open and propped on his legs as he searched for who knew what. Since he'd gotten his degree in forensic accounting he'd been working over here more than the Vail office where he was based. Duncan had had him working on a couple of things, and he knew Parker had as well. From a boss point of view, John felt like the change had been good for Brian.

John liked Parker. He was a no-nonsense kind of guy, and he would run his ship well. For a solid year he'd been working damn near alone, taking cases and building a customer base to prove to LNF there was a market for their services. The three partners had talked and agreed that a Columbus branch was a good endeavor and that if Parker made it a success he would have the option to buy it outright at a later date. Parker didn't know that yet, though. That was what this meeting was for.

"Have a good trip out?" he asked, shaking the man's hand.

Parker nodded. "I miss Denver, but I don't miss the damn snow. Makes my bones ache."

John lifted a brow. "I don't know. I hear you have someone to cuddle with now."

Parker barked out a laugh, the lines of his face deepening. "I do. Andromeda is an incredible woman. She came with me but she's working at the hotel right now. You'll meet her at dinner."

"Excellent," John murmured.

Zeke had shifted away to lean down and give Shannon a hug to welcome her back. John wasn't even sure what the big man was doing here. He'd been working the Frog Dog with Ember, taking less and less cases with the group. Zeke had always been a bit of a nib-shit, though. Maybe he was just here to be social. John turned to Flynn. "You get that kid you were looking for?"

Flynn nodded, running a hand over the bristles on his recently shaved chin. "I did, but he wasn't as much help as I'd hoped he'd be. I think I have to go digging again."

John frowned. "Okay, we'll have to talk about it after the meeting."

Flynn nodded once and motioned to his dog, leaving as silently as he'd surely arrived.

Duncan was at the back of the group, talking to Marigold. The young woman gave John a dark look, then continued her conversation. She had an iPad in her hand and was taking notes as she talked to the boss, stylus flashing across the screen. Duncan had his arms crossed and his feet planted, intimidating in a way that he probably didn't even realize.

Marigold didn't seem to have any reservations about talking to him though. Shannon crossed the room and gave the young woman a hug, then reached out and pulled Duncan into a hug as well. A couple of years ago boss man probably wouldn't have taken it, but he did now. Being with Alex and having their new baby had changed him for the better.

John glanced at Logan and held out a hand for the man to join him. "Let's go get something to drink, kid."

∽

LOGAN HAD NEVER SEEN SUCH an interesting, dangerous, eclectic group of people. At least, not since he'd left the burn unit.

There were about seven guys standing in the reception area off the elevator and every single one of them had injuries just as bad, if not worse, than his own, but they radiated power and self-confidence. The biggest guy in the room had a battered ball cap on, just like Logan, but Logan could still see the scars and misalignment of his face. What the hell had happened to him? The guy seemed to be moving better than Logan did, but, damn...

The guy in the muscle shirt also had a ball-cap on, but Logan couldn't see any scars beneath the bill. Something about him, maybe the wide, scrolling tattoos on both muscular upper arms, hinted at Marine. Oh, yeah, there was the Eagle, Globe and Anchor hidden in all the black. He seemed to be flanking a blond haired, muscular type. Was that his boss or something? Blond guy appeared to be fairly good-looking at first, but Logan could see the faint tracery of surgery scars around his right eye, giving him an uneven look. And he stood braced, like he was in pain.

The guy with the dog had seemed like a spook. He'd dealt with enough SEALs over the years to recognize them.

There was another guy sitting in one of the chairs to his left and the gleam of metal peeked from beneath his pant legs. Both of them. He clattered on a laptop like he was looking for state secrets or something.

The men appeared to be a group, but with individual little factions. Different shifts, maybe?

A flash of green caught his eye. A woman wearing a thick, hunter green sweater stood on the other side of the crowd, deep in conversation with Shannon. She was leaning over the shorter woman, nodding her dark head at something Shannon was saying, the tail of a braid hanging over her shoulder. As he watched, they tipped back their heads and laughed. For a moment, the young woman's gaze met his, and stuck. Logan waited for the moment when her face would crinkle up in disgust, but it didn't happen, and he was left wondering if she had actually seen him, or just glanced in his direction. Blinking, he forced himself to turn away, but the afterimage stayed on his mind. The woman had been beautiful, with wide-set greenish eyes set in a pale oval face. She seemed tall and strong, and even a little protective as she stood next to the much smaller Shannon.

There were other people milling about the room, and they obscured his view. It didn't matter because Palmer called him down a hallway. He couldn't help but glance back, looking for a final glimpse of the woman.

"Sorry about the crowd out there," John said, waiting while Logan crutched his way through the doorway to a chair. "We have a big meeting planned for today and it gives the guys a chance to catch up with their buddies."

Logan blinked, frowning, rethinking his deductions. "Did you all serve together?"

Palmer shut the door, blocking out the noise, and moved to a small fridge in the corner. "Nope. The only two that served together are Duncan and Chad, the guy that rode with us earlier. The three of us created Lost and Found after we got out of Walter Reed and had no fucking idea what to do with ourselves. Actually, Duncan created it, we just helped with backing. Water? Coke?"

Huh.. that was interesting. "I'll take a water. Everyone I saw was..."

"Wounded. Disabled. Yeah. We like to say combat modified, too." John said, handing him the bottle. "We prefer to hire other vets that can't find a spot anywhere else. Businesses say they like to have people with military experience, but they don't always realize how much a wounded vet has to deal with every day. We do. And we position them in jobs they'll excel at."

"That's...really something."

Logan's mind was roiling with all the possibilities. What a great idea, building a company to suit your own, and those of your workers', abilities.

Palmer rolled the wheelchair around behind a desk littered with electronic equipment and stacked papers. "So, let's get some background information on your family and we'll see what we can figure out."

He pulled out a tablet and swiped through a few screens. "So, tell me what you do know about the family left behind."

Logan related the details he was sure about first, but there weren't very many. His family name had been Vance, he believed, but there was also a family name of Walter in their history as well. He'd had a grandfather by that name, or maybe a great-grandfather. Logan knew that his father was one of four boys, but he thought the others had died, one at childbirth and the others later.

He knew his grandmother, his father's mother, had owned some kind of restaurant or something. Or maybe she'd just worked there. And his grandfather had been a mechanic. It was hard to remember all the details because his father very rarely spoke about his Colorado roots.

"Okay, hold on a minute."

John started pounding on the keyboard of his desktop, looking back and forth between the two screens. Logan appreciated the break in activity. His legs were aching like a mother fucker and he didn't look forward to getting up again. Tipping the bottle of water back, he drank it down.

It was just a few minutes later when John looked up,

scowling. "I thought this would be an easy search, but I'm not finding anything right off. Where are you staying?"

Logan rubbed his forehead. "I haven't really decided yet. I'll find a hotel or something."

John handed over a business card. "I'm going to have to dig, Logan. Text me when you settle. Do you have a ride?"

"No. I can grab a taxi or something."

John snorted. "Not out here you can't. This is the industrial park."

He dialed a number on the phone beside him. "Can you come in here a minute?"

Within seconds the woman in the green sweater Logan had seen earlier was standing in the doorway, pushing squarish-framed glasses up on the bridge of her narrow nose. Damn, she was something to look at. Her skin, something he was very aware of now, was flawless, milky perfection.

"Marigold, do you think you could drive Mr. Vance to wherever he needs to go?"

The young woman made a face at him. "I'm not an Uber." She glanced at Logan, and he felt the direct look hit him hard. She had very green eyes under those lenses, almost the same deep green of her sweater. "Sorry. No offense."

"None taken," he murmured, quickly turning his scarred face away.

Logan hated feeling defensive with women, but when you saw even the nurses wince at your appearance, you learned to look away from the reaction to salvage your pride. Something had made him stare at the young woman, though, and he glanced at her again. She was significantly younger than most of the other people he'd seen, but she didn't seem out of place here.

"I know this isn't in your exact job description," John said patiently, "but I would appreciate it."

She scowled, still looking unconvinced.

"I can take a taxi," Logan said quickly.

John acted as if he hadn't heard Logan, giving the woman a hard look. Then he seemed to sense some weakening in her stance, because he gave her a wink. "Bags are in the bed of my truck."

"Fine," she groused. "I'll be back in an hour. Come on... you. What's your name?"

"Logan."

"Come on, Logan."

She spun and left the office. With a final wave, Logan turned and followed her swinging hips, feeling like his life was not his own anymore.

"Let me grab my jacket and bag," she said, glancing back at him. She was gone for less than a minute, then they waded back through the still-milling group in the reception area to the elevator. She pulled on her jacket as she waited for the doors to open. Once on, she turned to him and stuck out a hand, smiling brilliantly, her demeanor completely open. "I'm Marigold Lee. Sorry about the tension in the office, there. Mr. Palmer made an ass of himself when he hired me on and I'm not letting him forget it. I'm going to drag it out as long as I can."

Logan barked out a laugh, more than a little taken off guard, but charmed. "No problem. I'm sorry you have to be my driver."

She turned and faced the front. "Oh, I'm not. They're having this big meeting in a little bit and it'll be boring in the office anyway. I was just about to break for lunch. Now that Shannon is back, she'll want to be in on the meeting. How long are you in Denver?"

Logan blinked, trying to follow her changing subjects. "Um, not sure. I guess the group is going to help me find any stray family I might have out here. Or at least figure out some history."

She nodded, glancing at him. "I will say, Gunny Palmer is thorough. If there's anyone out there, he'll find them for you."

Logan sighed, appreciating her easy manner. "I don't think there's anyone out here, honestly. My dad said most of them were dead, basically, or very old. I kind of just want to look at where I was born and stuff. Get a feeling for my roots."

She turned to look at him, and he realized suddenly that his wounded side was to her, on full display. His face started to heat, because he could feel her looking at him. "I can understand that," she murmured. "It's important to know your history."

The doors opened, then, saving him from a response. They headed out into the parking lot, and she strode toward Palmer's red truck. Once there she leaned over the side rail and drew out Logan's bags. Adjusting his crutches, Logan took one from her, and motioned with his head. "Which car is yours?"

Without fighting over the bag, Marigold led him to a deep navy-blue Volkswagen Beetle. Logan chuckled, eyeing the back seat. Could he even get his bags in there?

It took some finagling and both of them working from opposite sides, but they got the bags in. Logan settled gratefully into the passenger seat, his legs throbbing. It had been a long time since he'd been on his feet this much, and he was looking forward to getting to a hotel and just chilling out. Assuming he could even get himself out of the low-slung car.

Marigold settled in beside him, her shoulder brushing his own in the confines of the car, sending a shiver through him. When had he last even responded to a female like that? It didn't bear thought. He shifted his shoulders toward the door to give her more room. The sweet and tangy scent of oranges wrapped around him, and he wondered if she had an air-freshener in the car.

"Do you want cheap, moderate or expensive?" she asked, dark, sleek brows lifted as she turned the ignition. The diesel rumbled to life.

He snorted. "How about somewhere in between?"

"You got it!"

They headed out of the parking lot and down the street, the Beetle seeming to find every pothole to rattle his bones. Logan felt like he needed to fill the silence, which was odd. He wasn't normally the talkative one. "How long have you worked with the group?"

Marigold swerved smoothly around a slow turning semi. "Mm, about a month, now. I've enrolled at UC Denver for the fall quarter but it doesn't start for a few months, so I'm getting as many hours in at LNF as I can. And Shannon has needed help for a while. Holy crap, that woman is a machine."

"It sounds like it," he murmured. "They have twins, too, right?"

Marigold nodded. "Yeah, I think they're about two. I overheard Gunny freaking out when Shannon's flight got cancelled."

Logan watched the scenery roll by. They were getting into a more commercial area now, and he spotted several hotel signs. "Any of these will be fine," he told her.

Marigold put on her blinker and swung into the parking lot of a Hampton Inn. "These are usually decent. Their breakfasts can be a little weird with the powdered scrambled eggs, but it can't be any worse than what you ate in the military probably. Unless you were Air Force. They seem to get the good shit."

She glanced at him expectantly and he shook his head. "Nope. Good old Army. We had the best dog food the government could buy."

Marigold gave a throaty laugh as she pulled up into the check in area. Logan swung his door open and maneuvered his crutches out onto the pavement, then strained to get himself out of the car. His face heated as he struggled to get his legs and crutches going in the same direction. "Back in a minute."

The attendant gave him a considering look as he walked in, obviously trying to look at Logan's scars without appearing to. "Will you be joining us this afternoon?"

"Yes. Probably for several days, actually."

He had no idea how long it would take Palmer to dig into his background, but he needed to be close by, probably.

Logan handed over his credit card and took the room cards the guy handed him. When he turned to retrieve his bags, Marigold was just dragging them through the door. "I would have gotten them," he said defensively.

She grinned at him. "I know."

She let him take the handle of the roller bag, their hands brushing. Logan looked at her. The woman hadn't seemed curious or affected by his injuries, which was a refreshing change.

Reaching into her jacket pocket she retrieved her cell phone. "What's your number?"

Logan rattled off the digits, and he felt the phone buzz in his pocket with a text message. "If you need anything, let me know. I don't live too far away from here."

"I will, Marigold. Thank you very much for the ride."

She grinned at him. "Any time!" she promised, before turning to head out the door.

Logan watched her ass for a bare moment before turning to head toward the elevator and his room. Dragging the bags through the doors of the elevator, he turned around. His own face stared back at him from the reflection of the elevator wall, flushed and not nearly as handsome as he used to be. One of the hardest things to get used to when he'd been recovering had been the changes in his own appearance. The missing hair at the side of his head he could deal with. If he kept his hair long enough it wasn't really noticeable anyway. His face, though... It looked like he'd stood too close to a blast furnace, or something, the skin sagging and pulling on the lower edge of his right eye.

He missed just standing up without pain and walking across a room. Little things like that didn't even occur to you during day to day activities. Not until you couldn't do them any longer. Since he'd been injured he'd felt like he'd aged about forty years, and he didn't like it. The doctors said he might get a little better, but to not get his hopes up. More than likely he had a lifetime of pain pills ahead of him.

The elevator doors opened and he pushed through. Glancing at the placard on the wall he headed for his room. Of course it was all the way at the end.

Shoving through the final door, he threw his bags against the wall, locked the door and turned toward the bed. He needed to get off his legs for a while. As soon as his head hit the pillow, he was asleep.

MARIGOLD DIDN'T EVEN REMEMBER GETTING to the car. Her nerves were humming in a way that she'd never felt before. As soon as she'd looked up and seen the scarred man standing in the elevator doorway, and his incredible blue-green eyes, something had clicked inside her, some intangible recognition software suddenly activating.

Logan Vance had to be a bit over six feet tall. With the other LNF men in the reception area, he'd fit right in with the group, with broad shoulders and a strong upper body. Whatever his injury was, it impeded the locomotion in his lower half, but it appeared as if his top half had more than learned to compensate. Though he could have appeared weak with his arms in braces, he really didn't.

Logan seemed to realize that he fit in as well. There was a bit of a shell-shocked look on his face, like he hadn't expected to see so many vets in one place like this.

When Gunny Palmer had called her into his office, she'd gone quickly, anticipation humming in her blood. The new guy was standing to the side of the door and as she stood beside him, she realized that they were almost the same height. She wanted to step closer and look at him without his flinching away, study his brilliant eyes and the scars that meandered down the right side of his face, and the thick, dark curls that peeked from beneath his cap, but she didn't think that would happen. Even as she entered the room, he turned more fully away. She wanted to scream at him that she wouldn't reject him, but of course, that would be extremely counter-productive.

She put on the offended act for Palmer, but internally she was dancing up and down in excitement. There was some reason she was supposed to get to know Logan Vance, and she would do her best to do it.

Marigold had wanted to seem intriguing and sophisticated, but she was sure she didn't attain either. It just wasn't her. She thought she attained comfortable and girl-next-door, which would have to be good enough.

She left him at his door reluctantly. If she could have come up with some bullshit excuse to stay with him she would have, but she had seen the tiredness in his face. Logan needed to relax, so she'd left him alone.

5

"Are you ready?"

John looked up from whatever he was looking at on the tablet, snatching off the wire-framed reading glasses. Shannon didn't understand why he was so vain. As people got older, they needed to use glasses. It was no big deal.

Crossing the office and circling the desk, she retrieved the glasses he'd hidden in the drawer and slid them onto his face, then sat on the edge of the desk in front of him. "I think these make you look handsome."

Leaning in, she pressed a kiss to his frowning mouth.

"They make me look old," he grumbled.

"Sophisticated," she contradicted, reaching her tongue out to touch his lips.

John drew in a breath. "Senile."

She giggled. "Doddering."

"Hey," he protested. "You're supposed to be building me up, not agreeing."

"Sorry, baby," she laughed.

John grinned and pulled her across his lap, fitting her

ass into his groin. "I know this isn't the time or the place, but we really need to make time for us tonight."

"I completely agree," she sighed. "It was only a week but it felt so much longer. I can't wait to see my boys."

"They'll be all over you."

She rested her head on his shoulder. "Let's get this meeting out of the way and see if we can slip out early. Marigold did an excellent job keeping up. I don't have nearly the work I expected to."

And that was an understatement. The woman was a dream. She was very mature for her age but there was an inherent sadness to her personality. Several times over the past month Shannon had seen her watching the men a little oddly. When she'd asked her about it, Marigold had explained about her father. He would have been a little younger than Duncan. She watched the men because she could almost imagine one of them could be her father. Shannon had teared up, then, and wrapped the girl in her arms.

"I'm so sorry you lost your dad," she whispered.

Marigold had taken the hug, then pushed away, seeming a little embarrassed. Shannon wasn't quite old enough to be her mother but in that moment she'd felt like the younger woman had needed a hug from a parent. Shannon had been on the verge of asking about her mother when Marigold had sent the conversation into another direction.

Shannon had a feeling that she would be around for a long time, though, so they would have another chance to talk.

When they rolled into the conference room, it was almost packed. Duncan was seated in the middle of the far long side, with Parker Quinn to his right. There were stacks of paperwork in front of him. Lost and Found's attorney,

Calanthe Kemp, sat on Duncan's other side, looking beautifully reserved throughout the chaos, pointing out things with her Mont Blanc pen. Shannon liked Calanthe a lot, but she seemed a little lost when it came to interpersonal communications. The rest of the LNF crew sat along the length of the table, ready to plan the expansion. The guy that Parker had brought with him sat on the other side of him, rocked back in the chair, face under shadow. If she was asked what the guy looked like, she was sure she wouldn't be able to give an answer. His name was Brady? Brody? She would need to pin that down before he left.

Duncan already had a lot of the cogs in place for the business set up. Shannon knew he'd been planning this expansion almost as soon as he'd spoken to Parker last year, he'd had that much faith in him. There was plenty of work in Columbus. Statistically they were the larger city. Yes, the area had other investigative companies, but with Parker's connections to the prosecutor's office, he had a bit of an in with a lot of work. And as of right now, he was swamped. Even this meeting today was a quick trip. They would have dinner with the group tonight, then take the red eye home.

Shannon had worked on the details of the contract with Duncan and Calanthe, and Parker had been sent an early copy. It was potentially profitable for both sides, and she didn't think there would be any sticking points. Parker was being given a very large amount of company money to procure office space, a couple of vehicles and hire several investigators. Parker and Andromeda already had a lead on the office space, as well as two investigators they wanted to hire. They also had an office manager in mind.

Then he got to the section about buying LNF out. His silver eyes narrowed and he looked at Duncan. "Are you serious about this?"

The older man snorted. "Well, since it's in the contract..."

Parker's mouth worked, like he was trying to control his emotions. "Thank you, First Sergeant."

LNF Columbus would hire veterans, just like the Denver office, and Duncan would like some input into the people hired. If any of the guards at the Denver or Vail office wanted to transfer they would be given the option, on a short-term basis. If they wanted to stay long-term it would be up to both branches to agree.

Shannon knew that everything in the contract had been worked out ahead of time and the meeting itself was just a formality, but it was important to observe the protocols. Parker would need a lot of support when he did eventually start the company, which should be within the next few weeks. Parker already had a couple of clients lined up for when they did get to open their doors.

"I took the incentive and had some stationery printed up for you," John said suddenly, his dark eyes twinkling.

Oh, John...

Chad moved to the corner of the room and collected a white, cardboard box. He set the box in front of Palmer, then returned to his chair.

"We were thinking up names for the Columbus division of LNF. You know, a way we can differentiate between the groups. Officially you'll be called Lost and Found- Columbus, which is just incredibly ingenious," he rolled his dark eyes, "but un-officially, we thought we needed something a little more... interesting."

Duncan rocked back in his chair, smiling. Shannon knew the guys wouldn't have done anything without his knowing about it.

"We went through a bunch of options," John continued. "There was Arch City Investigations. Union Blue Security.

Did you know Columbus was known for blue jackets because they manufactured so many Union jackets during the war?"

John looked at him expectantly, and Parker shook his head, a bemused smile tilting his mouth. "I had no idea."

"But that wasn't quite right either," John told him, removing a stack of something white from the box. He held it in front of him as he posed thoughtfully. "We thought about calling you Chapter Three, or Cbus Brigade. But that just didn't sound right. Then someone came up with the Olentangy Pansies."

Zeke raised his hand, grinning crookedly. "T-that was mine."

John gave him a golf clap. "Excellent suggestion, Zeke. But Dunc said it has to be PG, so we settled on this."

He slid the bundle down the table to Parker. The other man looked at the stack of notepads in front of him, brows quirked over his dark grey eyes. "Seriously? The Buckeye Brigade?"

Snorts and laughter rippled up and down the table. Shannon grinned, straightening the papers in front of her. She might have had a small hand in ordering the stationery.

"What the fuck is wrong with you people?"

Shannon's eyes widened at Parker's angry bellow. How had that flipped so quickly?

"Do you think you're better than us?" he hissed, rising to his feet, his fists clenched around the notepads. "Better than me? Why the hell do you think you can talk down to me? Just because you're fronting the money it doesn't mean I'm going to let you Denver Dicks belittle me."

Shannon blinked, her mouth open. Had he just called them dicks?

The room erupted into howls of laughter. John turned

his chair to Parker and clasped his hand, laughing. "You crazy fucker."

Parker grinned. "The difference being, since it's only me and Brody right this minute, I can be as non-PC as I want to be."

The men crowded around the group, laughing, and Shannon snapped a few pictures with her phone. A new business had been born.

6

It was a damn party at work that day.

John didn't remember there being this much excitement when they branched off to Vail, but Vail was at least still in the state. Maybe that was the difference. Columbus seemed like a very long way away, and more of an event. Plus, it had been a long time since Parker had been in the offices, and he'd been missed. John had a feeling it would be a flourishing business in no time.

As soon as he could, he slipped away. The details of Logan's family had lingered with him, and he wanted to at least do a preliminary search before he went home. Tonight, they would be at the dinner and if he didn't do it now, it wouldn't get looked at until tomorrow.

Shannon came into the office as he slid behind his desk, and he smiled. Looking at her always made him smile, no matter the mood he was in.

"Are you back to looking for Logan's family?" she asked, moving to hover over his shoulder. She rested her other hand on his back.

"I haven't gotten that far, but yes."

John logged into his computer and started pulling up some of the sites he frequented to dig up dirt.

"I'm not going to lie, John," Shannon said softly, "I feel for Logan. And I worry that if we don't find him something, he's going to do something drastic."

He looked up at her sharply. "What do you mean?"

She shrugged. "Just some of the things he's said makes me think... well, I think he's thinking about suicide. This seems like some kind of checklist he's going through to let himself go. Some kind of bucket list, almost."

John blinked, looking back at the keyboard. The thought had occurred to him as well, though maybe not as clearly. There was something a little... lost about Logan. He felt a little sick as he wondered if John was helping him check off the list. "Well, maybe we can find him something to live for. Give me a little time and we'll go get the boys."

Shannon leaned down and nuzzled him, pressing a kiss to his cheek. "I'll be out at my desk. I love you."

"I love you too, babe."

He watched as she exited the office. Hopefully something would pop out at him to give him a direction, because he hadn't seen it earlier. It sounded like Logan needed some kind of connection.

An hour later he wanted to punch the keyboard in frustration. Nothing was coming out right. He'd done property searches and death searches, searched the genealogy websites, and tapped into a somewhat shady database. All to no avail. He didn't have enough information to engage the background check services he normally used, so he would have to hope he happened across something random. Actually, he needed to interview Logan again. Maybe they could invite him to the dinner. He wasn't part of LNF, but he was a vet alone in a town he didn't know anything about.

When he texted Duncan, his partner agreed immediately.

I would have suggested it myself if I had known. A lot going on today.

Definitely. Thanks. Hey, Shannon and I are peeling out early. She's dying to see the kids.

No problem. See you at dinner?

Absolutely!

Shannon grinned when he rolled into her reception area and snatched up her bag and coat. With a wave at the lingering men, they climbed onto the elevator.

"I feel like we're skipping school," she whispered.

John chuckled, loving the bright shine of her eyes. It made the disappointment he'd been fighting with the Logan search fade away. They had a few precious hours to savor together before they had to be at the dinner.

The boys were overjoyed, of course, to see their mother. Wyatt bounced up and down in her arms, but Caden curled up against her and pressed his face into her neck. Caden had always preferred his mother's arms, and there were no substitutions.

John wondered what would happen if they added another baby to the mix. Somebody would be mad. Displaced.

They packed the boys into the truck and headed for home. Shannon was twisted around in the seat as far as her seatbelt would allow talking to the boys and listening to their gibberish. It was adorable. John could decipher a fraction of what they were saying. Shannon seemed to be able to understand even the smallest of sounds. He knew she was guessing as much as he was, she just made it more believable.

When they got home, Shannon unloaded the boys to the driveway, then reached into the back for her suitcase. Caden stuck close to his mother and tried to help her with the bag. He was more of a hindrance than a help, of course, but Shannon still let him. John guided Wyatt ahead of him and unlocked the front door, shooing the boy in before he rolled into the room. They left the door open for Shannon and Caden to bring her bag in.

Carmella met them at the door, the golden flag of her tail waving. She gave Wyatt a long lick up the cheek, sending him into giggles. When Shannon walked in the door, Carmella went crazy. It had been just as long for the dog as it had been the family.

"I love all the love," Shannon laughed, ruffling the dog's fur. Then she gave John a critical look. "Or did you not feed her while I was gone?"

John made a face at her. "Do you seriously think I would forget to feed my own dog?"

There was no way in hell he was going to admit that he had, in fact, forgotten. There'd been food in her bowl the first night, but the second night, it had only been when she'd whined that he'd remembered to refill her bowl. He'd done the cats, then, as well.

"When are these kids going to be old enough to pull their own weight?" John huffed, removing Wyatt's coat. "Is it time to assign them chores, yet?"

Shannon laughed, as he'd wanted her to do. "I'd be happy if they'd just learn to go to the bathroom on their own. We'll have plenty of time to give them chores."

Shannon moved through the house, kicking off her high-heeled boots and slipping into a pair of house tennis shoes. The dog and the kids trailed along in her wake, waiting for some scrap of attention. The Pied Piper of the house who doled out loves.

John had a feeling he wouldn't be getting any personal attention in the near future. And he was pretty much okay with that, although his body was clamoring for some kind of touch. Yes, he'd been touching her ever since they picked her up at the airport, but they had to keep it PG at the office. It was a standing rule. There had been a few close calls in the break room and shower over the past few years. So, Duncan had put out a memo limiting PDA. John, since he was a partner, had been bending that rule a little bit, he admitted, but he and Shannon had never been caught *in flagrante delicto*.

Wyatt brought him one of his favorite trucks. John played with him for a little while and listened to Wyatt's chatter. The kid could spin a story, even if John only understood a little bit. It was fascinating listening to the rise and fall of the natural cadence of his words.

"Hungry, Daddy."

Wyatt held his arms up to John. He gathered the boy against him and rolled into the kitchen. Caden must've been hungry too, because Shannon had just given him small cup of goldfish crackers. She handed a second cup to Wyatt, and the boys sat on the floor together, munching and playing.

John caught Shannon's gaze. There was a soft, hazy expression on her face that was precious to him. It meant she felt like her heart was overflowing with love, and her home was complete. He loved making her feel that way.

And she made him feel that way as well. Yeah, he liked to be the bad ass in the group, but the past few years had really softened his heart. John knew that if Shannon wanted another baby, he doubted he could tell her no. He didn't necessarily agree with the timing, but he would go with what her heart wanted.

Besides, anything that would get him more sex would be a good thing.

The gods seemed to understand his need because after the boys ate some snacks, they started to get a little drowsy. Shannon slid a look his way, her eyes lighting with an internal fire. "I might have a chance to take a shower and get rid of the travel grunge," she murmured.

"And I might have a chance to make you retake your shower," John said, grinning.

Shannon grinned as well, and even more important, she didn't say no. In fact, she quirked one of her brows at him and gave him a sexy little hip wiggle.

John settled onto the couch with the boys and turned on their favorite YouTube kid. Who could have imagined the audience there would be for farm toys breaking down in mud, and phantom hands coming in from off-camera to fix the equipment and get it moving again? The kids could watch hours of this ridiculousness.

Within just a few minutes of settling down to watch the endless videos, both boys were nodding off. John knew that this nap would be a fairly short one, though. Eventually they would wake up and be ready to go again. Trying to plan ahead, he tucked light blankets around each of them and put a toy in front of them. Wyatt got the lion toy. When they woke up they usually did so slowly, playing for a little while before they rolled off the couch and called for them.

One afternoon when he and Shannon had been stealing some time alone, they realized that one of the toys, a hard, plastic lion with four piano keys, always went through the same series of songs when a certain button was pushed. The boys loved the lion, though the songs could drive he and Shannon to the loony bin. It really wasn't the best sounding machine, tinny and a little off-key, but the kids loved it, Wyatt especially. When they woke from sleep the boys always pressed the button to send it into the musical loop.

It ended up being a great alarm clock for John and Shannon. Or maybe, timer. The loop gave them enough time to get up and take care of their own morning business before they had to go care for the boys. Or, it gave them a warning when they were making love. When they heard the songs start, they knew they had a finite amount of time to get done. Pop Goes The Weasel was the last song on the loop.

Of course. Seemed appropriate.

John chortled as he wondered what the guys at work would think if they knew he made love to Old McDonald, The Wheels on the Bus, and Pop Goes the Weasel.

By the time he made it into the bedroom, Shannon was already stretched out on the bed, towel barely covering her. After having the kids, her breasts had settled into a fullness they hadn't had before. She worried about the stretch marks, or the slight sag, but John loved every inch of her. Her breasts could make him harden in seconds. And she knew that. It was why she was posed like this, just for him.

"You know it's harder than hell to get into the bed with a hard-on," he grumbled, setting his brakes and shifting himself up onto the mattress. Shannon helped him undress, sliding the jeans down his legs and the socks off his feet. John had long ago stopped arguing with her about the help, because it actually helped them both out. If he could be making love five minutes sooner, hell yes, he would let her strip off whatever she wanted to.

Once he was undressed, he rolled onto his side to peer

down at her. "You are stunning. I missed you like crazy, and not just because I had to take care of the boys."

Shannon's eyes darkened. "I missed you, too. I'm glad I went to the conference, but I missed you desperately. And when the plane was delayed, I about cried. I'm so used to seeing you every day..." She nuzzled at his jaw, running her nails over his chest. "We don't have long. Between the kids waking from their nap and the dinner, we only have a couple of hours to do everything we want."

He grinned, cocking a brow at her. "Well, I guess I'd better get going, then..."

Leaning in he kissed her like he'd wanted to all day, without others watching or being nearby. Shannon moaned into his mouth, her breath sweet with her own distinctive flavor. With one hand he traced his fingers down her bare shoulder, down her chest and over her nipple. Nudging the towel away he drifted over her tummy and to the patch of dark curls at the apex of her thighs. With a breathy little sigh, she lifted one knee, a clear invitation. John didn't need any further urging, his fingertip teasing along the seam of her lips. Shannon had already been thinking about this little interlude, because her own arousal eased the path of his finger inside.

John could have groaned at the feel of her wetness. His dick hardened to the point of pain, but he wanted to, needed to, make sure she was taken care of first. No matter what time constraints they were under. She deserved it and she needed it.

Leaning down to press kisses to her shoulder and chest, he slipped one finger inside her folds, finding her clitoris. Her body tightened around his fingers, a clear indication he was touching her the right way, and he stroked harder. With a breathy sigh her hips surged into his touch, arching in time with his movements.

Lowering his head, he took her lips again, moving with her subtle shifts and grinds. Then he began to vary his touch the way he knew she loved, going deep into her body, then shallower along her clit. Within just a couple of minutes her body began to twitch and quiver.

"Oh, John..."

His own body ached, but pride demanded that he satisfy her first. She had to find pleasure with him, every single time.

And when the orgasm gripped her body in a convulsive spasm, the shared pleasure was almost enough to push him over the edge as well. His cock swelled at the sight and sound and even smell of her pleasure. It was glorious.

It took her a few moments to come back to him, her lashes lifting as she looked up at him and smiled. "That was incredible. But I think I need more."

"Good," he chuckled. "I know I do."

She laughed, swirling her fingernails over the hair of his chest. He shivered, anticipating the pleasure to come. "I want you to ride me," he whispered.

Immediately, she shifted, going high above him. John rolled to his back, pushing his legs where he needed them. Then Shannon was lifting her own long, sleek thigh over his hips. No matter how many times they did this, he cherished the sight. She was a beautiful woman, and he was proud and humble that she had chosen him as her life partner. He never would have imagined he would be good enough for her and every day he tried to be the best man he could be, for her.

Because this is what he got in return; a hot woman who

craved his battered, broken body and found something to love about him.

Holding her softly rounded hips in his hands, he guided her onto his cock. "Fuck," he breathed as she sank down onto him. Her damp hair hung to the side, just brushing her breast. She felt so damn good. He adjusted his own hips on the bed, then pulled her close. He loved feeling the cushion of her breasts against his chest and looking down to see the depth of her cleavage.

"You are such a great piece of ass," he murmured, teasing her in for a kiss.

Shannon giggled. "Thank you for the compliment. Your peepee is pretty nice as well," she breathed.

"My big peepee," he corrected, drawing her hips tight to his own. They both gasped, finding that sweet, sweet position that they both loved.

Then Shannon went still, her head cocked toward the door. "What the hell...I think the kids are awake," she breathed. "I hear Old McDonald. Damn it."

Fuck... John focused on the feel of her body gripping his. They were on a deadline now, and she hadn't had her second orgasm. They started moving, each of them aware that their little interlude could be derailed at any moment. The door was shut, of course, but... Shannon sat up on his hips and her head fell back as she rode him, her breasts swaying and her fingers tightening on his chest spasmodically. She knew that he wouldn't come until she did again.

The Wheels on the Bus started to play. There were only three more short songs.

Shannon reached down and rubbed her clit as she rocked on him, and John could feel the beginning of her orgasm. Her grip on his cock tightened, and she began to moan. His own release was climbing, fast, and he prayed that she would get there quick, because he was holding his release back, deliberately not hitting that perfect spot. Then she was there, giving that sweet, high keen she had as pleasure overwhelmed her. She cried out and slammed down onto him, and John shifted that tiny little bit to find his release. He jacked up into her, his body no longer under his control, and let the pleasure take him. The final strains of Pop Goes the Weasel drifted through the house, and Shannon disintegrated into giggles.

7

L ogan snapped awake, his legs throbbing. Glancing around the room, he tried to figure out what time it was. A shaft of sunlight streamed across the bed, obliterating his vision. The alarm clock sat just beyond the light. Curling into a sitting position, he breathed through the pain. Obviously, he'd slept through his last dose of pain medication.

Lowering his legs to the floor, he wiggled his toes, trying to get the circulation running again. Finally, he was able to see the alarm clock. 603 pm. Marigold had dropped him off a couple of hours ago, and he must've immediately crashed.

Whatever. He could always use a nap, considering he barely slept through the night. Ever.

Feeling like his legs had recovered, he pushed to his feet and staggered to the bathroom. When he returned, he sank into the office chair and turned to face the plate glass window.

The jagged, snow-capped mountain skyline called to him. As they'd driven into the city earlier it had drawn his attention over and over again. Something about it appealed to his sense of alone-ness. From here there was no way he could see people on the mountain range, and it was easy to imagine he was the only one around. If he looked down, he could see the moving traffic and even some people on the sidewalks below, but the mountains called to him. Since this trip was open-ended, maybe he would take some time to explore those mountains.

Then reality crashed in and he looked down at his legs. Maybe not.

Before he joined the Army, he'd been an active kid. School had held no appeal to him, but he'd gotten through it. If he'd had his way, he would've stayed in Virginia tinkering on cars and hanging out with his buddies at night. Eventually he'd realized that he wasn't going to be satisfied staying in the same neighborhood and doing the same things. He wanted more. More than just spinning his wheels in the same town he'd grown up in and avoiding his home life. Any time he'd gotten a few bucks in his pocket, he'd traveled. No great distances or anything, sometimes just to the next state to see what he could see. The Army had seemed like a great choice to let him see some of the country and get paid. His father hadn't been happy about that, but the older he'd gotten, the less Logan had cared what his drug-addicted, abusive father said. Then one day his father had told him he would absolutely not be joining the Army. Period. Not after the way they'd treated him. Unfortunately, Chris had never learned that Logan very often did the opposite of what he demanded just to be contrary.

Logan had signed his life over to the US Army the following week.

The thought of deploying overseas had been a slight worry, but not enough to stop him from joining. Less and less people had been killed on deployment, though they were still in a war, the recruiter had made sure to tell him.

The injury rates, though, were still substantial, which he'd found out the hard way. At the end of the 6th year, mere weeks from going home, he'd been in his third IED attack. The difference being that this time, everyone in the truck with him had died.

And it had been his fault. The recon trip had been acting upon one of his hunches.

Even now, seven months later, when his thoughts landed on that day, his stomach hollowed out and he felt like he was going to throw up. A lot of guys completely lost the day they were injured, but that hadn't been his case. He remembered every single word, every single sight, every single smell, every single scream. He didn't have the luxury of forgetting.

Reaching Into his bag on the desk, he retrieved a small bottle of whiskey and took a swallow. It burned going down, which was good. It meant he was still here, still feeling something.

When his phone buzzed on the nightstand, he almost didn't bother to move from the chair. It probably wasn't anyone he needed to speak to right that moment. Something urged him to move, though, and he grabbed the phone. Not a number he recognized.

"Hello?" he rasped.

"I'm so sorry, did I wake you?"

It took a moment to recognize the husky voice. "Um, Mari, Marigold?"

The young woman with the startling green eyes and the curvy hips.

"Yup," she laughed. "It's me. Hey, I didn't know if you had a ride to the dinner tonight or not."

Logan frowned. "What dinner?"

"The big birthday dinner for the new branch in Columbus."

"Um, no. I don't have anything to do with that."

She sighed on the other end of the line. "I know, but John and Shannon thought it would be good for you to be there. And I think Gunny Palmer had some more questions for you. There's no sense in sitting in a hotel room alone when you could be hanging with other vets talking shit."

Logan chuckled a little. That's exactly what they did, talked shit. "I'm not even part of the company."

"I know that," she repeated patiently. "Are you dressed?"

He looked down at his boxers and t-shirt. "Kind of."

"You have five minutes. I'm on my way up."

"Wait, Mari..."

The dial tone rang in the silence of the room. Shit. Did he really want to go hang out with a bunch of people he didn't even know? Fuck...

She didn't give him time to take a shower, but by the time Marigold knocked on his door, Logan was mostly dressed and put together. "I don't know why I'm even going to this..." his voice drifted away as he caught sight of her.

Marigold had made an impact on him earlier that day. The name was distinctive, and she had the look of the kind of woman he normally enjoyed. Now she stood on his doorstep and something about her made him shut up and stare. She was, quite simply, beautiful. He'd thought cute earlier. Not classically cute like a petite little waif type, but cute in an athletic way. She was kind of solid, like she'd spent years playing softball. Strong legs, broader hips, slightly muscular arms, all revealed by the tight stone-washed jeans she wore and the long sleeved, shimmery dark gray blouse. Wow, that really worked with her dark hair.

She'd done something to her eyes to make them appear larger than they were, the lashes thick and dark. Her hair fell in a dark straight sheet down her back, and he wondered of it was as soft as it looked.

Logan blinked, then looked at her again. Her eyes were startling green, but there was a shard of gold in the center. Not hazel, but green and gold together. Or was she wearing contacts? Her glasses were gone, and her irises were a little fuzzy around the edges. Maybe they were enhancing the color? Even if they were, the color was stunning.

He blinked, realizing he'd been standing there not saying anything for way too long. "Sorry, you just took me by surprise. You look beautiful, Marigold."

Pink touched her cheeks, then her dark brows dropped, and she blinked. "Thank you. I think. Are you okay?"

"I'm fine. Really." He backed into the room. "Just give me a minute to finish up. I had settled down for the night already."

She glanced at the slim silver watch on her wrist. "It's, like, six o'clock. Are you eighty?"

Logan glared at her as he walked into the bathroom, trying not to limp too much. "No, I'm not fucking eighty, but I have had a long day today."

She waited, leaning against the hotel door, as he finished brushing his teeth and tucking in his shirt. He'd pulled on a pair of khakis and a button-down, solid dark blue shirt. He'd brought a tie, but he didn't think he'd wear it. Too stuffy. Using the wall for balance, he headed back to the open suitcase on the stand beside the TV. Unzipping one side, he drew out the brown leather loafers he had brought. They weren't as comfortable as his boots and didn't give him nearly the same support, but he could make do for a couple of hours. The brown suit jacket still had a few wrinkles from being in the bag, but there wasn't much he could do about it. He pulled it on and smoothed it down.

Logan was very aware of Marigold watching him get ready. He slid his forearms through the arm cuffs of the braces, settling them. Then he grabbed his wallet and hotel card from the dresser. He desperately wanted to snatch up his ball cap, but he'd already combed his hair, very carefully positioning some of the hair over his burns. As soon as he went outside the spring wind would blow it to hell, but he had to try. He very rarely went out without something on his head anymore.

He turned to stand in front of her. "Is this all right?"

Her gaze drifted over him. Was that appreciation he saw in her eyes?

"Yeah, you're good to go. Do you have your phone?" Marigold asked, jerking his attention back to her.

Logan paused and felt his front hip pocket. He must've slipped it in when she'd knocked. "Got it."

He followed her out the door, making sure it latched behind him. Then he walked down the hallway shoulder to shoulder with her to the elevator. Logan tried not to be self-conscious of the way he moved, but something had changed just now. She'd been pretty before, but now she was... relevant to him.

Which was ridiculous. He wasn't here for any reason other than to find the Walter family. He didn't have time for any personal entanglements. The awareness in his body apparently didn't seem to agree.

The scent of orange wrapped around him.

∾

MARIGOLD KNEW she could have called the man a cab, but that hadn't felt right. Logan deserved more than a generic ride from a potentially dangerous driver. Denver seemed to have more than its fair share. It had been an eye-opening experience the first time she'd driven Interstate 70 through downtown.

But it was more than that, too. John Palmer had never asked her to escort someone before, so that made her suspect that the guy was a little more important than the average joe for some reason. Before they left for the day, Palmer had asked her to make arrangements for Logan to get to the dinner. He had not specified that she was supposed to drive him. Marigold had taken that responsibility on herself, because she was curious. From what she'd heard, the guy didn't have anyone really, and he was out here on a ghost hunt.

Marigold knew she was too soft-hearted, but there was no way she couldn't feel for the lonely man. It was obvious he'd been through something devastating. The scars on his face had that pink, raw look, like they could still be incredibly painful. It made her want to reach for cream to soothe the hurt, but she knew the pain had to be beyond anything over-the-counter medicine would even touch.

Plus, he was younger than a lot of the guys at LNF. The original partners were in their late thirties or early forties. Duncan was at least in his late forties, if not a little older. Logan seemed to be barely into his twenties. Or maybe that was just the way he appeared to her. His brilliant blue-green eyes, which reminded her of sea glass, seemed much older, like they'd seen the worst in the world and returned to tell the tale. And maybe he had.

There was just something about the guy that called to her. Maybe fate had put them on a collision course so that she could help him find his family or something. She didn't know. What she did know was that the few minutes it had taken her to deliver him to a hotel hadn't been enough.

When he opened the door of his room, looking a little rumpled and hazy-eyed, she felt bad, but not enough to leave. Then she'd found herself wondering if that was what he would look like after making love, his dark curls standing out from his head. That shocked her, because she'd literally only known him a few hours. The last guy she'd slept with hadn't had it so easy. It had taken him weeks of dates and conversations to get into her bed, and as soon as they'd slept together she'd known it had been the wrong move.

So, why was this guy ringing alarm bells in her gut?

Her eyes lingered on him as he finished getting ready, and she imagined the reverse happening. Would he go through the same process to get undressed?

And then, as if she hadn't been struggling enough trying to keep her thoughts off her face, he'd asked for her opinion on his outfit. Holy hell, that had been hard, trying to sound so unaffected by his presence. Even with the scars, he was a striking man, with his height and dark hair and light eyes, hell, his presence. She didn't think he understood how much he affected her.

The pain she could see him struggle with made her heart hurt. He didn't appear to need the crutches moving around the room. Or maybe he was just acting like he didn't need the crutches for her sake. She certainly hoped he wasn't putting on an act for her. Eventually, he'd fitted the braces to his arms, and they'd left the room, walking side by side down the corridor. She wished she could save him the pain she could see him struggling with.

Her car was in the turnaround of the hotel. As he struggled to wedge himself into the seat, Marigold circled the car to get in. After working with so many vets for the past few weeks, she'd learned exactly what not to do with injured veterans. Number one was pity them, and a close number two was offer them any kind of help. If he were truly struggling, she would, even at the risk of having her head snapped off.

The VW cranked like she was supposed to, and they took off. The restaurant Duncan had rented was around the loop a little to the North, and they probably should have been on the way already. She shifted again as she merged onto the highway.

"This car is amazing," he said. "What year is it?"

"It's a seventy. My dad had it restored before he went overseas. It was his first car and he wanted to pass it on to me."

Logan ran his hand over the dash. "It's in amazing condition. He did a really good job."

"Thank you. It's a bit of upkeep, but I can't imagine driving anything else," she told him honestly.

"How does it handle the Denver snow?"

"You know, not too bad," she laughed. "As long as it's not ass deep she actually goes pretty well because of the front-wheel drive."

Logan nodded his head, turning to look out the window. The conversation seemed to be at an end, if she let it. No, there was too much to learn about him.

"How long do you plan to be in Denver?"

He shrugged, lightly. "I guess it depends upon how quickly Palmer finds anything, or if he does."

Marigold glanced at him. "Oh, he will. The guy can be a dick, but he knows his job."

That made him look at her. "That's your boss you're calling a dick."

Giving him a tight grin, she nodded once. "Yeah, and I would call him a dick to his face, too. He's not one of my favorite men."

Curiosity sharpened his expression. "What made you not like him?"

Marigold sighed. "It sounds stupid and petty, but he made fun of my name. The name my dad chose for me before he was killed."

Logan scowled. "That's not stupid. I'm sorry about your dad."

"Thank you." She waved a hand. "I don't really remember him. Just flashes and impressions."

Signaling a lane change, she shifted over to the off ramp. "Just to warn you, this is going to be hectic as hell because all these guys know each other. I've only been here a few weeks and I can tell these people really like to have fun."

He smiled slightly. "That's good to know. And who's birthday is this?"

"Oh, it's a company birthday," she said. "They just signed paperwork to create a new Lost and Found branch in Columbus, Ohio. Denver is the main office. Vail is the second office, and Columbus the third. I think they're maybe talking about Texas, too, but that's later on down the road."

Logan nodded. "Business must be doing well."

Marigold laughed. "You know, there's no end to jealous wives and husbands, I will say that. I think the Columbus branch will be more corporate stuff, is what I'm feeling. And criminal investigations. Our branch does a little bit of everything from forensic genealogy to corporate espionage and personal protection. I'm still learning everything we do."

"Job security," he murmured.

She grinned at him. "Definitely."

She turned right at the light and accelerated. "And what about you? What branch were you in?"

"Army," he said shortly.

"How long were you in?"

"Almost 6 years."

She gave him a sharp look. "You have a baby face, then. You don't seem that old."

He gave a bitter laugh, looking out the window. "Baby face. Right."

Maybe she shouldn't have said that, Marigold realized. It was too late to take the words back now.

Marigold didn't say anything else as they pulled up to the restaurant, a popular Denver steakhouse. Shannon had called last week and booked a banquet room for the group, knowing they would need the space. As they walked into the dark and intimate room, even she had to stop and stare at all the people inside. A lot of the men she recognized, but there were women that she didn't know. She just hadn't been here long enough to know everyone.

Alex, Duncan's wife, happened to be closest to the door, and she crossed to welcome them in. "Marigold, welcome! You probably haven't been to one of these little LNF shindigs, have you?"

Marigold shook her head, a little intimidated by the beautiful, auburn-haired doctor. She wanted to be Alex Wilde when she grew up. "I've heard about them, though. Alex, this is Logan Vance. Gunny Palmer is working on a background search for him."

Alex smiled beautifully and reached out a hand. Logan turned the damaged side of his face away from her but shook her hand. "Nice to meet you, ma'am."

Marigold watched Alex's face for any kind of reaction to

Logan's injuries, but she could only see welcome in Alex's pretty, calm expression.

"Duncan is holding court at the end of the room, near the fireplace. I think he's part reptile, or something, the way he always goes for the heat source. Dinner will be in half an hour."

Marigold looked down the room. Yep, there he was, leaning against the stone mantel of a giant fireplace. She was a little surprised that he could even stand so close to the flames.

Palmer was in his chair to Wilde's right, talking to a massive guy with a mostly shaved head. Marigold had no idea who that was, or what he did for the company. Actually, there were several men down there she didn't recognize.

She scanned the room. Shannon and a few of the women were seated at the long table, drinking glasses of wine or ice water. When she saw Marigold, she waved and called her over. "Go ahead," Alex murmured. "I'm the unofficial hostess tonight, so I'm stuck on door duty."

Marigold crossed to the table, Logan close behind her.

"Marigold, this is Willow, Ember, Rachel, Kendall, and I think you've met Lora."

All of the women were beautiful, in completely different ways, and made Marigold wish she had the tiniest bit of poise that these women had. She lifted a hand in acknowledgment. "It's a pleasure to meet all of you." She held out a hand for Logan to step up. "This is Logan, everyone. He's here for Palmer to investigate something for him."

The women all said hello, and she watched for any of them to react adversely to his injuries, but they'd all been around the group long enough to know when not to react. Hell, they all had their own injured warriors.

Wait. Their own? Marigold looked at Logan, wondering

when she'd gotten possessive over him. That really wasn't like her. Yes, she'd had the overwhelming feeling that she needed to know him, but did she need to claim him? She didn't think so. That really wasn't her style. The thought of dealing with a significant other right now made her tired. There was too much going on in her life. It was difficult to deny the tingle she felt when he was nearby, though. That was something she hadn't felt with anyone else before.

Logan seemed like a decent guy, and he was damn easy on the eyes, in spite of the injuries, but she didn't think John and Shannon would appreciate her hooking up with one of their clients.

Logan shifted away from the group like he wanted to fade into the background. Marigold caught Shannon's gaze and the woman shared a smile with her in understanding. Their group was a lot, and it could be overwhelming. Logan had the look of a drowning man. She would let him catch his breath for a minute.

8

Logan looked around the room at the people gathered there. What the hell was he doing here? These people meant nothing to him, and they were derailing his objective. He needed to get in, apologize to Miller's family, and get out.

Sounded easier than he knew it would be.

It was hard to stay on point, when he could see the joy and excitement bubbling around him. Apparently, this was a project they'd been working on for a while and it had just come to fruition. Logan felt like a voyeur, spying on their accomplishments. And then the women had welcomed him into their midst, for some reason making him feel like even more of an interloper.

It wasn't right, but he couldn't fight the ache that being with these people created in his chest. For months now, he'd resigned himself to dying alone on his terms, when he wanted to and how he wanted to, where he wanted to. Being here gave him a glimpse of what he would be giving up by leaving the world. He glanced back at Marigold and fought not to stare at her mobile face laughing with Shannon about something.

Could he even remember being that enthusiastic about anything? Maybe about joining the Army years ago. And he'd been excited about nearing the end of his contract. Until it all went to hell.

Moving to an open table on the far side of the room, he sat with his back to the wall. A floating waiter crossed to him. "Can I get you a drink, sir?"

"Beer, whatever you have on draft, please."

"Yes, sir."

Logan was glad the guy left without trying to ID him. That would have been more than he could handle right then. Usually the scars were enough to advance his age to the point that wait staff let him pass.

Baby face, my ass...

He glanced at Marigold. She'd drawn up a chair to sit with the women, and she was speaking in-depth to Shannon about something. The two of them were kind of lost in their own little world. The rest of the women talked around and over their heads, giving them a semblance of privacy.

It was awkward being here. Pulling his phone from his pocket he looked for his Uber app.

Movement out of the corner of his eye caught his attention. John Palmer was rolling toward him. Logan set his phone on the table. He took John's hand when it was offered.

"Logan, I'm glad you made it. I hope Marigold wasn't as rude as she was earlier."

Logan smiled. "Nah, she was fine."

John leaned back in his chair. "I'm coming up with dead ends right now, buddy, I'll be honest. Can you think of any other details that might help me narrow things down?"

Logan racked his brain, trying to come up with something. "I don't know. I believe I told you everything I can think of that might narrow it down. I mean, I was little when we moved to Virginia. I have flashes of faces but nothing concrete. That was before pictures on cell phones, and stuff. I'm just going by little things my dad said. Or my mom whispered. They got into a fight once. I remember my mom wanted to send 'them' a card for Christmas. My bedroom was on the second floor, but when my parents fought, I could hear it through my register in the floor. Anyway, she wanted to send the card and he said absolutely not, that they didn't deserve to know how we were doing."

John frowned, leaning forward in his chair. "Did they fight like that a lot?"

The waiter arrived then with Logan's glass of beer and a fresh bottle for John. Logan thanked the kid and took a swallow, needing the liquid in his throat. It was good beer. "They fought more than the average family I suppose. It wasn't great. My dad had a substance abuse problem most of his life."

"I'm sorry about that," John said quietly, and Logan could tell that he meant it. "My mother did as well. I assume that was why she left me at a church when I was five."

Logan winced and shook his head. "People can be fucked up," he murmured.

"Agreed." John reached out and clinked his beer bottle to Logan's glass, and they both drank. "But I will say, people can only fuck you up as much as you let them. My brother and I are figuring that out. We have families now, and we're building our lives in spite of what our mother taught us to fear."

Logan looked down into his glass. He was very aware his childhood hadn't been normal. His older sister Jana had done what she could to minimize the impact of their father's issues on the family, but it hadn't always been enough. Their mother had not been strong, but Jana had, so she'd taken up the slack. It had also painted a target on her back. Logan could remember the look on her face when their parents had come in, drunk off their asses, and Jana had failed to do a chore, or something. It had been terrifying. Jana had tried to take on the world for the three of them, little lion that she was, but she'd been too small herself. More than once they'd ended up in the emergency room, backing up a story that she'd fallen on the playground, or some other lame ass excuse his mother had come up with to explain away their father's indiscretions.

Clint, their youngest brother, hadn't helped matters. He'd looked up to Dad, in spite of all of the issues they'd had because of his substance abuse. Within just a few years he'd been out of school and out of control. By sixteen he'd pretty much moved out, running the streets as he wanted with no supervision. Logan knew that Jana had carried the weight of Clint's decisions on her heart, like she always did, but he had made his own decisions. Now he had the criminal record to prove it.

Jana had encouraged Logan to join the military as soon as he turned eighteen. She'd tried to build up the bullshit about dad being in the military, but in the end, Logan had decided that the Vance military history would end with him in an honorable service record, not the discharge for contraband his father had brought. That had been why he'd joined, to try to make better what his father had ruined.

The Army had done him well and he didn't regret a second of it. The service had given him something to live for, a structure he'd never had before. Though it had been a serious shock to the system at first, in the end he'd loved the life, and he'd excelled.

Logan thought of his father's anger when he'd first joined up. It had been an epic fight. Jana was the only one that knew he'd been seeing the recruiter and taking the test, but even she hadn't known when he was leaving. Logan made sure not to tell anyone until the day before, because he knew what the reaction would be.

His father had turned about ten shades of purple with anger, and his mother had immediately broken into tears.

"You're going to call that recruiter and tell him you changed your mind, boy."

Logan could remember the exchange like it was yesterday, though it had been years. He'd straightened, knowing what was coming. The anger on his father's face had been monumental. "No, sir. I'm eighteen, now, and you're done telling me what to do."

The punch had spun him off his feet, but it lacked the force to actually put him on the ground. The old man had lost a lot of his strength as his body wasted away from the alcohol. He hadn't been able to put them down for a long time.

Jana had been shocked, but secretly elated too. She'd been squirreling her money away for years, a few dollars here, a few more there, hidden very carefully beneath the carpet in her room. Logan knew she'd been staying in the house to protect him, but his joining the Army now allowed her to make her own break, because she didn't have to protect him anymore.

Logan had already packed his bag in preparation of leaving, so when his father kicked him out of the house, he was ready. Hugging his sister and promising to be in touch, he'd walked out of the house. His mother had cried in the corner, but she hadn't spoken up against his father. Logan had known she wouldn't. She'd never protected her kids. She'd been a weeping, cooking decoration in the background for as long as he could remember, and she'd become insignificant to him.

Jana had met him later at a friend's house, where they'd spent the night. For hours, they'd talked and reminisced, but only about the good things, and Logan had been so reluctant to leave her the next morning.

Jana had smiled that crooked smile of hers, her turquoise eyes shining with pride, and tapped his chin with a finger. "I'll be fine, Army man. Go make us Vances proud. Do what Dad couldn't."

To this day he could hear the words in his mind and see the way the wind tossed her dark, dark hair, standing there on the porch. It had been the last time he'd seen his older sister alive.

"Can you look up old military records? My dad was medically discharged from the Army. Maybe you can find some info there?"

John looked out at the crowd thoughtfully. "I might have to call in a favor, but I think I can. Give me a day or so to figure it out. In the meantime, enjoy yourself. The company is covering the tab. Most of us are Jarheads or Squids, but there might be the occasional Ground Pounder."

Logan chuckled. He hadn't heard that slang applied to the Army for a long time. "No Zoomies or Coasties?"

John looked outraged. "Seriously? We have standards at LNF."

And he rolled away. Logan chuckled and knocked back his glass, swallowing the rest of the beer.

"You should smile like that more often."

Logan looked up at Marigold, standing beside him. Man, her eyes were green... He shrugged, leaning back in the chair. "Palmer is pretty funny. I can appreciate his friendly fire."

She made a face as she looked after the man. "Yeah, I guess, in his own sarcastic, fuck-you way, he's all right."

Logan shifted his crutches out of the way as she dropped down into the seat opposite him. "Has he found your family?"

"Not yet," he said, running his thumb over the texture of the wood table. "The details I gave him are pretty sketchy."

"How did you lose track of your family?" she asked, propping her chin on her hand on the table.

Logan regarded her. Marigold wasn't being invasive, per se. He would be curious, as well, if he were in her position. "Not sure exactly. I think there was some falling out, but I can't say for sure. For some reason we moved away from Colorado. We lived in Indiana and Ohio for a while, before finally settling in Virginia. My parents were not the most reliable."

Marigold snorted. "Sounds like an understatement."

"It is," he admitted, "but it's what I'm willing to say."

"I can respect that."

A soft smile spread her lips as she propped her chin on her hand and looked at him. Logan glanced away to shield his expression. If given the chance he had a feeling he could completely lose himself in her eyes.

"I'm not judging you on your scars, you know," she said, startling him.

Immediately, his jaw clamped and he drew back. Why had he been leaning in toward her that way? "It doesn't matter if you are," he said softly. "I'm used to it."

Frowning, she tilted her head at him. "I'm going to call

you out on that one, buddy. You walk around like you have a swastika tattooed on your forehead and are trying to hide it. This isn't the group to hide in."

Logan frowned. "If you see the way most people react to my face, you would understand."

"No one will react to you like that here. I've seen how the public reacts to Zeke," she said, pointing to the huge man across the way. Even from across the room Logan could see the unevenness in his face, and the healed scars. But also, he was grinning like a mother at something John had said. "He works as a bartender with his fiancée. I'm sure he probably has the occasional issue but for the most part he just rolls with it. I think you have to own it and be above anyone else's expectations."

"Easy for you to say," he snapped, angry now, probably because he knew she was right. "You've got the world on a platter. You're beautiful and you have a great job, as well as a brilliant future. I have a feeling your home life was kittens and rainbows. I don't need your patronizing attitude."

Logan sat back in the chair. Marigold, conversely, propped both arms on the table as she leaned across toward him. "Yes, I had kittens and rainbows when I was a kid, thanks to my grandparents. I also had a suicidal mother and a father that was killed in action. No one here has treated you as if you're lesser. Period. We all have issues, Logan." Then she frowned. "You think I'm beautiful?"

Logan blinked, ready to lash out again, until he heard the uncertainty in her voice. Her eyes were hooded, like she didn't want to be looking into his face when he tore her down.

"You have to know you're beautiful," he said, voice gruff. "How can you tell me to be secure in myself when you aren't?"

She gave him an ironic look. "Yeah... what's that saying about doctors being the worst patients?"

Narrowing his eyes, he stared at her. "What do you mean?"

She shook her head. "Nothing," she murmured. Flagging down the waiter she ordered a rum and coke. "John have any more info about your family?"

Logan sighed, knowing that he needed to let go of his aggravation. "No, nothing really. The info I gave him is pretty slim."

"Do you have brothers and sisters?"

He lifted a brow at her question and she shifted uncomfortably. "Sorry. I'm curious."

"It was my dad's family out here. My dad, my mom, my younger brother and older sister all left here back in the late nineties. I just know there was some kind of falling out, and we drove away in my dad's craptastic car. We broke down in Indiana and stayed for a while, before finally making it to Virginia. I was like, six at the time, and I just remember being hungry and cold in the back of the car as we drove. And fighting over space with my sister."

By the end of that trip, though, they'd been friends more than enemies. Jana had been just as scared, he was sure, but she'd cared for him like the lion he always thought her. Their mother had concentrated on taking care of the baby, leaving Logan with Jana.

"We settled around Bowling Green, Virginia. My dad was familiar with the area because he'd been on the Army base there years ago. I think even after he was discharged from the Army he hung around and worked for a while, before he went home. It was familiar to him."

He played with his empty glass, wondering if Bowling Green still looked the same. There had been changes, he was sure, but he wasn't curious enough to ever go back. Just talking about it was too much.

"So, what are your thoughts on finding your family?" she asked him softly. "Do you think you'll want to reconnect with them?"

Logan had thought about this for a long time. "Assuming there is any family, and that's a huge IF, I'd like to reconnect and find out what went wrong. My job was in intelligence, and I've looked for anything I can find about my family, but I just don't have enough to go on. I've looked in all the obvious places, now I guess I need help looking for the un-obvious places."

Marigold nodded her head. "John will help you with that. It's impressive you came all the way out here for that. Where do you live now?"

"Virginia, just outside of Richmond. It was just a stop after I got out of the hospital. And I didn't come out for John to work on my case. Shannon pretended to be a damsel in distress, but she helped me out at the airport and one thing led to another."

Marigold grinned at him. "Yeah, things do that around here. My suggestion is to just enjoy the ride and be patient. John will find something."

Must be nice to have someone have that kind of faith in you.

"So, you came all the way out here from Virginia to *maybe* find your family?"

Logan blinked, not surprised that she realized there was more to it than that. "No, I have other business. Army business."

Her dark brows lifted a little. "Ah. Fun."

Logan clenched his jaw and fought the trepidation in his gut. "Not really."

She seemed to sense that there was more to what he was saying, but he wasn't going to fill her in. "I'm sorry."

"Nothing to be sorry about," he told her softly.

"You know," she said softly, leaning forward to park her elbows on the table. "A couple years after my dad was killed, we had a guy come to our door. I was old enough to remember my mom crying when he left. When I asked about it, she just said he had been one of my dad's friends from the Marines. I never found out exactly what he said, just that he made my mother feel better. She'd been in a fog for months, kind of drifting through. I made us dinner most of the time, and I was only six or seven. But I remember her changing after that. She started to be more like my mom again."

A chill went through him as she related her story. How had she known that was why he was here?

She smiled softly, twisting a silver ring around her pinky finger. "I can admire what you're doing, looking for the family. It might really make a difference in their grief."

Again, he was fighting emotion. He never told her he was looking for a family. This woman understood him in a way he never expected. "Thank you for telling me your story," he said. "Did you ever find out who it was?"

Marigold looked up at him and grinned. "Yup. Can you keep a secret? It was a young Marine by the name of John Palmer."

Logan barked out a laugh. "Seriously?"

Marigold nodded. "It had been his first command and my father had been the first man he'd lost, so he felt he needed to come talk to the family. He doesn't know who I am, so don't say anything, okay?"

He nodded, feeling bemused, and thoroughly curious.

"So, where are you from? And how did you come to be here?"

Grinning, Marigold rocked back in her chair. "I'm from Arizona, originally. Tucson. My mom died a few years ago and I wasn't sure what to do with my life. I'd taken care of her for so long, I was a little lost. We'd done everything together. She never married again and never seemed completely happy after my dad died. It was sad, really. It was like I was the only reason she was living and once I started looking at colleges out of state, it was like she gave up."

"Did she commit suicide?" he asked, horrified for her yet morbidly curious at the same time.

Marigold frowned, her eyes going dark. "I don't want to think that, but I do, yes. She was a diabetic, so it was very important that she monitor her sugar. I think she just let herself go. I know she was drinking; I could hear it in her voice when she talked to me."

She turned her face away, but not before he saw tears glimmering in her eyes. Logan knew she had to be feeling incredibly guilty. He could see and understand the emotion because he lived with it every day of his wretched life.

"You know it wasn't your fault," he said, leaning forward. Surprising even himself, he reached forward and touched her hand, lightly, before drawing back. Marigold caught his scarred fingers before he could pull away completely.

"I think we're both carrying a lot of needless guilt," she murmured, her gaze hitting his for a long, timeless moment. Squeezing his fingers, she let him go.

Yes, they probably were, but he didn't know how to release the albatross. Reaching blindly for his glass he tipped the remainder of the liquid into his mouth, relishing in the coolness.

Marigold watched him for a long moment and some

understanding passed between them. Logan suddenly felt more connected to this young woman than he had anyone else in the past year. And it scared him. Once he found Miller's family, his list would be complete and he would be free to do as he liked. That didn't include tying himself to another person who would have to eventually take care of him.

Looking away, he flagged down the waiter for another beer. One was usually his limit, but he didn't know what else to do with himself while she sat there.

As if in answer to an unspoken prayer, Duncan drew everyone's attention.

"I want to thank you all for being here. I know we don't really need a reason to get together and drink, but I think this is an especially good one. Parker and Andromeda," Duncan raised a glass of beer to the beautiful couple, "welcome to the Lost and Found family. Again. I look forward to doing business with you."

Parker pushed to his feet and limped close enough to shake Duncan's hand, then they did a shoulder press and back slap. Both men were grinning, and Logan had a feeling they liked each other a lot. Duncan had to be a stand-up guy to run a business like this, so Logan assumed Parker was a good guy as well. And his fiancée or wife was stunning, beaming proudly as she watched.

The solidarity in this place, with these people, was really something. If he didn't have a different objective in mind, he would like to be a part of this group as well. Who wouldn't?

Several waiters came through in a wave to take food orders, and Logan realized he would be dining with Marigold. That was fine. He could do it. He just had to remember to keep his emotional distance.

MARIGOLD FELT it was fortuitous that she was still sitting at Logan's secluded table when they started to order food. "We can join the group if you'd prefer..."

Logan shook his head. "I'm good here. I don't know anyone enough to be good company."

"I disagree. I think you're fine company."

He grimaced. "Then you'd better stay here."

She took it for the invite it kind of wasn't.

Colorado was a natural topic of conversation and Logan seemed genuinely interested in the state. Marigold didn't try to gloss over the things she knew he wouldn't be able to do with his disability, she told him about everything. "And honestly, I'm still learning. I moved up here to go to school, so I haven't done a whole lot yet. I'm looking forward to summer, though, and hiking."

His brilliant sea-glass eyes narrowed. "What are you going to study?"

Sigh. She was hoping he wouldn't ask. "I'm going to the University of Denver Graduate School of Professional Psychology, with a focus on Military Psychology."

Logan drew back, as she'd expected him to, and his battered face seemed to close down. Marigold was afraid of this. She didn't want him to think that she was hanging with him just because of professional curiosity. It was quite the opposite, actually. She was very definitely *personally* interested in him.

Which was actually even worse. The guy was from Virginia and would be returning to Virginia once they'd found his family. Nothing that developed between them would ever go anywhere.

Maybe that could be an advantage, too, though. If they

knew there was no long-term commitment, maybe they could just have fun.

The damn flip-flopping her mind was doing was going to make her sick.

Had Logan been with anyone since his injury? *Dangerous thoughts, girl...*

The waiter arrived with their food and it gave them a little breathing space so that they didn't have to talk.

"Kind of ruined the vibe, huh?" she asked eventually, after they'd tasted their entrées. "I don't want you to feel like you're under scrutiny. I haven't even started classes. I've been working and saving my money. Mom left a lot of hospital bills. My grandmother promised to help, but she doesn't have a lot either."

Logan glanced up at her. "It's okay. It just took me by surprise. It's actually a very worthwhile path of study. I've talked to more than my share of psychologists and they have helped me with some things. It's just hard to open up and be vulnerable."

"I completely agree," she said softly. "I've talked to my fair share as well. Between Mom fighting her demons and being the child of a war casualty I barely even remembered, I've had more than my fair share of crap fall on me."

She gave him a sardonic look as she took a drink of soda. "I think everyone could benefit with a little objective insight into their issues."

Logan's mouth crooked into a smile. "You're probably right."

They ate the rest of the meal companionably, talking about inconsequential things. When Logan mentioned that he wasn't sure how long he was going to stay, Marigold debated with herself. Something had occurred to her earlier, but she wasn't sure if she should throw it out there.

Then she decided hell with it. "If you think you're going to be here longer than a week or two, you might think about finding another place to stay. And I have to mention that my landlady is a doll. A bit of a dirty-minded doll, but easily the nicest landlady I've ever met. And I'm sure she would give you a better rate than what you're probably paying at the hotel."

Logan stared at her thoughtfully. "Thank you for that. I might give her a call."

"I don't know what your finances are like, but she might even make you a deal for a shorter amount of time. We can run by there on the way back to your hotel tonight if you want." She could tell he was thinking about it. "We'll see where the night goes."

She shrugged like it was no big deal, but internally, she was jumping up and down at her brilliance. Though she'd only known him for the day, she had a feeling if he gave her a chance, they could connect.

And she strove to build that connection through dinner. Logan was a fascinating guy, insightful about world events in particular but knowledgeable about a whole range of things. Even without knowing his job in the Army, she would have suspected that he was in some kind of Intelligence position. Marigold had a feeling he could name everyone in the room he'd been introduced to, because he never hesitated or looked confused when she mentioned people. Eventually, the topics moved to the more personal. They talked about growing up in their respective states. Virginia sounded beautiful. She'd never been that far east before, so she couldn't imagine the amount of green he described.

"Arizona was amazing and beautiful, but I think Colorado is even more so," she murmured. "I love it here."

And she did. There was no connection to Arizona anymore, other than her grandmother who traveled more often than she was home, now that she had time and freedom. So, when Marigold had started looking at colleges, she remembered one of the few family vacations she'd taken with her mother and grands, when they'd all been a family. It had been to Colorado. They'd toured ghost towns and ridden a railway line. It also had a fantastic college graduate program, so she decided Colorado would be a perfect home for her.

"Not leaving a boyfriend behind?"

Marigold was stunned that he asked. "No, unfortunately not. If there had been a boyfriend, I may not have left."

"Hm."

"How about you? No significant other?"

He snorted derisively. "Fuck, no. Not anymore."

She waved a hand. "You can't leave me hanging. What happened?"

"What do you think happened?" he snapped, his beautiful eyes narrowing in fury.

Marigold held her hands out. "I have no idea. Why would I?"

Color raced under his damaged cheeks, and she could see he was gritting his teeth. "I don't understand," she whispered.

Logan pushed up from his chair and left the dining room, anger radiating from him. Marigold stared after him, wondering what the hell she'd said. Her eyes stung with tears and she glanced around, wondering who had seen them. Everyone seemed to be enjoying their meal. Had none of them seen Logan storm off?

Should she go after him? For some reason she felt like

she'd done something wrong, but she honestly couldn't say what...

Her internal monologue was interrupted a few minutes later when Shannon joined her. "Everything okay?"

"Not sure," Marigold murmured, "I think I just pissed Logan off."

Shannon's eyes widened. "How did you do that?"

"I don't know," she cried. She related the conversation. "I can only assume someone left him because of his injuries."

Shannon nodded. "Sounds like it," she murmured sadly. "Unfortunately, it happens a lot. You'll hear about it repeatedly when you're a military psychologist. Duncan's fiancée did it to him when he was in the burn unit at Walter Reed. He would tell you that himself. It motivated him like nothing else."

Marigold frowned, looking toward the door. She'd been waiting for Logan to return and laugh it off, but if he didn't, she would have to go find him.

"Veterans, especially combat veterans that have seen action, are very different animals," Shannon continued. "I don't think Logan has been out of combat for a full year, yet, so he'll probably react to things a little more aggressively for a while. They find offense quicker and are willing to fight sooner. It's probably nothing you did, just a perceived slight that feels more hurtful than it actually is. They need time and understanding to work through their emotions, because they've been taught by the military to turn them off for so long."

Damn. The insight and understanding in this woman's heart was something it would take her years to learn at school. Sighing, Marigold looked toward the door. "Should I go after him?

Shannon smiled. "It's up to you. John and I didn't expect

you to babysit Logan so thoroughly. We appreciate it, of course."

"I'm not babysitting because I have to. I like him."

Shannon gave a single nod of her head. "Then maybe you should go after him. Just be aware that veterans, especially those that have recently come back from combat, are more sensitive to situations and words. We've thrown a lot at Logan today."

Marigold snorted. "I know. I may or may not return. I'll see you tomorrow, Shannon. I'm glad you're back."

Shannon waved her off and Marigold left to find Logan.

"What's going on?" John asked her, rolling up beside her chair as she sat down.

Shannon grinned. "I think there might be something going on between Logan and Marigold."

John's eyes went wide, and he glanced at the door. "Seriously? He just got here."

Shannon smiled and leaned over for a kiss. "I know, but I think he's been searching for more than his family for the past few months. You should try to find him a job, because if the look in Marigold's eyes is anything to go by, she's not going to want him to leave. And I'm not sure Logan is going to try to get away very hard."

John shook his head. "What the hell did you do to us, Shannon?"

She smirked and reached out to run her fingernails through his black beard. "Nothing you wouldn't do yourself. I know how you are."

"You've ruined me with good food and good sex and incredible children."

"I did," she agreed, grinning. "And you love it."

"I love you. More than I ever could have known. I was thinking about this earlier." He glanced around to make sure they were out of earshot of the rest of the group. "Years ago when I was in Walter Reed recovering I contemplated throwing myself off the balcony to the pavement below and getting it over with. I didn't think I was high enough to actually kill myself, though. With my luck I figured I'd just fuck up my arms in addition to my legs, and I would have been seriously fucked. I'm very glad I didn't go through with it, or eating a bullet later, when I had the option. I'm not sure why exactly I stuck around to deal with the suck of my life, but I'm very glad I did now."

Shannon's eyes filled with tears at the thought of the despair he had to have been in. "I'm very glad you didn't as well," she whispered, her throat tight. "I can't imagine you not being in my life. Or my kids," she sighed, blotting at her eyes with a napkin. "I think Logan might be dealing with some of that right now. I can tell he feels inadequate being here, but it's deeper than that. I think he's suicidal, and I worry now that if Marigold is growing attached to him, if he leaves it's going to wreck her."

John frowned. "If he is, there's not much that we can do about it. We'll express to him that he has options, but he's a grown, apparently sane, man. If he decides to end it, there's nothing we can do."

Leaning forward he pressed a line of kisses along her jaw and into her hairline. "Let's make our goodbyes to the group and go see those incredible kids."

Shannon nodded and they turned to say their goodbyes.

9

Logan didn't go very far. He knew he was probably overreacting to Marigold's words. She was young and had no idea how many men were left by women in the military.

Amber, his ex, had texted him that they were breaking up. At first, he'd laughed. The laughter had faded when she'd reiterated her position that they would be better off apart. Logan had been in Walter Reed at that time, unable to walk from the injuries to his legs. He was, quite literally, about to undergo his tenth surgery at the time. Logan had been in shock for the better part of a week, not understanding how the woman he'd loved had turned on him so thoroughly. It wasn't until a week later that he realized how royally Amber had fucked him. When he'd been deployed, he'd given her access to his accounts for shared living costs. They'd been living together at the time, for more than a year. By the time Logan had realized she was still using the account, she'd taken almost thirty thousand dollars. Logan had immediately messaged her, asking her what the hell she'd been thinking. Her response had been that the money had been for pain and suffering as she got over their broken engagement.

Logan had had to have a hospital liaison investigate whether or not he could file charges on her. He could, but it would have been an uphill battle proving that she wasn't allowed to have the money since he hadn't taken her off the account when he'd returned to the states, regardless of the fact that he was drugged into a coma because of the burns on his legs. Rather than engage in a lengthy civil court battle, he wrote off the money as a hard learning experience. The retirement account was untouched and he had a small savings account she hadn't known about. He would be fine as long as didn't live beyond his means. The biggest expense he had right now was the hotel.

Logan wasn't surprised when Marigold slipped onto the stool beside him. Of course, she chose his damaged side. Logan knew she deserved an explanation. He'd kind of gone off on her.

"My fiancée screwed me over when I came back from deployment," he admitted. "It's still a little raw. Sorry I snapped."

"I'm sorry I probed," she murmured. "I didn't know."

He shrugged, drawing on the straw of his ice water. He'd realized when his head started to swim that he needed to lay off the beer. It was a bad idea to drink it anyway considering some of the pain meds he was on, and the company he was in.

His father had always complained that the Army had done him dirty, looking for a reason to discharge him for being injured on the job. He'd thrown out his back lifting a crate, or something. The reasoning just didn't hold water, though. The military dealt with thousands of soldiers injured on the job. What was one more? According to his father, when they'd done a random search, they had found a pain pill in his pocket. Logan had always thought there was more to the story, though.

Logan thought they discharged him because of the addictive personality he had. At home, when Dad ran out of pills to treat his 'bad back', he'd moved onto alcohol. And their lives had been hell. They'd always struggled for money and food because first priority had always been liquor to control their father's pain. Because when he was in pain, he was an abusive asshole.

Logan did not want to follow in his footsteps in any way, shape or form.

"I need to clarify, too, though," she continued, voice hesitant, "that I don't believe your scars are as bad as you think. So, I didn't honestly think it would be enough reason to cause a breakup."

Logan felt his face flush and he clenched his jaw. Why did she have to keep at him?

"They're bad enough," he snapped.

One of her hands rested on his right wrist. "They're not. I promise you."

Logan was shocked speechless as she leaned against him and rested her lips against his rough cheek. Her warm breath tickled the hair at his ear. "I promise," she whispered.

Her voice and movement sent chills up the right side of his body. It made the skin on his lower leg and thigh hurt as it tried to respond the same way as the rest of his body. Logan drew in a sharp breath and glanced at her out of the corner of his eye. "Why did you do that?"

If she gave him some bullshit response about his ego or some shit...

"Because I wanted to. You smell..." she paused, her nose

burying behind his ear. "Well, you smell like something I want a candle of."

Those damn goosebumps erupted in another wave down his body, sending sharp awareness throughout. Logan closed his eyes as he savored the reaction of his body. It was startling, feeling something so pleasurable. His life had been made of pain for so long, he'd almost forgotten what it felt like to feel excitement, and arousal.

It scared him how much that single touch rocked him.

Pull away, damn it, he pleaded with her, then was almost gutted when she did. Her brilliant green eyes had gone dark and she blinked a few times before she met his gaze. "Sorry," she murmured, her voice husky. "I don't know why..."

Marigold sat back in her chair and her hand left his wrist. Logan didn't know whether to curse or cry in relief. His body was ricocheting from pleasure to fear to pain and excitement. It had been so long since he'd felt a woman's touch... even before his fiancée had thrown him over, he'd been on deployment for almost a year.

Logan was intrigued in spite of himself. That was desire he'd seen in her expression, he would bet money on it. Did cripples turn her on? Or was she one of those few people actually able to look past the exterior. She was so young...

"How old are you, Marigold?"

She snorted. "Think I don't know what I'm doing? I actually do. I'm twenty-four."

Fuck. She was a year older than he was. He frowned, trying to reorder his thoughts. The arguments about her age just went out the window and he wasn't sure what he was left with.

"If you want to get out of here we can," she said eventually. "I can take you back to the hotel or we can swing by my apartment building and talk to my landlady.

That had been one of the things he'd been out here mulling. His money wasn't going to last forever and if he could save a few bucks on the hotel, it might be worth it. "If you don't mind, can we swing by your place? I'll pay for gas."

She waved a hand, her naturally painted nails catching the light. "I'm not worried about that. I'll charge it to John," she grinned, leaning in to brush his arm conspiratorially.

Slipping off the stool, she pulled on her jacket. When she struggled a little, he reached out and adjusted the arm for her. That shocked him a little, because he'd been in his own head for so long that other people's struggles never even occurred to him. Why was he so conscious of her?

Logan shifted from the stool and settled his crutches. He'd never taken his suit jacket off, so he was ready to go. He was glad for it as he walked through the restaurant door the hostess held open for him and he walked into the brisk air. "When does it normally warm up here?" he called as they walked across the lot.

She gave a bark of laughter. "I have no idea. I just know my power bill has been outrageous because I can't get used to the cold." She fingered the faux-fur collar of her thick wool coat. "Yeah, we could get cold in Arizona, and even some snow occasionally, but nothing like this. It's been a shock for my system, too."

They climbed into the beetle and she cranked the engine. Logan had to laugh when she dragged a blanket from the floorboard of the backseat and spread it across their laps, with the gear shift exposed. "Virginia doesn't have snow like this either, does it?"

A shudder racked him, and he tucked his hands beneath the blanket. He kind of wished he could wrap the damn thing around himself. "We get cold and some snow, definitely, but not so late in the season. Right now, Virginia has grass growing and flowers sprouting."

Marigold nodded, blowing into her cupped hands as they waited to pull out of the lot. "Well, you'll be happy to know she'll be warm by the time we get to the house," she laughed. "Sorry. I've upgraded everything I can in here but the heater is original."

Logan wished he had three more blankets piled on him. As she'd predicted, the car was just beginning to get warm when they pulled into the driveway of a charming three-story Victorian. There were whimsical turrets on each corner, and a massive wraparound porch. He leaned forward, peering through the windshield. "That's a lot of lights. She must love Christmas."

Marigold nodded. "She does, but those aren't the Christmas lights. Those are the all-year lights."

He frowned and squinted. "Is it purple?"

"No," Marigold told him firmly. "It's called Magnificent Merlot. You'll love it even more in the daylight."

Logan turned his head to look at her, not sure if she was joking or not. In the glow from the dash lights he could see the twinkle in her eyes. "Seriously?"

She shrugged as she pulled into a small paved lot in the back of the house. There were two other cars there, a Subaru wagon and a Ford truck. Marigold turned off the ignition, but before he could get out she rested a hand on his arm. "Listen, Mrs. Marshall is a little... different. But she's lovely. Really. Just...smile and nod and try to go along with what she says. She's harmless, I swear, and I love her to pieces. She made my transition up here so much easier."

Logan was a little alarmed, but he nodded. "Okay."

They left the car and went up the back steps. The porch was decorated with cute little statuary and furniture, and he had a feeling it was beautiful in summertime. Marigold crossed to a heavy oak door with a stained-glass inlay of tall flowers. He thought maybe they were orchids, but he didn't know much about plants. It was stunningly beautiful. There was a modern keypad on the door, and Marigold keyed in the code. Pushing open the huge door, she stepped inside.

"Mari, hang up your coat and come in here," a voice called from the depths of the house. "I could hear that damn car of yours coming all the way down the block."

Grinning, Marigold hung her coat on the wall near the door, and offered to take his, but he shook his head. It was much warmer in the house, but he was still fighting a bit of a chill. When most of your bottom half was burned, it was hard to regulate body temperature. When too hot, it was hard to cool because sweat glands had been burned. Too cold and the muscles didn't always contract in shivers the right way. His body was broken and he had to consciously take care of regulating his own temperature. So, the jacket stayed on because he was cold. And damn, he missed his hat...

Logan followed Marigold down a short hallway. It opened up into one of the most beautiful kitchens he'd ever seen, with white granite countertops and dark gray cupboards. There was an older woman standing at the stove, leaning over and looking at a tray of cookies on the stove top. The cookies were flat and a little toasty on the edges. He could only see the woman wore a light purple sweater-set with matching pants, and had bright white hair, a little mussed in the back like she'd been napping in a chair earlier. She turned to Marigold and pointed at the cookies. "What did I do?"

Marigold leaned over the pan and poked at a cookie.

"Not sure, Grandma. Did you put baking powder in it? Maybe the butter was too soft."

"Well," the other woman admitted, "I did fall asleep in my chair watching the news earlier. So, you think it's the butter's fault?"

Logan could see the grin Marigold was fighting. She motioned to him. "Grandma Nancy, this is Logan..."

"Oh, Mari, you found a boyfriend," Grandma interrupted, her face lighting up. "I didn't like the last one you had... man-buns just don't do it for me."

"No, Grandma," Marigold laughed, her cheeks flushed. "This is Logan Vance. The Lost and Found group is investigating something for him and he's in town for a little while. I told him your third apartment space might suit him better than the hotel, even if it's just for a week or two."

Grandma seemed disappointed that he wasn't there as Marigold's boyfriend, but she moved toward him with a smile, peering up into his face. "Oh, Marigold, he reminds me of my W.C." She lifted an arthritic hand and Logan made himself hold still as she rested a palm on his scarred cheek. "Look at those eyes. My W.C. had eyes as beautiful as yours. They swept this girl off her feet so fast my mother and daddy didn't know what happened," she giggled. "Looks like you got into a tangle with something nasty. Gives you a devil-may-care look." She winked at him and grinned, a silver crown shining on her canine.

Logan couldn't help but smile back. He looked at Marigold. Her expression was wary, as if she were worried that Logan would rebuff Nancy's advances, but he could tell the older woman meant no harm. And she didn't mean to be condescending. The memories were there in her expression. He could hear the sincerity in her voice.

"W.C. was your husband?" he asked.

"For seventy years," Nancy breathed. "He was my partner in everything. A part of me died when he did."

Logan stared at her, incredulous. "You were married for seventy years?"

Nancy gave a nod of her head. "Married in 1947. We had seven children, seventeen grandchildren and..." she started counting on her fingers. "At last count thirteen great-grand-children."

"That's so impressive," Logan told her. "I don't know how you even keep track of them all."

Nancy grinned and tapped her temple. Her finger was bent with arthritis, but the nail was painted a deep maroon. "Ninety years young," she told him, grinning. She picked up a tall thermal, glitter-encrusted cup. Ice tinkled against the aluminum on the inside. "Jesus juice. Keeps you young."

Logan lifted his brows in surprise. The right didn't work as well as the left, but he thought he pulled off the expression. "That's incredible, Nancy."

She waved a hand, then tucked it into his elbow. It was a bit awkward maneuvering that crutch away, but he handed it off to Marigold, then tightened his grip on the other side. He let Nancy lead him from the room.

"Now, this rear apartment gets a lot of sunlight in the morning," she said brusquely. "You'll have to deal with some kitchen noise, but it's cozy and warm. You're welcome to it for as long as you need it."

She named a figure that seemed incredibly low. "That's for the week?"

"Month. I believe it's fair, because it isn't a full-sized apartment. You're responsible for your own space. I have a girl come in once a week to clean the common areas. If you want her to do your space it's an extra twenty-five a week, but she'll do everything."

"That sounds fantastic," he murmured, looking around.

The rooms were decent sized with hardwood floors, just like what was running through the rest of the house. It looked like there were just two rooms, the bathroom through the far door and this bigger space, sectioned off into areas by the furniture. In one corner was a large bed with a heavy wooden headboard and matching dresser. There was a sitting room area with a decent looking couch and chair, and the two areas could be separated by a folding wall partition if he wanted some privacy. On the far side, near the exterior door, was a compact galley kitchen. The appliances seemed newer. There was literally nothing wrong with the space.

Logan thought about his end goal. When he'd headed west, he hadn't really had much to live for, merely a mild curiosity about his family history and a need to explain himself to Miller's family. He wasn't sure he wanted to invest in this cozy, way too welcoming space. Or these incredible, fascinating women.

Anxiety began to churn in his gut. There was too much coming at him too fast and he needed to back off.

"I'm going to have to think about this, Nancy. I'm not sure how long I'm actually going to be here and I don't know if it's worth moving my stuff."

Nancy looked a little crestfallen, but he made himself turn away, grabbing the crutch from Marigold as he went. He'd known the elderly woman for five minutes. It wasn't his business to safeguard her feelings.

Then he caught sight of Marigold. Her clear green eyes were narrowed and her berry colored lips that had sent shivers up his body were pursed. Logan made himself walk away. It wasn't his responsibility to keep them happy. Period.

"Can you drive me back to the hotel?"

Without waiting for an answer, he went through the doorway. He heard her murmuring to Nancy, her voice cajoling, but he left without a backward glance.

The car was unlocked so he climbed in, wedging his crutches in beside his legs. Within a few seconds, Marigold was climbing behind the wheel. She didn't say anything as she started the car and pulled away from the house.

Logan scowled as he looked into the dark, cold night through his side window. It wasn't his job, damn it, to ensure their happiness. He didn't know them. Period. They weren't his relatives or lovers.

The thought of Marigold as a lover made him pause. Well, he'd pretty much nixed even the chance of friendship, now.

MARIGOLD WAS ANGRY, but his silence gave her a chance to think about why he had pulled away so sharply.

It had to seem too good to be true, everything that was going on. John was finding Logan's family and now she was offering him a place to call home, even if it was temporary. Grandma Nancy was amazing, and if he hadn't had anything like her before, maybe he could feel threatened.

His total aloneness worried her, and she'd rushed in to try to change that for him.

"I'm sorry if you felt like Nancy was too much," she murmured. "She tends to adopt anyone that lives in her house. And I'll admit, it's been kind of nice having someone to worry about me again."

"She seemed like a nice lady," he said softly. "Wine and all."

Marigold grinned in the dark car. Yeah, Nancy was definitely a different kind of bird. "Don't let the wine or the age fool you, Logan. She's sharp as a tack. She loved her husband like crazy till he died a couple years ago. They've lived in that house all their married lives."

It was incredibly sweet, the way the two of them had been together. Marigold had seen the pictures, and all the little nick-nacks around the house with their initials together. In all of their pictures, they were sharing love-filled glances. It was so sickeningly sweet.

And she wanted it. She wanted that same devotion she could see spilling from W.C.'s eyes, the way he touched Nancy's shoulder and held her hand to make sure she didn't fall. In a way she even wanted the heartbreak she could see in Nancy's eyes, because it meant she had loved deeply and completely.

Marigold hadn't felt that kind of love, yet, and she wasn't really in a hurry to. School would be taking a lot of her time, coming up, and it wasn't fair to half-ass a relationship. She'd refused to allow herself a pet for the same reason. It wouldn't be fair to the animal if she wasn't there to care for it. Her heart ached for something to cuddle and love, but she wasn't going to allow her need to eclipse another being's emotional health.

"I can't imagine being married that long," he murmured.

She didn't say anything, though it was the perfect opportunity to bring up the ex. If he wanted to talk about her she would let him bring her up.

For most of the ride back to his hotel she held her tongue. It wasn't her business if he wanted to rebuff their offers of friendship. She needed to quit expecting more from him.

When she dropped him off at the front entrance,

though, she wavered. "If you need a ride anywhere, just let me know. Obviously, I'm just a few minutes away."

He turned to look at her for a moment, his stunningly bright eyes dimmed in the shadow of the car. "I'll think about it."

Marigold knew that he wouldn't call her, and that hurt her heart. It was his choice though. She watched as he made his way into the hotel, then she pulled away. She couldn't worry about every guy/client that came through the LNF doors.

10

On Monday, Logan called John in the hopes there had been a breakthrough in his investigation, but there hadn't been. He'd been hoping that he would have some reason to go down to the office and see Marigold. They hadn't parted on the best of terms and he'd had a long, boring weekend to regret that. Several times he'd picked up his phone to call her, then changed his mind. What exactly would he say to her?

Oh, hey, sorry I was a dick. You were just too nice and it freaked me out because I don't want to get attached to anyone in case I decide to kill myself.

How lame, metaphorically, could he be?

If he had any sense at all he would take her up on the housing offer, if it was still available, and hope they didn't see each other at the house or something. Yeah, right. He'd seen the look in her eyes. The one that made awareness rattle his bones. If he had any balls at all he would test that look and allow his life to take a different path.

And the kiss on his ear... Fuck. The scene kept replaying in his mind, and he wasn't sure what to make of that, exactly.

All he knew was that it kept him up at night, replaying through his mind. Wondering how far she'd go.

Man, it hurt when it didn't work out, though.

A relationship wasn't for him. There was no way he was going to allow himself to stick around and be a burden on someone. He looked down at his legs. Since he was in the hotel room he hadn't bothered to dress in more than boxers and a T-shirt, though he should have. He hated looking at himself. Scars crisscrossed his legs in every direction, and there were chunks out of his thighs. All shrapnel wounds. Just like the divot out of his right calf and the missing toes on his right foot. His right knee had been replaced because it had been completely shattered. Sometimes he wondered if that wouldn't have been better to have amputated the damn thing. It gave him more trouble than anything else. The IED had blown up beneath their vehicle, and the same metal that had protected most of his vital organs had destroyed his lower extremities. The doctors had said that they couldn't do much more for him, although his physical therapy guy thought he could do more than he already was. That was hard to believe just because of the level of pain he dealt with daily.

Pain pills barely controlled the agony. Logan had been trying to wean himself off of them, but sometimes the pain was just too much, and he would have to take one. Or even a few of them. It made him feel weak to need pills, and he hated it.

At least he was here, though. Wasn't that what they'd told him at Walter Reed? You made it back when others died.

In his mind, the ones that had died had gotten off easy.

Guilt gnawed at him. He didn't like thinking that way. Miller and Harrison and Stafford hadn't deserved to die. If they had any say in the matter, they would probably all be here, no matter how wounded they would be.

At least they weren't in unending, uncontrollable pain, though. Every day was a trial, and he wanted to get off the fucking merry-go-round. It was what he was living for. Force himself to go see Miller's family and get the fuck out.

He still wasn't sure how he wanted to approach them. He'd called the number to the house, then hung up when someone young and female had answered, probably Miller's younger sister. Logan didn't feel like he was strong enough to go out yet. The address was mapped on his phone, marking the place eighteen point three miles away where his best friend's family lived.

In a way, he was excited to see them again. Several times over the years he'd spoken to the family and visited, and they were on a first-name basis. He'd been to Miller's home. Eaten their food. Joked around with his mom, a single parent, and his sixteen year-old sister. The thought of looking into Lisa Miller's face and trying to explain to her why her boy was gone absolutely gutted him. They'd been notified officially, of course, but it was his moral responsibility as Miller's commanding officer and best friend to explain to the family why their boy hadn't returned home.

What answers could he give? He was still wondering what the hell had happened himself.

One minute they'd been joking around like they always did and the next, he'd been swiping pieces of brain matter off his face, trying to understand why his ears were ringing. Just that quick their lives had shifted and gone in a different direction. Most of the time Logan felt like his compass needle was still spinning.

He missed his battle buddies. They'd done everything

together and now that he had the toughest mission before him, they weren't here to support him.

Walter Reed had released him last October. In February, just a few months after he'd gotten out of the hospital, he'd talked to Harrison's family in Florida. They hadn't known what to do with him standing on their front porch. In the end they hadn't invited him in, which he was okay with. Rex Harrison had been his friend, but he hadn't been as close as Miller.

After Florida he'd flown directly to Milford, Kansas, where Charles Stafford had been from. Charlie's father had railed at him, calling him every name in the book for not bringing his only son home. Charlie's mother Charlotte had cried and melted into her husband's arms, and Logan had felt like he'd hurt them unnecessarily. They'd received the official notice months before, and his presence had only resurrected more pain.

The next day, though, when he'd been packing his bags, Charlotte had invited him out for coffee. The situation had been stilted and painful, but in the end, they'd been able to laugh about some of Charlie's antics. He'd been the joker of the team and Logan felt like he'd been able to leave Charlotte with some good memories of her handsome son.

Miller's family was completely different. In a way, Logan felt closer to them, even now, than he did the remnants of his own family. He knew that Lisa had a volatile temper, and that she could quite literally beat him for losing her son. Logan didn't want to hurt her. Didn't want to hurt either one of them. He'd rather get blown up again than cause them any more pain.

He had to talk to them, though. Putting it off wasn't going to make it any easier.

The weight of the guilt he was carrying was going to kill him before he could do it himself.

For a moment he allowed himself to feel how utterly alone he was in the world. If he killed himself now, literally no one would mourn him. His father had disowned him, his mother was too hung up on his father, his brother was probably tweaking in jail and his sister...well, she was gone.

Marigold might miss him, a little. But she'd probably chalk it up as just another veteran suicide, eventually. He would be one of the twenty, or whatever the number was now, a day that just disappeared from life. No more pain, no more loneliness.

A small voice inside him wondered if that loneliness wasn't partially his own fault. After he'd gotten out of Walter Reed last year, it had taken a while for him to even leave his efficiency apartment. It had been so hard adapting to life after the military. People just ran around like idiots, feeling self-important as they carried their designer coffees into jobs that no one cared about. There was no place for him to fit in.

There was counseling, of course. He'd gone a few times, trying to get what he could out of the experience, but it left him feeling even more isolated. They wanted to pump drugs into him, saying that his childhood issues, his combat trauma and survivor guilt were what they called Complex Post-Traumatic Stress. C-PTS. He'd never heard of it before, and he wasn't sure he believed in it. Certainly not enough to take happy pills. Logan realized very quickly that he would rather be clear-headed and morose than drugged and oblivious. It was bad enough he had to take pain pills.

Marigold came to mind, with her bright green eyes and dark hair. Logan had a feeling that she would have a field day playing in his brain once she got through school.

Sighing, he swiveled to face his laptop, but those eyes taunted him. The hurt he'd put there didn't sit well with him, but he wasn't sure how to approach her to apologize.

He looked at the phone on the bedside table. It was silent. It was always silent. The most excitement he'd had recently was when a telemarketing company had added him to their roster. Though he hadn't driven for more than a year, and had no vehicle, he listened to the warning that his car warranty was about to expire.

TV sucked. The one time he'd turned it on he'd gotten so sick of the political ads he'd turned it off immediately.

When there was a knock at his door, he almost didn't believe he'd actually heard it. The knock came again, motivating him up out of the chair. He crossed the room and peered through the peephole.

Those brilliant, smiling green eyes he'd just been thinking about looked back at him. Fuck, what was she doing here?

"Hold on," he said, shuffling back enough to open the door. He peered around the edge. "Marigold. What are you doing here?"

She lifted her brows, looking curiously at the door. "Well, it's a beautiful afternoon and I thought I'd get you out of the crappy hotel room. Have you moved at all since I left you here Friday?"

He scowled, not liking how transparent she thought he was. "Yes, I have, actually."

She rolled her expressive eyes. She wore her glasses today, as well as a pair of blue jeans that seemed painted on her they were so tight. "For more than getting ice down the hallway?"

His face must have revealed guilt because she laughed.

"Come on. If you're going to be out here you might as well see the city."

Logan stared at her for a moment. "Do you mind waiting for me downstairs? I'm not dressed."

The humor faded from her expression and something more aware settled in. Her irises dilated and he wondered, somewhat regretfully, what she thought he looked like without his clothes. "Believe me," he said quickly. "You're not missing anything."

She blinked and her cheeks flushed with color. Quickly, she backed away from the door. "I'll be downstairs in the pick-up loop. Take your time."

Logan shut the door firmly, wondering what the hell he was going to do. The woman was stirring emotion he didn't want to deal with, let alone have.

MARIGOLD THOUGHT he had agreed to go with her, but it took him a while to get downstairs. The front desk clerk kept giving her the side-eye through the big window to the left, but Marigold wasn't moving. There was plenty of room for other vehicles to get around her if they needed. Maybe he just didn't like her car.

When Logan eventually appeared, her heart thudded with excitement. Though he was too old in the eyes, there was something about him that drew her. She had been praying for John to find out information as much as Logan had, just so that she had a reason to see him again. Then, she thought, fuck it. She was a grown ass woman. If she thought Logan actually meant what he'd said, she wouldn't have bothered, but she truly believed that he had fears of becoming attached, then being hurt again. He had told her as much with the no commitment crap. And if she put herself in his shoes, so to speak, she would probably have fears of being a burden on someone. Without his even speaking the words she knew his injuries were catastrophic and would be something he would have to deal with the rest of his life.

The blue ball cap shaded his face as he settled into the car, the crutches going alongside his legs. It was cold out and he'd bundled into his gray wool coat. There was a navy-blue sweater beneath the coat, and blue jeans. He wore those brown boots a lot, and she wondered if he needed the support for his ankle joints.

"We can put those crutches in the back if you need more room," she said.

"I'm okay," Logan told her, glancing out the side window at the attendant, then back at her.

Marigold didn't think he turned his head away to hide from her as much anymore, and she appreciated that. The scars on his face were bad, but not hide away from the world bad.

"I'll admit, I'm surprised to see you," he said. "I thought I made my position clear."

She looked him in the eye. "No commitment, I know. But I was worried about you. I doubt you've eaten anything decent for a while, so I thought I'd take you to a local watering hole. It has incredibly good food, and you'll be supporting a veteran."

His jaw tightened, and he stared at her for a long moment, before eventually giving her a reluctant nod. "Fine."

"But before we do that, I thought I'd show you a few highlights of the city." She smiled at him and lifted her brows, trying to lighten his mood. She'd jerked him out of his lair and he wasn't necessarily happy about it, but he could lighten up a little.

"I'd appreciate that. Not sure I'm up for hiking the mountains yet, but maybe another day."

She snorted, appreciating the attempt at humor, though it was self-denigrating. "That's fine. This is a car tour. No hiking needed unless you want to get out and look around."

Marigold turned toward downtown first. They were only a few blocks from the capitol building. When they idled by, she pointed. "If you stand on one of those steps you'll be exactly one mile above sea level."

"Ah, very cool," Logan murmured. "I always wondered where that point was."

Marigold huffed out a laugh and waved a hand. "Now you know."

She turned down a couple of streets and began to head north. "Denver is a very artsy city. You'll find so many different art museums, from fine art to street art. This is one of my favorite areas so far. It's called RiNo, for River North."

The little car purred her way through traffic and Marigold thought that Logan might be appreciating what he was seeing. A couple of times he craned his neck to keep something in sight as long as possible. Then she slowed and flicked on her blinker, waiting for cross traffic to pass. "I think this is my favorite street in Denver, so far. It's called Art Alley."

They idled down the street, looking at design after design on the walls of the buildings. "Okay," he breathed, leaning forward in his seat. "This is pretty cool."

Marigold grinned, so glad that she'd brought him here. "Supposedly there's a street festival in the fall. New artists come in and paint new murals. Sometimes they go over the existing ones, so I've taken pictures of all of these before they're lost."

"This really is amazing. I admire anyone with creative inclinations. I definitely don't have them."

"I do a little bit," she admitted. "I love that there are classes everywhere, here. I'm signed up for a couple this month."

They drifted along with the rest of the traffic, not in a rush to get anywhere.

"Do you like books?" she asked. "There's an amazing bookstore not too far from here."

"I do like books," he admitted. "You?"

Marigold appreciated that he was at least responding to her. "I love them, though I tend to read a lot of fiction, urban fantasy in particular."

He gave a nod like he actually knew what urban fantasy was. Maybe he did.

They drove for a few more minutes until she pulled along a street and pointed out a series of windows. "This is the Tattered Cover Lodo, or Lower Downtown. It's an amazing store. Would you like to check it out?"

He gave her a nod. "I would, actually."

She maneuvered close to the front doors and idled. "Can I drop you off here?"

"Find your parking spot, Marigold. There are cars behind you."

Sighing at his obstinacy, she turned down the street. There were several pay lots nearby, but she wanted to get as close as possible for Logan and his stubborn ass. She managed to snag a compact space about a quarter of the way down from the store. Damn, that was lucky.

Marigold was surprised that he even wanted to go in. Logan seemed to be in his own little isolationist bubble.

Maybe this was his attempt to placate her, or something. She wasn't upset that he hadn't wanted to move into Nancy's house, just disappointed. It would have been good for him.

She slowed her gait to stay beside him as they walked toward the front door. Surprisingly, they were the only ones on the sidewalk at that moment. She watched the placement of his crutches on the ground, watching for stray ice patches. It was pretty clear, and the sun was shining, melting what was left on the sidewalks. When he paused and turned to her slightly, it took her a second to realize what he was doing.

"Marigold, I want to apologize for the other night. I'm not... that felt like a commitment to me. The house was fantastic and Nancy seems to be a doll, but I'm just not ready to engage further."

She shrugged, trying not to show her hurt. She scuffed at the sidewalk with the toe of her boot. "That's fine, Logan. I was just trying to help a guy out. No commitment stated, inferred or requested."

He nodded slowly, dark brows furrowed under his ball cap. "Roger that."

They took off walking again, but she couldn't help asking, "What if you find family, though?"

Logan gave her a narrow-eyed look from beneath the cap, crutches swinging. "I guess I'll see when and if it happens. As of right now, I don't think John will find anything."

The massive bookstore was not especially crowded, though Marigold knew it was a matter of time. When they entered through the front door and went up the steps, Logan had to stop and stare. It was a beautiful old building, and her favorite of the four locations. It called to her heart.

Union Station was a popular shopping area, with some

fantastic restaurants nearby. Marigold had come here on a few dates. The excellent food helped make up for the not-so-excellent companionship. And the bookstore was to die for. She spent a lot of time here, in this particular store. Sometimes she brought her laptop just to sit and soak up the calm ambience. She had a feeling when school started she would be here even more.

"Okay, you weren't kidding," he said softly. "What a cool space."

Crutches planted firmly on the hardwood floors, legs moving, he headed toward the history section. Marigold didn't feel like she needed to babysit the man, so she headed toward the magazine section. Shannon had sent her down several times with petty cash to load up on gun magazines for the reception area and the guys' break room. No Vogue or Good Housekeeping for the LNF offices, she thought with a snort.

Then she headed to the urban fantasy section. Logan was also in fiction, now, and she wondered what he liked to read. Looked like westerns. Hm. She watched as he walked down the hardwood aisle, crutches hanging from his arms. He could walk without them, but his gait was stiff, like he'd been sitting in one position too long. But he could move. The crutches appeared to be insurance when out in public.

That was good to know.

They hung in the bookstore for almost an hour and a half, settling at the coffee shop to peruse what they might buy. Marigold had picked up a new Ilona Andrews book. She couldn't help but roll her eyes when she saw the book on genealogy. "John will find your family," she promised. "Save your money."

Giving her a crooked smile, he set the book aside and

pulled a different one from the stack in front of him. "Do you know if this is a good one?"

It was a book on the Denver art scene. "It is, but I suggest you get a second one, as well. Or I can loan you mine."

"If you don't mind," he murmured, lifting his coffee cup and looking at the rest of the stack.

She nodded mutely, wondering if he considered a book loan a commitment.

Don't stir the pot, Marigold!

The thick, dark hair at his ears flipped out a little, like the band of the hat was constricting them. If she had even the slightest encouragement she would run her fingers through it, putting the waves in order. That was way too familiar, though. Glancing down, she watched his hands flip through the books. They were broad and obviously strong, though looked like they'd been through hell, just like the rest of him.

They each left with a bag of reading material. When they got back to the car, he let her take his bag of books so that he could get in the car. He braced the door when she would have shut it and looked up at her. Even in the dimness of the evening his eyes were beautiful. "Thank you for dragging the bear out of the cave. Honestly, I was going a little stir crazy."

"No problem," she murmured, doing everything she could to hide her joy at his words. With a trembling breath, she circled the car and settled in behind the wheel. "It's going on seven. Are you getting hungry?"

"Not too bad. Maybe we can drive around a little more?"

"Absolutely."

They left the parking space and she turned right, then another right. "This is Coors Field, where the Colorado Rockies play." She drove for a few blocks. "And this is the

Central Market, a trendy shopping area. The Denver Zoo is that way," she pointed, "and it's fantastic."

Marigold drove him around for almost an hour, showing him landmarks and highlights of the city she'd grown to love in the few months she'd been here. "The snow is pretty epic. I will say that. But there are as many winter festivals and excursions as summer. Bike paths criss-cross the city."

"I won't be using those in the near future," he said shortly.

"Well, you might," she said carefully. "There are a lot of trikes and even hand bikes out there as well as regular bikes. There's no reason for you to be trapped in your room, or in a city you know nothing about."

His jaw tightened at her gently chiding words. "Let me tell you something, Marigold. You may be a little older than I am, but you're very young and idealistic. After you have to hear a child cry out because your face scared them, or have a guy ask you if it was worth the damage, being over there in the war he didn't agree with, only then can you tell me how I should live my life. If I want to stay in my hotel room the entire time I'm here, it's my choice. If I decide I don't want to deal with the bullshit anymore and put a bullet in my brain, it's my choice," he gritted, eyes narrowed in anger. "There's no walking in my boots. They were blown off me in Afghanistan. Stick to your lane."

Marigold blinked rapidly, not used to anyone barking at her that way. It hurt her heart, the things that he'd said, because they were surely something he had experienced. "You're right," she said eventually, breathing through her watering eyes. "It's not my place to tell you how to live. I can encourage you to live the life you've been given, though."

Then the bullet-in-the-brain bit sank in, and she turned

to glare at him. "And don't joke about shooting yourself. It's not even funny."

"I know," he said, voice low. And he left it at that. Which scared her even more.

Marigold was a bundle of nerves when they finally pulled into Frog Dog. The parking lot was somewhat crowded, so she had no doubt she would recognize a bunch of the people here. How would Logan react, coming to a place so densely packed with other disabled veterans? She hoped he didn't think she was messing with him after he'd snapped at her.

"This is a popular little spot for LNF, and they have fantastic food."

They left the car and headed for the heavy oak front doors of the bar and grill. She held the door open for him and stayed behind, determined to let him choose where they sat. He hesitated, and she could tell he was scoping out the room. For those uninitiated to the Frog Dog, it could be a bit shocking, seeing the obvious veterans crowding the room. There was an older crowd that were regulars, with their black memorial Vietnam Veteran or Korean War hats and even a few old uniform jackets on display. The younger crowd was more dispersed, and there were a few hats, but not a lot.

Logan picked a direction and she followed, not surprised when they ended up in the farthest, darkest corner, out of the line of sight of the many TVs broadcasting sports. Logan took the seat against the wall, leaving her with her back to the room. Marigold knew that was a coping mechanism to deal with unfamiliar surroundings, so she didn't say anything. Within just a few seconds a waitress approached them, handing them menus.

"Hi guys. Welcome to the Frog Dog."

It was Ember, Zeke's fiancée. "Hi, Ember."

"Oh, hey, Marigold, right?" Ember's face lit with a smile. "What a unique name. My mom used to love Marigolds. I'm glad to see you again. What can I get you guys to drink?"

"I'll just do a diet-Coke for now."

She watched as Ember turned her bright expression to Logan. She was a knockout, with long dark hair and dark, seductive eyes, and an amazing empathy. The woman didn't even blink at the scars on his face, and Logan seemed a little shocked. "Uh, something draft."

"IPA or domestic," she asked.

He frowned, considering. "Something IPA. Light."

"Gotcha. Zeke has a couple he likes. I'll have him bring them over. Do you guys want an appetizer?"

"Oh," Marigold said, "fried pickles, please!"

Grinning, Ember nodded. "You got it. I'll be back with your drinks."

Marigold leaned forward on the table. "In case you missed it, Ember is Zeke's fiancée. They've been engaged for a good while, I think. Not sure when they're getting married. Anyway, her dad built this bar so that he and his friends could have a place to hang, but I think Ember and Zeke have pretty much taken over the running of it. Her dad has a new love interest so he hasn't been paying as much attention to the business."

Logan gave her an understanding nod. "I don't think I've met either of them."

"Zeke is... a former Marine, I believe. Most of the people at LNF are Marines, with a few former Navy SEALs thrown in."

He nodded again and glanced up. His eyes widened and Marigold assumed Zeke was on his way, all six foot five of him. The dude was built like a heavy-duty football player, with broad, muscular shoulders and trim hips. She'd seen more than one woman preen with interest before they saw his ravaged face. As much as she felt for Logan and the healing scars he was dealing with, she'd never seen anyone so harshly damaged as Zeke. His entire face was a mass of old burn and surgery scars, some faded white, a couple still angry red. It was obvious he'd had a devastating injury, and the doctors putting him back together hadn't necessarily been successful.

Logan looked at him, obviously shocked. Then he jerked and seemed to come back to himself.

Zeke, bless his big old heart, set the flight of pale amber beers down in front of Logan and the diet Coke in front of her. "Hi guys. Marigold, good to s-s-see you again."

Zeke thrust his scarred hand out to Logan. "Zeke Foster. I think I saw y-y-you at LNF the other d-day."

"Logan Vance. Yes, I saw you, as well. John is helping me track down some family."

Zeke nodded, grinning crookedly. "He's good at that. Mind of I j-j-join you for a minute? I'll tell you about the b-b-beer."

Zeke pulled up a chair and started pointing at each of the beers on the flight of glasses. Marigold wasn't much of a beer drinker, so she didn't pay a lot of attention, just watched the men interact with each other. Zeke was one of the most self-assured men she'd ever seen, and she knew working at the bar was probably a big part of it. Ember was another part of it. She'd seen them together, laughing and touching. The love between them was obvious for anyone to see. Though she hadn't been around them a lot, she'd seen Ember stroking his rough cheeks and the lines of his surgery scars.

Maybe Zeke's self-assurance would filter over to Logan.

Ember came back at one point to drop off their appetizer and take their food order. She smiled crookedly as she watched the men sip from the glasses, and leaned down to Marigold. "Zeke is really loving some of the local IPAs coming out right now. Sorry if he's horned in on your date."

Marigold snorted. "This is not a date. Believe me."

Ember looked between her and Logan, her dark brows raised skeptically, as if to ask, *you sure?*

Marigold watched Ember go, wondering if the other woman was seeing something she herself couldn't. Even when she'd kissed his ear the other night he hadn't seemed especially moved, so she'd drawn back. Then he'd given her the no-commitment spiel and distanced himself from Nancy's. She was done making advances and being shot down.

11

Logan didn't like the derision he'd heard in Marigold's snort. He tried to listen to Zeke go on about the Lion's Head IPA, or whatever it was. The beer was good, and the information had been interesting, but when Ember had asked Marigold about this being a date, he'd been too interested in the answer. Then inordinately disappointed at the disdainful snort. Why had she done that? Was he not good enough to go out with?

Then Logan realized how hypocritical he was being. He proclaimed not to want commitment, but when she disavowed it he was peeved.

Make up your damn mind, already.

Plus, she'd kissed him. Kind of. And he'd basically shut her down.

The previous version of himself, the guy before he'd been blown to hell, would have loved to date Marigold. She was unique and beautiful and didn't seem to mind looking at his ugly mug. Hell, if the flush earlier at the hotel was anything to go by, there was attraction there as well. He doubted she would move on it again, though. It would probably be up to him.

Marigold excused herself to go to the restroom, and he watched her walk away, unable to help himself.

Zeke had obviously asked him a question, because he was staring at him expectantly. "Sorry, Zeke. What was that?"

Zeke smiled softly. "Nothing, buddy. I'll get out of y-your hair and let you en-en-en...have fun on your date."

"This isn't a date," he denied, repeating Marigold's words.

Zeke hesitated, then turned to look at the dark-haired woman behind the bar. "Let me give you a w-word of advice, Logan. Even if you don't want to, if every p-p-part of your b-being wants you to curl up into a ball and fade away from the world and commitment, d-d-don't. Take the chance on the girl. And have faith that she knows what she wants."

Logan frowned. "I appreciate the advice, but I've only known her a couple of days. We're not dating."

Zeke shrugged his broad shoulders, glancing back at him. "Ember and I n-n-never really did date. But she is the core of my heart." He pushed up from the chair. "I'll get y-y-your food and another beer."

"Thanks, Zeke."

Logan watched the man leave, envying him his ease of movement. The guy looked fighting ready, and he wondered if there were ever any scuffles in the bar.

He watched Zeke cross to Ember. By the way her eyes widened and she shifted, Logan thought Zeke had stroked her ass beneath the line of the bar. They grinned at each other, and Logan felt a moment of remorse that he wouldn't ever experience that kind of relationship. Once he talked to Miller's family and found out what he could about his own family, good or bad, he was done. He would be exiting stage left and getting the fuck out of here.

The thought wasn't as reassuring as it had once been, though. In point of fact, it chafed.

When Marigold returned to the table, he tried a smile on her, feeling like an ass when she blinked in shock. Maybe he had been a prick to be around, he realized. Or maybe his face just looked especially bad when he smiled. Shit.

Marigold returned his smile, though, as she slipped into her seat. She seemed a little flustered as she took a sip of her cola. "Zeke is a good guy."

"He is," Logan agreed, reaching for the basket in the middle of the table. He popped one of the golden bundles into his mouth and jerked. "What the fuck is this?"

Marigold giggled, reaching for one as well. "Deep-fried pickles."

Logan made as much of a face as he could, pushing the basket toward her. "They're all yours."

He glanced around the space, looking at the memorabilia on the walls and hanging from the rafters. "This is a neat place. Again, thank you for getting me out of the hotel room."

"No problem. I know I would go nuts cooped in a little room like that. And even with your mobility issues, there are other things that you can do and appreciate."

"Yeah," he said, softly, appreciating that she hadn't let him shove her away. Marigold had been nothing but kind to him. Everybody had been. Zeke's words rang in his mind, nagging at him. Abruptly, he came to a decision. "I'm going to take that room at Nancy's."

Marigold's mouth dropped open and she blinked, obviously shocked. "What about your no commitment, thing?"

He shifted, feeling uncomfortable under her probing

look. It had been less than two hours since he'd said that and he hated to be called on his shit. "I still don't want any commitments, but I'm sick of the hotel room. Depending upon what John finds, and another task I have to do, I'll be here at least another week or two. Might as well be more comfortable during that time."

Smiling broadly, Marigold reached out and touched his hand on the table. "I think you'll enjoy it there. And though Nancy appears effusive, she knows when to give you space. Plus," she said considering, "since you look like her W.C., I think she'll appreciate having you in the house. As long as you're willing to stay."

Ember brought their food, then, with Zeke trailing behind with drink refills. "Enjoy, guys," she told them, dropping an extra stack of napkins on the table before they left.

The food was upscale grub and Logan realized how hungry he was at the first bite. They'd had the coffee earlier but obviously it hadn't been enough. He plowed through the food, honestly surprised at the quality. Bar food tended to be fried and unhealthy, but his steak tacos were freshly made and loaded with vegetables. The steak was so freaking tender.

"Ember does most of the cooking," Marigold said around a mouthful of grilled chicken, "and I will say her Friday catfish fry is out of this world. I'll have to bring you sometime."

He nodded. "I can go for some good fried fish."

What the hell. If life was handing him opportunities, maybe he needed to start taking them.

So, when she asked about his other task, he looked at her, debating, and let some of his tightly-held control go. "I have to talk to my best-friend's family."

"Oh!" she looked confused. "Are they local?"

"Boulder," he said. "On the north side."

"That's not far away. Is he going to come down and get you?"

Logan stared at her for a long minute, then blinked and looked down at his uneaten food. He wiped at his forehead, as if he could still feel... then he used his napkin to wipe his forehead, not understanding when he didn't see the blood he could feel rolling down his skin. Miller... Miller was nowhere to be seen. He wouldn't be grinning at him again or punching him in the shoulder... Flashes of a monochromatic sandy landscape pinged through his brain, with the guys laughing and joking and shooting and fighting. He'd been with Miller since he'd been deployed and they'd fallen into such an easy, brotherly relationship. It had been like nothing he'd ever experienced. Miller had been the brother he'd literally dreamed of having.

But he'd died. And Logan hadn't. It was so unfair, giving him a brother, then taking him away.

Logan drew in a ragged breath and closed his lids, his eyes dry from not blinking. Then they flushed with too much liquid, and his throat tightened. Tightening his jaw, he turned his head. Marigold had moved her chair. She was now sitting right beside him, with her arm around his waist. He hadn't seen her move or felt her touch until now. Stiffening his shoulders, he drew away. And she let him.

Dropping his head, he wiped his eyes and cleared his throat. Embarrassment washed through him. "How long was I gone?"

She was watching him carefully, her expression not giving anything away. "About ten minutes. Long enough for your food to get cold." She forced a smile, but the corner of her lips quivered.

"I'm sorry, Marigold. Did I say anything?"

She tilted her chin up. "You asked for Miller a couple of times. Is he your friend?"

Logan nodded, glancing around the bar.

"Don't worry," Marigold said. "I think Zeke knew something was going on, because he cranked the volume on the far game TV and started pulling attention that way."

Logan looked at the big guy behind the bar. Yep, he was looking at him now. Logan gave him a slight wave and received a nod in return. Since this was a veteran's bar, Zeke had probably seen a few guys slip off the edge of reality.

"I'm so sorry, Logan," Marigold whispered. "I should have thought about your words. I just didn't connect the dots."

He shook his head. "Not your place to connect the dots. That doesn't happen very often and I didn't expect it to happen just now. I don't think I ever told you what exactly I was doing. It was my fault and I apologize."

"God, quit apologizing. It was my fuck up."

Logan reached for his beer. Even though it was warm, it felt good sliding down his throat. "He was my best friend," he told her softly. "I didn't like him at first. He was too nice. Too... goody two-shoes. You know what I mean?"

Marigold nodded, leaning forward enough to prop her chin on her hand. "Was it the way he was raised?"

"Oh, yeah... he was the son of a single mother. He has a sister about five years younger. Lisa took her job very seriously, raising her kids, and didn't spare the love or the discipline. Miller felt responsible for his little sister a lot of the time, and he had to be the example she followed. You always hear stories about kids following in their father's footsteps, going into the military. Miller actually followed in his mother's footsteps. She'd been a staff sergeant in the Army and had deployed to the Persian Gulf. And her dad had deployed as well years ago."

"Incredible."

"He planned on staying in the Army long enough to retire, carrying on the family line."

Logan stared out the dark window, watching a car turn into the parking lot. "So, my task is to go see my best friend's family. That was the main reason I came out here. Three of my men died that day. I talked to Harrison's family in Florida and Stafford's family in Kansas. But I left Miller's family for last."

"Because it's the hardest," she said softly.

Logan gave her a crooked smile. "Yeah, I guess. I've only been procrastinating for months, since I was released from the hospital."

"I don't think you've been procrastinating," Marigold said, touching his hand. "I think you've been healing. And preparing."

Logan downed the rest of the beer. Almost magically another one was set in front of him. Zeke didn't say anything, just rested a hand on his shoulder for a moment and left. That solidarity rocked Logan and it took everything in him not to tear up again.

He dragged in a breath, realizing how wrung out he was. The flashbacks always took it out of him. "I think I'm about ready to go, Marigold."

She nodded and turned to wave at Ember. Before she could drop a card, Logan handed his over. "You hauled my ass around all day and listened to me whine. I'll get dinner."

After a few minutes, Ember returned his card, and they slid out of the chairs. His joints had stiffened and it took him a minute to get moving. With a final wave at Zeke and Ember, they left the Frog Dog.

Logan appreciated having a driver. Marigold turned on a soft rock station on the way back to the hotel. "I'll let them know I'm checking out in the morning. What's the actual address of the house."

"I can come get you. Shannon probably won't need me till afternoon."

"I'm taking up a lot of your time, it seems like."

She shrugged, her face lit by the dash lights. "I'm not really doing a lot right now anyway."

"Okay. If you're sure."

They didn't say anything else as she drove downtown. When she pulled into the loop to drop him off, she rested a hand on his arm. "I think Miller's mom will be happy to see you."

Logan hummed in his throat. "We'll see. Thanks, Marigold. Good night."

"Good night."

Gathering his bag of books, he pushed up out of the car, using his crutches to brace himself. Then, slamming the door, he walked into the hotel. Glancing back, he caught the flare of her tail- lights as she pulled away.

12

J ohn rocked back in his seat, frustration gnawing at his guts. It wasn't very often that he was unable to unravel a mystery, but this could possibly be one of them.

For three days he'd been milking every resource he had to find Logan Vance's family, and he'd hit dead end after dead end. There were people with the same name, of course, and he'd actually resorted to cold-calling a few, but none matched the exact details Logan had given him. The kid was coming to the office in a couple of hours, and he didn't know what to tell him.

He looked up at a knock on his open door. Aiden stood there, frown marring his lean face. John smiled. "What's up, brother?"

Aiden's face eased into a matching smile, but within seconds the worry returned. "Do you remember Shannon having a lot of morning sickness?"

Nodding, he swiveled to the left to the coffee machine Shannon had brought in a few weeks ago. He plugged a K-cup into the reservoir and watched the coffee stream into the clean cup. When it was done, he added some creamer and handed it to Aiden. "Yes. For the first three months it seemed like she lived in the bathroom. Not always throwing up, but nauseated. Angela still struggling with it?"

Aiden nodded. "She's lost more weight than she should. The baby is growing, but it's almost like it's eating her from the inside."

Grimacing, John turned back to the desk with his own cup of coffee. "It's a stereotype for a reason. Ginger Ale and saltines. That's all I can tell you. I bought tons of the stuff for her. If Elizabeth thinks she's losing too much weight they'll hospitalize her. Shannon's mother also made her ginger rice, which seemed to help."

Aiden pulled his phone from his pocket. "Do you have the recipe or is it something I can find?"

"I think it's on the net," John said slowly, turning to his keyboard. "Yep. I'll email you this recipe. It has almost five stars. Ask Shannon on your way out. Maybe she'll have a variation, too."

With a few keystrokes he sent the link to Aiden's email. "I wish my other cases were that easy."

Brows raised, Aiden settled into the chair across from his desk, coffee cup balancing on the arm. "What's not going well?"

Sighing, John looked down at the notes on his desk. "This Logan Vance thing. I'm trying to find this kid's family but I'm really striking out. I've checked the newspapers, the PVA, the DMV, every public access option I have. I've logged onto the public library system to scan their older microfiche, which has not all been computerized yet. I even called in a favor from a friend looking for Christopher Vance's military record and there is none. I've completely tapped out my options. I don't know what else to do, or where to search."

He handed the file he had over to Aiden and watched as his brother flipped through page after page of information. "Are you sure the old family name is Walter?"

John scowled. "That's the name he gave me. A few other things popped up for other names and I researched them a bit, but I didn't deep dive yet. That's my only option left."

"I feel like..." Aiden frowned, and his mouth skewed to the side, "it's not Walter. It's something else. Walken. Walker. Showalter."

John jotted the notes down, having learned that his brother's gut feelings were often on the money and not to be discounted. "I'll check those out. I have nothing to lose. I feel like I'm disappointing this kid, and I don't like feeling like that."

"None of us do," Aiden said softly, handing the folder back to him. "As soon as I get back to Arlington, I'll try the ginger rice."

Damn. He'd forgotten Aiden was leaving tonight. He'd come out to Denver to pack up Angela's apartment. They were both working at the Silverstone Collaborative now, with Wulfe and Fontana. They were trying to develop a program for the men that were recovering from the illegal testing the company had put them through. Aiden had wanted to be here to see the paperwork signed on the new partnership, though, and to catch up with everyone for a bit. Angela had chosen to stay in Arlington and let Aiden pack up the apartment for her. She must really be sick, John realized.

"The sickness should ease the further along in her pregnancy she is," John told him hopefully.

"I know. That's what everyone has said, but she's six and

a half months now. I don't know if it's because it's my baby and there's something... not right, or..."

John wheeled around the desk to look his brother in the eye. "You know that's not the case."

Aiden shook his head, looking down at his clasped hands. "It could be. There have been no other babies born to any of the Dogs of War. How do I know that the ayahuasca in my body hasn't done something to the baby?"

John flinched internally. This had been a concern Duncan and Alex had brought up at one of the meetings, but no one had wanted to voice it to Aiden. Instead, Alex had called Elizabeth, Wulfe's wife and the new owner of the Collaborative. She was a doctor and had personally taken over the care of the former prisoners.

Elizabeth had already been preparing for the issue, stocking the Elton Recovery Building with everything they might need for a baby, including an on-call OBGYN. Duncan felt like Angela was under the best care possible.

That didn't ease the worried father's mind, though. John reached out, resting a hand on Aiden's shoulder. "It will be okay," John said bracingly. "He's going to be a Palmer, kind of. There aren't twins, are there?"

Aiden went pale at the thought and swayed in the chair. John held on to him just to be sure he didn't topple over, truly alarmed. "Aiden, I was joking. They would have seen it on the ultrasound. She's had one, right?"

His younger brother nodded, eyes devastated. "Yes, they have. Several of them."

"Then she's probably okay. The morning sickness is just one of those things that goes along with pregnancy."

Aiden sighed. "I know you're probably right. I just worry. She's led a healthy life, but I've had so much shit pumped into me over the years. I don't know what I might be cursing my child to."

John's heart ached for the guy. "But you've recovered from everything. Literally. If anything, I think this kid will be stronger than any of us," he laughed.

Dragging in another heavy breath, Aiden nodded. "Yeah, you're probably right. I just can't shut off my brain, though, you know? And I don't get any of my normal feelings when I'm with her."

Ah, that was part of it. Aiden was known to be especially sensitive, and if he got one of his 'gut feelings', ninety-nine percent of the time it was right. If there was a wall there that he couldn't break through, John could understand why he would be worried. "I think you're spoiled," he joked. "You're so used to having the upper hand you're not used to being normal."

Wincing, Aiden gave him a smile. "Maybe a little," he admitted. "Well, I'm going to tell my gorgeous sister-in-law that I'm heading out. I'll text you when I make it home."

"Thanks for that," John told him seriously. "I like to know where my little brother is and that he's okay."

Aiden pushed to his feet, then leaned down and gave John a back-slapping hug. "See you, brother."

John waved as Aiden stepped out of the office. He hadn't been joking about knowing where he was and that he was okay. Now that he'd located his brother, he wanted to make sure that he stayed healthy and safe. Even the former prisoners could be a danger to him, but John had to have faith that Aiden knew what he was doing. He wasn't a child. Hadn't been for a long time.

Forcing his attention back to the screen, he started chasing possibilities. Within seconds, he latched onto a possibility. Thank you, Aiden, John thought, laughing to himself.

WHEN JOHN ROLLED out to Shannon's desk almost two hours later, he was bursting with information. "I thought Logan was supposed to be here? I have news for him."

Her vivid hazel eyes lit up. "Did you find his family?"

He gave her a nod and leaned in for a kiss. "I did. And even better, they've been looking for him."

Tears filled her eyes. "Oh, my gosh! He needs that. I don't know a lot of his story but life has been crapping on him, bad. He needs hope and connection, and an anchor. He needs community, because I can tell he feels so alone."

John nodded. That's exactly what he'd gotten from the guy, too. "We can't force it on him, but we can offer it. Even though I've found the family, he may not follow through on connecting."

Shannon's face fell. "That would be such a waste."

John shrugged, not liking the thought either. "He has no one else so I hope he'll latch onto this. Has he called or messaged you?"

She nodded. "Marigold messaged me. She's helping him move his stuff into Grandma Nancy's house."

"Fucking Fudge," he breathed. "It's hard to tell when he'll be here, then."

Shannon gave him a narrow eyed look at the language. "Marigold promised she'd be here by noon to help me with a few things, and I'll make sure she'll give Logan a ride."

John blinked, tilting his head. "Are they..."

Shannon shrugged, but he could tell by the shine in her

eyes that she hoped something would happen between the two younger people. She was such a damn romantic. Just one of the many things he loved about her. "I love you, Shannon."

"I love you too, babe," she breathed, leaning forward for his kiss.

"Come on, you two. Don't you have a house to do that?"

They looked up at Duncan standing in his office doorway. "Yes," John said, "but it's overrun with mouthy critters and it's hard to get my wife alone."

Duncan laughed. "They're your critters. And if they're mouthy I'm sure that's your fault as well. "

"I know," John growled, pulling back from Shannon. "Hey, I've had a break on the Vance case."

John explained about Aiden's theory and the path it led him down.

"So, Aiden broke the case," Duncan murmured, giving John a probing look over the top of his glasses.

John scowled. "No, he didn't fucking break the case. He might have given me a little insight, but he didn't break it."

Duncan laughed, leaning against the door jamb. "Whatever you say, John."

He looked at Shannon and remembered what she'd asked. "Hey, Dunc, any chance we need another investigator? Or an intern or something?"

Duncan didn't hesitate. "Sure. What's he good at?"

"Military intelligence. Don't know much more than that yet, but he needs something. I, we," he said, glancing at Shannon, "think he needs community. Sounds like horse shit coming out of my mouth, but I've learned to appreciate it myself."

"I think we all have," Duncan said, eyes flicking back through the line of busy offices.

Yes, they'd all grown in the past several years.

"We'll be a little short-staffed anyway with Rachel going off for maternity leave," Shannon reminded them.

John felt better about offering Logan the job then. "Where is this fucking guy? I want to change his life today."

They laughed, but John actually meant what he said.

AN HOUR LATER, Logan knocked on John's open office door, leaning heavily on his crutches. He knew he looked a little rough around the edges.

"Come on in," John told him, frowning. "You okay?"

"Yeah, I'm all right." Logan half-walked to the chair. His arms were killing him, but not as bad as his right leg. "I took a header earlier. I don't know if Marigold told you but I'm staying at Nancy Marshall's apartment house. Anyway, my crutch caught on a rug and down I went."

John groaned sympathetically. "Been there, done that. Rugs were created by the devil. Knowing Nancy, she'll have every single rug out of there by mid-day."

"You know the Jesus juice lady?" Logan asked, settling to the chair seat. He forced a grin for John, though his thigh blazed like fire.

John, looking bright-eyed and disgustingly healthy, nodded once. "We did a job for her a few years ago. Since then, we've called on her occasionally to house a guest. She's a sweetheart."

Logan knew she was. The woman was the epitome of the grandmother every boy dreamed of having. Marigold doted on her and just from listening to their conversation, he'd realized that Marigold didn't have a lot of family either since her mother had died in Arizona the previous year. Her own grandmother was traveling overseas, somewhere.

Nancy doted on Marigold as well, calling her Mari, and she'd insisted to them both that they were welcome to call her Grandma.

That had taken Logan off guard. It felt like she was adopting him, almost. And the way she'd looked at him... like he was a long-lost grandson or something. Throat tight, he'd nodded, but he hadn't been able to answer her. He'd turned to go into the room and his crutch rubber had dragged on a floor mat. Down he'd gone.

Nothing like crashing to the floor in front of two women, because of course Marigold had been dragging in his bag for him.

One glowering look and they'd left him alone to get to his feet by himself. Marigold had skirted around him and lifted his big bag onto the bed so that he could unpack. Nancy had picked up the pretty, cursed rug and whisked it away.

He'd gotten to his feet, but he was sure it hadn't been pretty. Two pain pills later he was still pissed at that fucking rug. Marigold hadn't said a word about him crashing, though, which he appreciated. She'd focused on other things and eventually left to let him settle in, closing the door behind herself.

Half an hour later Marigold had come back, a broad smile on her face, telling him that Shannon had messaged her and that John had news. So, they'd hopped in her Beetle and headed to the industrial area where the LNF offices were located. The entire time he'd been fighting anxiety, his brain racing through possibilities. He could just say fuck it and have Marigold take him somewhere to forget.

He felt...discombobulated sitting here. Part of it was the pain pills, but his emotions were kind of pinging around as well. There was trepidation and excitement as he waited to hear what John had found. He was afraid to get his hopes up, because he'd been disappointed so many times before.

"Can I get you a coffee?"

"Yeah. With sugar if you have it." Anything to delay.

John spun his chair around and retrieved a cup of coffee, setting it on the edge of the desk in front of Logan with a couple of packets of sugar and a short straw to stir it with. Even though it was scalding hot, Logan stirred in the sugar and took a sip, praying that the caffeine would kick in as quickly as possible because he seriously needed the boost.

"Okay, I'm ready," he said, mentally bracing himself.

John set his own cup of coffee aside and pulled a manila folder in front of himself. "Okay, so, my brother stopped in and he has to get a bit of the credit. He didn't feel like the name was right."

Logan frowned. "What do you mean? It's the name my father gave me."

John shook his head. "It's a long story. Not important right this second. Anyway, I started searching variations on the name you gave me. I was striking out completely with Walter. I literally searched every public and a few not-so-public databases for the name. It just wasn't there. When I searched SHOWalter, though, I started ringing brass. Everything matched up. But this is the important part."

He handed over a paper. Logan took it, not understanding what he was looking at.

"That is a message board post connected to a popular ancestry website. Someone in the family has been looking for you," John said softly.

Looking for my grandkids, two boys and a girl. Son and I had a falling out October of '99 and he left. Haven't spoken to him in twenty years. Kids names are/were Jana, Logan and Clinton.

The message gave their dates of birth, as well as the

names of his mother and father. There was an email address.

"Did you email them?" Logan demanded.

John shook his head. "No, not yet. I thought you might want to do that."

Logan slumped in the chair, the paper shaking in his trembling hand. After all these years... he looked at the date on the message. "This was posted ten years ago. Do you think it's still a viable email?"

John shrugged. "It looks viable, but I guess we won't know until you try it."

Logan looked back down at the paper.

"I have other information. I just thought that was the most direct link, even though it's older."

Logan set the paper aside. "What else do you have?"

"Arthur and Eugenia Showalter have been married for almost fifty years. They own and run a restaurant in Arvada. They had four boys and one girl, and I can find records for most of them. Your father..."

He reached for another paper in the stack and handed it over. Logan read carefully, recognizing the Army discharge paperwork. For Christopher Alexander Showalter. There was a post-it note attached, listing several penal code numbers. "What is this?"

"It's your father's DD-214. And the list of charges he went to prison for before he was dishonorably discharged."

"Wait," Logan said, leaning forward in shock. "Dad said he was released under a bad conduct discharge, for having a pain pill in his pocket, or something. Contraband."

John shook his head, his dark brows furrowed. "Your dad had a court-martial for drug offenses and embezzlement from the Army. He was sentenced to three years in prison, served his time, then was given a dishonorable discharge."

Blinking, Logan stared down at the papers, his mind reeling. Dad had always given the excuse that the Army had been out to get him because he'd been injured in service, and he had a lifetime of care coming. He looked at the details on the paperwork, and the attached passport sized photo. It was definitely his father. Just with the Showalter name.

"What the hell..." he breathed.

Was that why he'd stolen them away from Colorado?

"Did you see if any of the other Showalter family had military service?"

"All but one of them, and one is still in the Army, stationed at Ft. Bragg. One brother was KIA in the Persian Gulf."

Ah, hell. Logan blinked, realizing that he'd come from a true Army Gold Star family. They'd lived and died by their service.

"So, my dad was the only one in the family that had problems."

"The only one I can find. Everyone else appears to be true red, white and blue."

John shuffled through his papers. "I also found this and confirmed it with the cop that found you. He's a captain, now, and I have his number if you'd like to talk to him."

It was a police report, detailing a crash scene a rookie cop had found on interstate 70, which ran through downtown Denver. Logan's analytical brain appreciated the clear, concrete details at the top of the report. His gaze drifted down to the narrative section.

The report was dated right after the discharge paperwork, and it painted a picture of a man struggling. The driver of the car carrying three children, ages 6 years, 3 years and 13 months had supposedly hit black ice, struck a guard rail and crossed a center median, making another vehicle swerve to avoid the crash. The second vehicle went off an embankment and struck a bridge support. The man was killed upon impact. Drug paraphernalia was scattered throughout the first car and the driver was found to be critically impaired by LSD.

"Holy fuck. He got high with us in the car and killed a man?"

John nodded. "That's what I'm inferring. The cop called children's services and you were taken away. Your father was taken to a local hospital with a broken arm and a concussion. You kids were all fine."

"Where was my mother," Logan breathed.

"It looks like she was at work at the restaurant your grandparents owned."

Logan sank back in the chair, his mind trying to cope with everything he'd learned. It was... horrifying. And it made a terrible, maniacal kind of sense. Even when he was a child, he remembered family members. He had no idea who they'd been, but he remembered playing in a big ranch house with other little kids. His parents had always claimed that that had been at a babysitter's house.

He could understand his father lying, but his mother? Why had she gone along with all this?

Because she loved her husband.

Logan had lived a life of lies that his parents had created.

"Is that all of the information you have?" he asked finally, looking up at John.

He handed over one more piece of paper. "That was where your father filed to have his name officially changed." His eyes kind, the older man leaned forward on the desk. "If you want I can approach the family on your behalf and confirm what I've found, but it seems pretty cut and dried."

"Yes, it does," Logan murmured. He shuffled the papers, putting them in order. "I think... I'll deal with this."

"That's completely your right. And it's not something that you have to move on right now. You know? They've waited twenty years. They can wait a few more weeks. Chill out, explore Colorado and Denver. Maybe take out a girl..." he grinned.

He couldn't quite return the good humor. "Yeah. Thanks, John. I know Shannon was taking pity on me in that airport, but I'm really glad you talked me into accepting your help."

"I am, too, Logan. You had the look of a man on the edge."

He barked out a laugh. "You have no idea."

John leaned even further forward across the desk, staring at him intently. "Logan, I want you to listen to me very carefully. I do have an idea. I contemplated ending it all more times than I dare say out loud, but I kept rolling along, knowing that I was at the bottom of the barrel and that I couldn't get any lower. And I was right. Duncan showed up with a job offer, which was a huge thing. Then I met Shannon. She is my salvation. And my kids..." his voice went rough, and Logan could see how much he loved them. "They are miracles. Both of them. And I don't deserve them but it doesn't matter because I'm never giving them up."

The fierceness in his eyes said everything, and Logan smiled. Then he made the harsh comparison to his own father. "I'm glad you love them that way, Gunny. Not every kid has that."

"I know. I have no idea who my father was. So," John said, taking an expansive breath. "Before you pull that trigger or pop those pills, you need to remember that there are people here for you. You have my number and Shannon's. I'll give you the whole directory to the LNF crew, because it's occurred to every single one of us, but we found our way through. You will too."

The stark words meant a lot to him. "I'm trying. it just feels like I'm drowning, sometimes."

John nodded. "It does. But there are people and processes in place to ensure that you don't. If you let them in."

Logan thought about that. It had been so long since he'd let anyone in, or even dared hope that anyone would be there for him. Miller had been the last one he'd relied upon, and he'd let him down. Fuck, and now Logan was letting him down by not being there for his family.

"There's also a job if you want it."

Logan blinked, not sure he'd heard him correctly. "What?"

"You heard me. We have an investigator going out on maternity leave so we're a little short-handed. If you don't mind starting with basic stuff while we get you certified, we have a place for you."

Logan couldn't even process what he'd said. "Why would you offer me a job? You don't know me."

John tilted his head, smirking. "Consider it my good deed for the year, taking on a Ground Pounder. And I do know you. You're a former intelligence officer and a veteran. You came to my wife's rescue even though you thought it was a ruse. I'd be a fool not to hire you."

Logan scowled. "I didn't do very good as an intelligence officer finding my own family."

John shrugged. "And you wouldn't. You were too close to it. You never would have believed that your dad changed his name, and your whole family's name. It wouldn't even have occurred to you. Lucky for you, you had us," he grinned.

Shaking his head, Logan didn't even know what to say. John was probably right. About everything, actually. "I need to think about all this."

John nodded, circling the desk. "I would expect you to. You have a lot to absorb."

Logan reached out and shook John's hand, but John pulled him into a shoulder-hug. "Don't let it overwhelm you," he said firmly.

Logan nodded, pulling back and bracing his crutches to get up. His body ached and he needed some time alone. "I'll give you a call," he told John, before he left the office.

When he entered the reception area Marigold glanced up and she seemed to sense that he needed to get out of there. She murmured something to Shannon, grabbed her coat and bag and met him at the door.

"Come on, I'll take you to the house."

Logan knew she was just as curious as he'd been, but she didn't say anything as they bundled into the Beetle and drove back to the house. When she pulled into the lot, he rested a hand on hers on the gear shift. "I'm okay from here, Marigold. I need some time to wrap my head around some things."

She nodded, her brows furrowed. "Well, if you want to talk, I'll be home in a few hours. Or you can text me."

Without saying anything else he pushed up out of the car and headed inside. Nancy's maroon station wagon wasn't in the lot, so she must be at the store or something. He was glad to make it to his room without seeing or talking to anyone.

Once inside, he headed straight to the shower, cranking the heat to high. Though he was dressed in a t-shirt, flannel shirt and jacket, he was still fighting the cold. He wasn't sure how much was mental and how much was physical, but he felt like he needed to bathe.

Logan stepped out of the shower, then shaved and got dressed, a plan beginning to form in his mind. He sat in the chair in the living room area and studied the contents of John's folder.

13

"So, what did he say?" Shannon whisper/shouted as she leaned into John's doorway.

Her sexy husband glanced up with a smile, rocking back in his chair. Looking self-satisfied, he crossed his arms over his chest, a pose she especially loved because it made his chest and arms look so big. "He's thinking about some things. There was a lot to go over and a lot of information he had no idea about, even about his own direct family."

"The poor guy," she breathed. "I hope he can figure it all out. And you offered him the job?"

John nodded once, hands moving to the wheels of his chair as he rocked back and forth. "Again, he has to think about everything. I dumped a huge amount of information on the guy."

"He looked a little dazed when Marigold took him home," she sighed.

"Yeah. I think once he has a chance to figure out which way is up, he'll be on board."

John's dark eyes roved down her body and Shannon

cocked her head, giving him a smile. "Yes..." she drawled. She wore an especially cute little purple business outfit today, with sparkly heels.

John grinned and shrugged. "You look good to me, what can I say? Why don't you come in here for a minute and lock the door. Leave the shoes on when you straddle me."

Shannon laughed, her cheeks going pink. "Yeah, not happening buddy. I know you. Duncan has already warned us once this week."

John scoffed. "What's he going to do, fire me?"

She shook her head, backing out of the doorway. "Love you, babe. Talk to you in a bit."

"Shannon," he growled.

She giggled as she headed down the hallway, away from temptation. There would be hell to pay tonight for telling him no, but she would be ready for it.

MARIGOLD WANTED to go downstairs and bang on Logan's door, but she would allow him his privacy. Shannon hadn't given her all the details, just told her that she needed to be patient with him because he had a huge amount of information to digest. And he had kind of said the same thing. So, she cracked open a fresh bottle of wine later that evening, turned on the TV for background noise and surfed her social media sites. Next week she had a pottery class and she was supposed to be looking for ideas to try to match, but her brain had been on other things.

Namely, the hunky guy downstairs.

Not that he thought he was hunky. She shook her head at the thought that someone would dump him because he's been injured. What bullshit.

Marigold worried that he would feel overwhelmed by everything he'd learned today, but she didn't want to rush down there unless he actually needed her. She needed to have enough faith in him to trust him to reason things out on his own, and not to take the drastic way out.

The thought terrified her, though.

Logan was better than that. Yeah, he may have hit some rough patches, but she didn't truly believe he would kill himself. But then, she'd thought her mother would never leave her either.

Unable to help herself, she sent him a text. *You doing ok?*

It was a while before he responded with a *yeah.*

Well, that was better than nothing.

She was into her second glass of wine and watching a British cooking show when there was a knock on the door. Grandma Nancy usually texted her so that she could avoid the stairs, and the third guy staying in the house was on the other landing, so Marigold knew who it was before she swung open her door.

"You didn't have to come up all this way. I could have come down."

Logan shook his head and gave her a slightly rakish grin. "No challenge to that. Mind if I come in?"

Marigold stepped back, waving him in. "I was just enjoying a bottle of wine. Would you like to join me?"

"Yes," he said absently, glancing around her space.

Marigold loved her little mini-apartment. It had everything she needed. The aqua colored comforter on the bed was one of the color focal points, and she'd built off of it, with pale blue scattered throw pillows, the drapes in her turreted office space, and some of the rugs all varying shades of aqua.

"You have a blue jean couch?"

She grinned and swept the gray fur throw blanket she'd been using into her arms. "I do! Blue jeans match everything so I used the same reasoning when looking at couches for the space. I think it worked beautifully."

He nodded. "It does, actually."

Sinking into the cushions, he sighed. "Comfortable, too. The one I have is a little well-used."

"Yeah," she said slowly. "That used to be up here. I told Nancy I would buy my own. Sorry," she laughed.

Marigold sank into the opposite end of the couch, propping her elbow on the back as she looked at him. "So, you had some revelations today, I hear."

Logan grimaced, running his fingers over the top of his arm brace distractedly. Then, as if he realized what he was doing, he set the crutches to the floor. "More than I ever could have expected."

"Anything you want to talk about?"

Logan heaved a great sigh, and she could see the lines of worry around his eyes. Shifting his arm to the back of the couch, he shook his head. "Not just yet. Tell me about your family."

Marigold's brows popped in surprise. "My family?"

"Do you have family? Other than your grandmother, I mean?"

She nodded. "A few members. Mostly cousins. My mother was older when she had me, and after my father was killed she never really recovered. I think I told you that. She never found her balance. Her mother and father were at the house all the time, picking up after her or making sure I had clean clothes. Eventually I just moved in with them. We both did. Life was...not good, but better for a while." She smiled softly. "Mom always worried about me, though. If I was late coming in from a date or school activity, she would be calling around looking for me. It was irritating, but I knew it was a coping mechanism.

"And then, a few years ago, my grandpa died," she sighed, her lips turned down. "Mom kind of... broke down, because he had been the sole man present all her life. When we should have been there for Grandma and her pain, my mother lost it, basically. She took a handful of pills in a suicide attempt and was in the psych ward while we were at the funeral."

She gave him a sad smile. "Whatever John handed you on the platter today, it can't be as crazy as my family."

Logan gave a bark of laughter. "Oh, I bet it can."

Marigold listened raptly as he reported what John had found. They split the rest of the bottle of wine. When he finished speaking, she had to consciously unclench her fists and her body. At some point she'd curled up into a tense knot on the cushion. What utter gall the man had! "So, your father basically ruined everything. He ruined his family by being the black mark on the perfect Army service record, and he ruined your family by lying about it all. And he dragged you all through hell because he didn't have the balls to own up to what he did."

"Correct," Logan said, sighing heavily.

Marigold reached out and gripped his hand on the back of the couch. "None of this is your fault. It can, literally, all be laid at his feet."

"I know. I just feel... ashamed. To have a family record like that is an incredible accomplishment. I wish I could have finished my deployment. Maybe it would have erased some of the blackness he spread."

She crawled closer to him, looking him in the eye. "Listen to me, Logan. You were injured in the line of duty. I have a feeling you have a Purple Heart hiding around somewhere. Am I right?" She could see in his face that she was. "You have nothing to be ashamed of. If anything, I feel like your service record will make up for your father's lack."

His brilliant blue-green eyes grew luminous. "I hope so," he admitted, voice hoarse. "Because I have nothing else to offer them."

She scrunched up her brow, her wine-lazy brain trying to react. "Why do you have to offer them anything? You didn't screw them over. It was your dad."

"I know, but..." he shook his head, obviously searching for words. "My brother Clint is a druggie, probably still in jail. Jana... Jana was killed right after I enlisted, by a drugged-out boyfriend. And I am just mobile enough not to need a wheelchair. That's not a great family line."

She huffed in exasperation, shaking her head. Her dark hair hung across her shoulder and she pushed it away. "Can you look at it from the other side, my side, for a minute?"

He looked at her, mouth tight. "How?"

Sinking back onto her heels, she pulled his hand down to the seat between them. "With you they get the best of the family back, a war hero. Someone who served the way the family expected in spite of his setbacks. Hell, you served the way the family wanted you to, and you didn't even know the family. That right there speaks to your genetics motivating you. You were bred to serve in the military, and you did," she said firmly, grinning.

Logan stared at her for a long minute, then looked down at their clasped hands. Marigold's thumb had been stroking over a burn scar, but she hadn't even noticed. The emotional hurt she saw in his eyes was more important than the physical in that moment.

"You are worth having," she continued. "Just you. Even

with the scars and the crutches and the PTS. You sell your-self short, Logan, and you need to recognize your own worth. I see it, John sees it, Shannon sees it. I have a feeling your buddy Miller did too. The family that you left behind will be overjoyed to have you. I can almost guarantee it. They've lost a son to a war. They'll be happy to get a grandson back."

"You're fucking me up, Marigold," he growled, voice hoarse, pulling away to swipe at his eyes.

Marigold grinned at him and pushed into his shoulder, pressing a kiss to his jaw. "I have just enough wine in me to tell you that I would love to really fuck you up."

He barked out a laugh, turning to look at her. There was something in the look, though, that demanded explanation. "You say when and I'm there," she breathed, her lips moving to press a kiss against his ear. It was the same thing she'd done in the bar, letting him know she was interested without being too forward, she thought. But this time, some-thing changed. She felt his breath catch, and the subtle loos-ening in his shoulders. Marigold didn't know what to think when he turned to look at her, cupped her face in his hands and took her mouth with his own.

Nerves shot through her belly as he called her bluff, his lips moving gently against hers. Marigold groaned, his taste sending a bolt of awareness down her spine and into her core. Oh, damn... angling her head, she let herself absorb everything she could about him; the scent of whatever he used in the shower, the abrasiveness of the patch of beard on the left side of his face.

Then he did something unexpected. Strong hands under her armpits, he turned her to lay across his lap, looking up at him, dazed. Marigold didn't know what to think. She'd never expected him to manhandle her so perfectly. Grinning, she reached her hands up to cup his face.

The scars didn't bother her in the least, but she could tell he was aware of her touching them. Rather than pull away, she touched him even more strongly there, running her hands up his cheek and into his hairline.

With a gasp he pulled back enough to look down at her. "You can't like touching that," he said softly.

"Am I hurting you?" she whispered.

He blinked down at her. "No."

"Then let me touch you," she whispered.

"Marigold," he growled. "You have no idea what you're getting into. I'm not..."

"Logan, look at me."

His mouth tight, he looked at her. "You are wanted," she said slowly. "You need to take those words inside yourself and feel them. I want you," she said firmly, again tugging his head down to hers.

Logan resisted her touch, but only for a moment. "What have you done to me, woman?" he whispered, pulling her tight against his body. They were chest to chest, mouth to mouth, and Marigold forgot everything as she lost herself in his taste. Oh, wow... wine and tangy freshness, like he'd brushed his teeth before coming up here. And holy hell the man knew how to kiss, angling her face to diagonal his, fitting their mouths perfectly. His tongue slipped out to tangle with hers, and Marigold melted. Her body responded in a rush, harder and quicker than it ever had before. She needed to be even closer. She didn't want to hurt him, though.

"Can I straddle your hips?"

His breath stalled, then he nodded. Marigold moved off the couch, then stepped close, planting a knee on either side of his hips. She could see the length of him behind the zipper of his jeans and she wanted to go there, but a few things needed to happen first. Sitting on his lap, she was almost at eye level with him, just a little lower, and the closeness was...startling. And stimulating. For the first time, he didn't automatically turn his head away from her gaze, letting her look her fill. She grinned. "You're very handsome, you know. Without the hat and looking at me this way... The burns are not as devastating as you believe them to be. I promise."

He heaved a huge breath. "You're the only one that's ever told me that. I think you're partial."

She grinned. "Maybe," she admitted, leaning forward to take his mouth again. She wrapped her arms around his head, enclosing them in together. She waited to feel his hands on her body, but he seemed to be trying not to touch her. "What are you doing?"

"I'm trying to give you an out. I'm not going to hold you against me."

Marigold drew back, frustrated. The wine was clearing from her system and she desperately wanted to feel him wanting her. "I'm not going anywhere, Logan, so you'd damn well better grab my ass and start enjoying yourself."

Jaw clenched, he fought himself internally, then seemed to give in. He did as she instructed, his broad hands spanning her hips, his fingers clenching. His eyes fluttered shut and she could see the arousal roll over his slackening face. When he dragged her against his groin, Marigold gasped, rocking against his hardness. Oh, damn...

"I have to...fuck, Mari, you're going to kill me. Stop, just a minute. It's been a while for me and I don't think... I'm not gonna last with you grinding on me like that."

Marigold laughed, loving the way he'd shortened her name. "Um, hello, you pushed up into me, buddy."

Logan snorted, taking her mouth with his. Then he skimmed his hands up her ribs to her breasts, his thumbs finding and stroking over her nipples. "Oh," she breathed, the tips pulling tight. More...

Pulling back, desperate for his touch, Marigold crossed her arms and pulled her shirt over her head, dropping it to the floor. Then she reached behind and released her bra, tossing it in the same general direction. When she looked at Logan, his gaze was fixated to her breasts. Cupping them, she split her fingers over her nipples, pinching them, and he groaned. Pushing her hands away he replaced them with his own, then pushed her torso back enough that he could lean forward and wrap his lips around the tips of her breasts.

Marigold trusted him to hold her secure as he worshipped her breasts. She just didn't want to hurt his legs with her weight. Surely, he would tell her if she was too much...

Logan moved between both breasts, his tongue stroking strongly. Then he began to suck, and Marigold groaned, feeling her body get wetter. It was if his mouth was connected directly to her clit, and it was preparing for him. "Oh, that's lovely," she whispered. Then he tweaked one nipple as he suckled the other, and something about the combination sent a pre-orgasm shudder through her. If he would only stroke against her jeans...

As if he heard her thoughts, he reached a hand between them, stroking her through her jeans as he tongued her nipple to the roof of his mouth, the edge of teeth on her skin. The orgasm hit her hard, sending her spinning through space. Marigold twitched and moaned, head rocked back on her shoulders as Logan held her, grinding against her.

IF LOGAN ever could have dreamed that her satisfaction would push him right to the edge of his own, he would have made sure to at least be undressed and in a bed. Fuck. As it was, he didn't dare move. His body quivered, needing release. His dick was cranked behind the fly of his jeans and he needed to stretch out and release.

Logan watched Marigold open her dreamy green eyes. The look of satisfaction in her expression was so worth the pain in his screaming legs. At first, her weight had been okay, but the bouncing around had made him ache in a distracting way, completely counterpoint to the good ache in his dick.

"You," she whispered. "Are dangerous. I've never come like that before, with a man sucking my breasts."

Cupping her head in his hands, he brought her mouth to his own again, trying to feel the truth in her words. There was no doubt she came, so, he would have to trust her honor. Her tongue darted out, stroking against his own and sending another delicious thrill of need through him.

Then Mari was gone, shifting carefully off his lap. He watched as she grabbed a pillow from the couch, dropping it to the floor, then kicking it into position between his legs. It took Logan a moment to understand what she was doing and he sat up, trying to push her away.

"No, don't..." he started.

"I know I don't," she said firmly, dropping to her knees on the pillow. "But I want to," she grinned, reaching for the fly of his jeans.

Logan snatched at her hands. "Mari, listen to me. I'm not... there was damage."

That stilled her hands and she glanced up at him. "Okay, well, we can go slow."

Logan grimaced. "I've got burns over most of my lower half, and my dick wasn't spared."

"Okay. Does it still cause you pain?"

"No, not anymore. It's just... there's scar tissue."

She lifted a brow at him. "And you expect me to stop because you don't look right?"

It sounded a little ridiculous when she said it like that. With effort, he removed his hands, stretching them along the back of the couch. Then he curled them into fists.

It seemed like he had given so much recently, emotion-wise, that he was just kind of done. If she wanted to see his fucking dick, he'd let her, then, maybe he could retreat to his cold little world again. If she got him off, great. If not, he'd do it later. And the lines would be drawn.

Her fingers brushed against him again. While they'd been talking, he lost interest, a little, but within seconds he was hard again. What he hadn't told her was that the scar tissue had a bit of a dampening effect on him. It took harder touches and strokes to get himself off. He hadn't been with a woman since the ex, so he had no idea how his body would respond buried inside a wet woman.

The feel of her orgasming on top of him sent a fresh roll of heat down through his body. If he could have ripped those jeans off he would have, just to feel her body's release. He had a feeling she was very wet, and the thought of sinking into that, into her, excited him.

She released the zipper on his jeans and spread the sides wide, exhaling loudly in the silence of the room. One of her hands flattened against his cock, then wrapped around him. He still wore his boxers, but the fabric was thin. Thin enough that he could feel the entire length of her hand against him, even over the scars on the lower side.

Marigold slipped her hand beneath the fabric of the boxers, fingertips finding his crown. Her touch danced lightly around it and he breathed through his nose, feeling her find the moistness at the tip. Her forefinger circled his head, spreading that wetness and teasing lightly.

Logan watched her face as she played. There was sensuality there, like she was actually enjoying what she was doing. Surely, she'd felt the scars when she'd flattened her hand against him...

Marigold leaned forward, bracing her arms over his thighs, in a way holding him still as she pulled the fabric away from his penis. Logan clenched his jaw and watched her, unblinking, as she surveyed the damage. As if sex wasn't hard enough, he had to display his most private damage. She didn't flinch, though. A softness entered her eyes as she flexed him up along his belly, looking at the worst damage. The crown and the top three inches, or there about, were fine. There was a strip up along the right side of his dick scarred as well, but it was narrow. It was only closer to his body where the burns were more pronounced, along the pipe beneath, circling around his shaft and up his belly, around his right hip and down his legs. His scrotum had been burnt as well, and when he'd been in the hospital, they'd very nearly removed it. One of the doctors thought it was salvageable, though, so they'd fought the infection with hard antibiotics.

"This had to have been so painful," she murmured, leaning forward to press a line of kisses along his length, her tongue swirling around his head again.

"It was really painful when I'd get a hard-on, which you just can't control sometimes," he admitted.

"Hm," she responded, lips spreading to wrap around his crown.

Logan suddenly couldn't breathe as he watched her. It had been one of his greatest fears, not being able to have sex again. Since the injury, almost seven months now, he hadn't had sex at all. He'd been too afraid to see revulsion in a woman's eyes when she looked at him. Jacking off worked well enough.

Strong fingers wrapped around his shaft and Logan lost track of his thoughts. His orgasm had been forced back earlier, but he could feel it rising again. The foreignness of having a hand not his own on his flesh was enough to amp him up. The sight of her lips on his body... she licked him in twenty different ways, up and around, through the slit, finding exactly where he was most sensitive. Then she nibbled her way down his shaft, finding and caressing the scars like they were no different that the rest of him. The feeling here was different. In some places it was more sensitive, in others much less so, to the point that he barely felt her touching him at all because the nerves had been burned away.

Marigold understood the reactions of his body better than he did because she concentrated her attentions higher, around the tip of him, drawing him closer to that edge. Logan was amazed that she hadn't run screaming from him, so he let himself relax a little. Looking down at her paying homage to his beat up dick, he let some of his closely guarded control go, again. It had been okay last time, so he would have to hope that it would be okay this time as well.

Marigold shifted on her knees, bringing her pretty breasts higher. She kind of wrapped the warm mounds around the base of his cock as she tongued him, and the graphic visual was too much for him. Yet not enough. The orgasm slammed into him, waves of pleasure making him arch up off the couch and deeper into her mouth. She pulled back enough for her hand to take over, pumping hard at the base, and he watched his release coat her breasts and fingers. Logan panted for breath, his body moving in ways it hadn't for a long time. Marigold had found a level of pleasure for him that he hadn't been able to himself.

And he hadn't even fucking been inside her. His head dropped back to the couch cushion as the aftershocks rippled through him.

MARIGOLD WAS VERY careful of the skin on Logan's penis. As delicate as it was on a normal man, it seemed even more delicate on him, even with the addition of the scars. And they seemed to impede his pleasure, a little. She rubbed her forefinger and thumb together, feeling his release and wondering if he had the energy to join her in the bed.

Maybe this had been enough for tonight. They'd each gotten off and though her body still hummed with need, it wasn't as sharp as it had been before. It could either be fanned or banked. Logan looked like he needed to chill for a little bit. She had a feeling this had been exceptionally emotional for him, because he hadn't let anyone else see him this way. She felt honored that he had trusted her enough.

"Come lay down," she offered impulsively. Reaching for her discarded t-shirt, she wiped her breasts clean, then his penis.

Logan looked at her bed and she could see the indecision. "I don't know..."

"No commitment stated, inferred or requested."

He barked out a laugh. "Oh, really." He rubbed at his face. "Fine. Just for a little while."

When he got to his feet and tucked himself away, she decided it was a good thing she'd asked him to stay. He was obviously in pain. "Are you okay? Did I break you?"

He winced, straightening his hips and back. "No. It's just...a little more exercise than I'm used to. And the fall earlier. It might be good to lay down."

Marigold swept ahead, swinging the comforter, blanket and sheet back for him to climb in, but he detoured toward the bathroom. "Back in a minute."

Marigold stared at the closed door, wondering what the hell she was doing, inviting him to stay. Logan could probably make it to his own apartment, but it might be nice just sleeping in the bed with him. What a great ice breaker before sex.

Oh, hey, yeah, you snore like a freight train. What was that? My feet are ice blocks? Yeah, I could have told you that.

Actually, the thought of just wrapping her arm over his chest and nestling in was very appealing to her. Realizing she was still naked from the waist up she crossed to her dresser, looking for a clean t-shirt to sleep in. Then, moving through the space, she picked up a few things as she waited for him to return.

Marigold picked up his cell phone from the coffee table. It was in a black, heavy duty case and the screen lit when she moved it. Nineteen percent. She set it on the bedside table and plugged it in since it took the same charger her phone did.

When she didn't hear anything from the bathroom for a

while, she snapped off most of the lights and climbed into bed. Her apartment was warm, but it was still cold outside, so it was nice to snuggle into her flannel sheets.

The bathroom door opened and Logan stepped out, leaning heavily on his crutches. When he saw her in bed, he paused, glancing toward the apartment door. Marigold didn't want him to leave, but she wouldn't force him to stay. He seemed to weigh her with his gaze. Eventually, he swung to the side of the bed and leaned his crutches against the wall.

Thinking she would give him some privacy, Marigold rolled over in the bed to face the dark living room area.

"If you don't want to look, that's fine, but if you're turning over on my account, you don't need to."

She looked at him over her shoulder. "I know you've had a lot going on today, so I didn't know if you were up for a reveal, or whatever."

He shrugged as he unfastened his jeans and pushed them down his legs. "I'm kind of numb, right now, so I don't think I really care what you see. It is what it is."

She hated the defeatist tone in his voice. It reminded her too much of her mother.

As his jeans were pushed away, though, dismay swept through her. She tried to control her face before he looked up, and it was one of the hardest things she'd ever done. His legs were a canvas of pain. She couldn't even imagine the trauma that had caused all of the scars running the length of his legs. Some appeared to be man-made, with straight lines and an odd pattern, like scales. Those must be skin grafts or something. The rest of his skin looked okay in patches, and thin and painful in others. His right leg...

"My God," she murmured, "How are you even standing on that?"

She crawled across the bed, incredibly curious, and reached out to run light fingers along the heavy divots into his muscle. One, in his lower calf, was almost down to the bone.

"Luck and bitter determination, as well as a lot of pain pills. Might be a few plates and screws in there as well. A wheelchair would be easier, but I'm going to stay on my feet as long as I possibly can."

Marigold looked up at him, feeling proud of him when it really wasn't her place. She gave him a nod. "I would as well. What did that? Do you know?"

He drew in a deep breath. "When we hit the IED, it blew up right underneath us, completely blowing apart the bottom of the MRAP. They build the machines super heavy to withstand the blast, generally, but this was a huge IED. It obliterated the truck, as well as the one in front of us. I was in the far corner, farthest from the blast, but I got hit by shrapnel. A lot of it."

She ran her hand down his right leg again. He was missing two toes on this foot. If his legs had matched the rest of his big body, he would have had good, strong thighs. His left leg seemed to have escaped structural damage, just had burn marks running the length, from the thigh to the foot. The skin looked paper thin. Marigold couldn't even imagine the pain he'd gone through. One of her greatest fears was burning to death, and in that moment in time he probably thought he was going to.

"I assume you were knocked out," she said, hoping.

With a bitter smile, he shook his dark head, a couple of curls falling over his forehead. "I was completely lucid until I was evacced. I felt every burn, but I couldn't put them out. I felt... I felt what was left of my friends sliding down my face.

My helmet was blown off, my toes cut off by shrapnel. I can't even tell you all the shrapnel spots."

She stared at him in horror, not even able to comprehend... Tears filled her eyes and she looked at him with new respect. "Logan," she said, swinging her legs off the edge of the bed and sitting in front of him. "I have mad respect for what you survived. I'm so sorry."

Pushing to her feet, she moved forward enough to wrap her arms around him. For a moment he held himself stiffly erect, as if to repel her pity, then he seemed to sag, exhaling into her neck. His arms wrapped around her back, holding her to him. A subtle shudder rippled through him, and he gasped in a breath, and she realized he was really struggling.

"It's okay, Logan. You're all right."

His legs seemed to sag and he staggered to the bed. His eyes were wet with tears, but none had fallen. He wouldn't let them. His face was contorted with remembered trauma. "I remember screaming from the pain and praying that I would just die, because I could literally feel my skin sloughing off. It took a while for the guys behind us to find me. They thought we were all dead."

Marigold sat beside him, rubbing his back, feeling more scars beneath his t-shirt. The absolute desolation on his face made her heart ache. She wondered if he'd been able to talk to anyone about this. The ex had dumped him, she knew that much. And his family was shit. Had he had anyone to release to?

"Did you have anyone for you at the hospital? Your family?"

His mouth turned down, and he snorted. "My mother called me a few times, but Dad wouldn't let her take the trip to see me."

"Fuckers," she breathed.

The lines around his mouth deepened in a slight smile. "Yeah."

The poor guy looked whipped. His shoulders were slumped, but he wasn't broken. He seemed more defeated than she'd ever seen him. No, not defeated. Beat down. It worried her.

"This has been a hell of a day for you, but I want you to realize how strong you are. If that day didn't destroy you then nothing will."

He smiled at her again slightly. "I don't know. Still have a couple of pending issues I'm not sure about."

She shook her head, determined to make him see what she saw. "Those are small potatoes, seriously. Not to minimize what you have to do but it will be nothing compared to that day."

Logan propped his elbows on his knees and scraped his hands over his face. "Yeah, okay."

"And I'll be here for you. Whatever you need, Logan. Okay?"

He rocked his head to look at her. "Okay."

Marigold gave him a brilliant smile. "But for now, I think you really need some beauty sleep."

Brows furrowed, he stared at her incredulously. "Beauty sleep? Really?"

She pressed a kiss to his quirked lips. "Yes. Crawl in."

Moving off the mattress she lifted the sheets for him to settle in, then she draped the blankets over him. Very quickly she ran to the bathroom and used the facilities, then came back. Circling the bed she slipped into the other side, snapping off the light, her tummy fluttering at being so close to him this way. She wasn't normally one to invite a man to spend the night, but Logan was different. Very different.

Rolling to her side, she looked at him in the darkness of the room. His profile was just barely visible.

It seemed a little ridiculous considering she'd given him a blow job less than half an hour ago, but this seemed so much more intimate. Reaching out, she wrapped her hands around his right bicep, feeling the strength, and the history of pain, there. "What are you going to do with the information John gave you?"

Logan blinked up at the ceiling. "Not sure, exactly. Want to go get lunch tomorrow with me?"

She was surprised by the offer, and thrilled. "Sure. Where at?" She grinned at the question, knowing the answer.

"I hear there's a great little restaurant up in Arvada," he murmured, his voice beginning to slow. "Maybe we can check it out."

"Sounds good to me," she agreed, her own lids growing heavy. "I think they'll be amazing people."

Sighing heavily, he turned his head and pressed a kiss to her hair. "We'll see."

14

The kid was fit to be tied.

John watched Wyatt throw the mother of all tantrums on the hard living room floor. They were just getting ready to head out the door to daycare and work, and the kid had just melted down. Shannon started to pick him up and baby him, but her chin had firmed and she'd stepped back, arms crossed beneath her breasts as she watched him. John sat back as well, though he wanted to rush forward and appease his son. Caden sat quietly on his lap, waiting to go to daycare. He had a toy in his hand and didn't seem concerned with Wyatt's antics.

This had been happening more often recently and when they'd asked Flynn and Willow about it, because Raven was a little older, they'd both laughed.

"Oh, they have you guys pegged," Willow had murmured. "I bet the first time he did it you rushed forward, thinking that he'd hurt himself or something. And you babied him. When something is happening that they don't like, he's learned what to do to get you to respond. So, say, leaving the toys to come eat dinner, which is Raven's flash point. She flung herself on the floor and cried the big crocodile tears, which is his weak spot." She pointed a blunt finger at Flynn, who made a face in agreement.

"She's a little terrorist," he grumbled. "Trained by some super-secret baby development group before we get them, or something."

Willow made a face, swinging her dark hair behind her shoulder. "Hm. Whatever. Mr. Hero here would go pick her up and cradle her and give her her favorite toy to play with, and dinner would get pushed off. Exactly what Raven wanted in the first place."

Shannon shared a look with John. They'd been guilty of that as well.

"Parenting is hard," she'd told Shannon, then she'd leaned over and hugged her. "I know, babe, but you wouldn't rather have it any other way. Next time they throw a tantrum, let them, and don't feed the little emotional beast. He's just being a drama-dick."

"A what?" Shannon had asked, laughing.

"A drama-dick. There are drama queens and drama dicks."

John remembered those words as he watched Wyatt check to see where Shannon was. The little bugger was checking to see if she'd caved yet.

Shannon must have seen the look as well, because she raised an eyebrow at Wyatt, then turned to head into the kitchen. Caden slid off John's lap and toddled over to Wyatt, patting his brother on the head. He babbled at 'Wy', and Wyatt seemed to get tired of his own histrionics. With a trembling breath, the tears evaporated and he sat up to talk to his brother. They had a language only they seemed to understand and it was interesting listening to them babble back and forth.

Caden seemed to be telling Wyatt that they needed to go, because he got to his feet and waddled toward John, who still held his winter coat. Without fuss Wyatt allowed John to put his coat on, then he took the toy Caden had been playing with.

"Shannon, I think we're ready."

There were no further issues as they loaded the boys into the truck and drove to the day care center. Wyatt started to snuffle when he realized his parents were going to leave him there, but Nene, a tall, willowy young woman with a bright smile, offered him a piece of candy, even though it was just after seven-thirty in the morning.

Thoroughly distracted, John and Shannon made their escape from the boys.

"We need to get smarter with these kids," Shannon murmured. "Can you imagine how bad they'll be when they're teenagers?"

John winced. "I think we need more playdates with Joe Flynn's family."

"Agreed," she sighed.

John reached over, taking her hand. "We're getting it. I don't feel like we're bad parents."

"Oh," Shannon looked at him, startled. "I don't either. Not at all. I think we need to stop underestimating them," she laughed.

He winced. Yeah, definitely. "I need to be writing all this stuff down for Aiden. Poor guy has no idea what's coming."

"I don't think you should stress him out anymore than he already is," Shannon murmured. "Angela texted me this morning to thank me for the rice recipe, and she says Aiden is freaking out, worse than she expected him to. They've talked about the stress, but I'm not sure it's easing him at all."

John scowled. "They've got a couple more months, yet."

"I know, but I was thinking..."

He gave her a narrowed-eyed look. "Thinking what?"

"My parents will be back in a couple of months. Maybe we can slide out and be with Aiden and Angela when the time is close."

John pursed his lips. It wasn't a terrible idea. If there was a way he could be there for Aiden he absolutely would be, because at this point it sounded like his brother was having more of an issue with the pregnancy than Angela was. Hopefully Wulfe and Fontana were helping to keep him grounded as well. "I'm not averse to the idea. Let's see where we are a little closer to the time."

"Agreed. After seeing everything Marigold did while I was gone, I'll have no hesitation in leaving her alone again."

Nodding, he flicked the blinker to turn into the parking lot. "I thought she was doing good, too, so it's good to hear it from you. Any word from her or Logan this morning?"

Shannon shook her head as they pulled into a parking space. "Not a word. But, maybe that's a good thing. I think Logan will go see his family sooner rather than later."

John leaned in for a kiss. "I think you're right. But then, you're always right, recently."

Shannon snorted. "Not. Just a little lucky."

LOGAN WOKE FEELING AMAZINGLY RESTED. He was warm. Incredibly warm. It was so nice. Then he realized there was a heavy weight against his right side. That was where the heat emanated from.

Marigold. Some of her hair was draped across his arm, and it smelled luscious. She smelled luscious. Scenes from the night before rolled through his mind and his body responded, hardening quickly. His dick knew that relief was mere inches away.

Marigold must have been half awake as well, because she turned her head up to blink at him in the morning light, smiling. Logan was struck by the innocence of her look. She had makeup smudged beneath her bright eyes and morning breath, but it didn't matter, because that look was turned in *his* direction. And there was something there, something that he didn't dare name in case it drifted away.

At some point in the past few days, something had shifted within him, and he had a feeling this woman was primarily responsible. The feeling of oppression that he carried on his shoulders every day seemed to be lighter. Hell, maybe it was just a mental shift in his own mind.

"Back in a minute. I have to pee," she grinned.

Logan watched her go, the cheeks of her ass peeking from beneath the hem of her T-shirt. The sight did not help his erection. He debated whether or not to get out of bed, but he really didn't want to. The mattress was so comfortable beneath his sore bones.

The toilet flushed in the bathroom and he heard water running in the sink. Then Marigold returned, her hair brushed, makeup wiped away. "Good, I'm glad you didn't move. It's a little chilly out here," she laughed, sliding back into the sheets, then tight against him. "How did you sleep?"

"Like a rock," he admitted. "Better than I have since I got here."

And that was the truth. Normally, he got a few hours, then was up the rest of the night, pacing and aching. Dreams woke him regularly. He didn't remember anything from last night, though.

"Good," she breathed, stretching her arm across his chest.

That put her breast in direct contact with him, and he could feel her nipple. Or maybe he just imagined it. What would she do if he rolled on his side and kissed her?

He had a feeling he knew. So, he did it.

Marigold's eyes widened as he loomed over her, but she grinned. She'd brushed her teeth while she'd been in the bathroom so he didn't think this was as spontaneous as he'd like to believe. "Thank you for last night," he murmured.

"And this morning?" she grinned hopefully, brows raised, eyes guileless.

Logan laughed, shifting his hips toward her as he leaned down to press a kiss to the corner of her lips. "If you don't mind some virgin-like fumbling, you might be able to thank me for this morning."

She made a face at him. "There was no fumbling last night."

"No, but grabbing your ass and fucking you are completely different things."

Her irises darkened, and she grinned. "As long as we're both happy at the end, I don't care how we get there."

Yeah, he was kind of the same.

Deepening the kiss, wishing he'd had his own toothbrush, he brushed his fingers over her body, thrilled to have access. Her nipples were peaked beneath the soft cotton of the tee, and he circled one several times, then held her entire breast in his hand.

Marigold's eyes fluttered and she sighed. Logan tugged the hem of the shirt up, baring her breasts for him to see. Her nipples were flushed a dark pink with arousal, and he leaned down to press a kiss to each one. Aware that he needed to shave, he lightly brushed his cheeks against the smooth skin of her belly.

Marigold reached up and cupped his face, scraping her thumbs over the dark bristles of his beard on the left side. The right side was bare of hair, but patchy down around his chin. He could feel her touch in some spots, but not really in others. "This must be hard to shave."

"It is. And it itches beneath the skin sometimes, like a hair is trying to come through."

She danced her fingers up the burns on the right side of his face, then stroked her thumb over his eyebrow. His eyelashes were thick and dark, and he'd been teased more than once about wearing makeup. "You know women would kill for these lashes, right?" she murmured.

His mouth quirked. "I've been told that many times. It's the only decent thing my father gave me, his eyes and lashes."

Marigold let her fingers drift down his cheek and neck to the collar of his t-shirt. "You might as well get rid of this."

Moving a little vertical, he whipped it over his head, tossing it away. Marigold stared, but it didn't strike him as a disgusted stare. Her fingers danced down his body, and over his abs. Some of the places she brushed he could feel, others he could not. When she reached his waistband, she tucked her fingers beneath the elastic, just barely brushing his cock, and looked up at him.

"Seriously? Why would you hide this body? I think you just need to be naked all day long."

He made a face, not sure how to take her words. "I don't

know. The cold doesn't always help a man's ego, if you know what I mean."

Marigold giggled, a light, carefree sound that he had a feeling he could grow to love.

"Well, someone," she batted her eyes theatrically, "will just have to warm you up occasionally."

Logan grinned. "Know anyone that would be crazy enough for the job?"

She shrugged, drawing attention to her exposed breasts. "If there are perks, maybe…"

"Oh, there are definitely perks," he murmured, licking the tip of her breast. Marigold sighed, her fingers running into his hair to hold him to her. Logan had a flash of insecurity, but she didn't even pause at what she felt, just tightened her hold.

Fuck it.

Pushing up, he levered himself over her, shuddering as her thighs fell wide to accommodate him. He worried about the replaced knee joint, but it bent exactly as he needed it to. When he lowered his hips to her cradle, they both gasped. He was hard as a rock, and even through his boxers and her panties, he could feel the heat rolling from her body. That hot spot called to him, and he needed to be inside her with a desperation that shocked him.

Reaching down he tucked the boxer elastic beneath his balls, releasing his aching dick. Then he pushed up into her, relying on the panties to keep them apart. Theoretically it would excite her more, teasing her like this, but she already felt soaked. "I…"

She reached down, jerking the gusset of her panties to the side, and before he could change his trajectory, she pulled him into her. "Oh, fuck…"

He paused for a moment, shaking, feeling how his body

felt inside the grip of a woman's body. "Give me just a second," he whispered. It didn't feel like it used to, years ago, but he'd expected it to be different. The heat was still there, and the pressure, but the sensation on the lower part of his dick seemed a little muffled. He withdrew his length, then surged forward again, losing himself in the sensation.

A tiny little part of his brain reminded him that they needed a condom, but the more visceral, instinctual part of his brain was urging him to feel and enjoy every second he could without the added barrier. The added layer might be what kept him from his pleasure.

Marigold sighed and shivered beneath him, her eyes fluttering open to meet his. They were dreamy with need, and Logan had to take a split second to realize that he never expected to see that look in a woman's eyes again. Her mouth sought his and he kissed her like he'd never kissed anyone before, trying to let her know what he felt.

"Oh, Logan," she breathed, arching her body up into his.

He tried to stay under control, he really did, but it had been so long since he'd done this. Reaching down, he lifted her thighs up over his hips, changing the angle. Marigold made this odd sound in her throat, a cross between a moan and a gasp. "Oh, my god, Logan. Oh..." she breathed, nipping at his earlobe. "Condom," she hissed, pushing at his shoulders.

It was one of the hardest things he'd ever done, stopping the rolling momentum in his body, but he did it. Bracing himself above her, he withdrew, panting, and let her scramble out from underneath him. He watched with slitted eyes as she circled the bed and ripped open the drawer of her bedside table. She held up the little foil square triumphantly, and tossed it to him as she bent over to shuck off her panties.

Logan struggled to move, but he managed to get the condom rolled on tight as Marigold returned, completely nude. She'd gotten rid of the t-shirt and panties and he could see her body completely naked for the first time. It staggered him. And humbled him. Thrilled him. In the morning light her skin almost glowed, very fair, with rosy pink highlights. The tips of her nipples and her lips were almost the same deep salmon pink, and he could only think of tasting her again. She was completely bare of pubic hair and he wanted to explore her body there.

Her strong thighs flexed as she crawled onto the bed toward him, and her eyes narrowed teasingly.

"You take my breath away," he admitted, cupping her face in his hands and giving her an open-mouthed kiss.

Marigold sighed and melted into him, her sweet tongue gliding along his. With a bounce, they moved back into position and she guided his cock deep, rocking her hips up toward him. Logan lost himself in the ride, pushing and grinding the way he needed to to find that euphoria he hadn't had for so long. Masturbation was fine, but there was nothing better than being balls deep inside a woman.

Marigold began to pant against his neck, her teeth nibbling the skin. "Do you know how good you feel inside me," she whispered. "You're going to make me come. Right there, Logan, right there..."

Logan maintained the pace with iron determination, needing her to find her release so that he could, but it got incrementally harder as he felt her unraveling beneath him. Her body loosened even more and her pants grew more excited. Just as he was worried he was going to come before her, she screamed out, her head arching back on the pillow and her body jerking with hard convulsive shudders.

Then his own release hit. Unable to muffle a groan, his

body went supernova with one of the hardest climaxes he'd ever experienced. Logan arched back, his legs digging into the mattress as he tried to get deeper than was physically possible. One moment he was kissing Marigold, then the next his head was buried in the pillow beside her and he was trying to drag in oxygen, his arms braced around her. Had he passed out? His body still contracted and rolled with light aftershocks.

Her strong arms held him tight, breast to chest, and she was whispering something into his hair. Gathering his strength, he lifted his head to look at her.

There was a smile on her face and a look in her eyes that told him he'd done a damned good job. "Are you okay?" he growled.

She nodded, grinning. Her legs were still up around his hips. Reaching down, she dragged the covers up over his shoulders. At some point they'd pushed them away. He appreciated the warmth immediately, though he knew he should move. Shifting, he readied to pull away, but she held him tight.

"Just stay here for a minute, please," she whispered.

Logan was more than happy to stay. He planted his head against the pillow again. "Just tell me when you need to breathe."

"I don't think I ever want you to go. Damn, dude..."

Logan grinned and had to pick his head up to look down at her. Anxiety churned. "You enjoyed yourself?"

She tightened her brows. "Um, yeah... I have a feeling Nancy heard that scream downstairs. Maybe she didn't hear it over The Price is Right. Do you realize you are ribbed for her pleasure?"

"What?" he asked incredulously, not sure he'd heard her correctly.

"Those scars seem to muffle your pleasure a little, but I'll have you know they do just fine for me."

She blinked her stunning green eyes up at him and grinned, and Logan couldn't help but grin back at her. "Ribbed for her pleasure, huh?"

A wicked light entered her eyes. "Yeah, like the condom commercials, you know?"

Logan laughed, rolling to the side, but he kept eye contact. "Not sure what to make of that, exactly."

"Take it for the compliment that it is," she said, giving him a smacking kiss. "I'm going to go take a shower. You're welcome to join me."

She rolled out of bed with no modesty whatsoever and headed toward the bathroom. Marigold Lee had such a beautiful shape.

"What sports did you play in school?" he asked, following her.

Marigold glanced over her shoulder as she turned on the faucet, grinning. "How do you know I played anything?"

"You're strong, solid. I'm thinking, softball."

She laughed softly, turning back to test the water temp. "And you'd be right. My grandpa coached, actually, and I played my entire high school career. I have a small scholarship I'm using for school, even, for going to state for a couple of years."

Logan nodded, gratified that he'd called it. "That's awesome. You have a beautiful body."

Brows lifted, she kissed him again before she stepped into the steaming shower. "Thank you. I think you do, too. Are you joining me?"

Logan stepped in behind her in the stall and slid the glass door shut. It was so strange to imagine anyone thinking of him as anything other than hideous or deformed, like he saw himself every day in the mirror. He'd gotten used to it, but it didn't please him. The thought that anything about his body could please anyone was... intriguing? No, confounding. Because it was so opposite of how he had viewed himself for so long.

Marigold turned, tipping her head back into the water and wetting down her hair. Then she nudged at him to switch places with her. Logan moved under the hot water and reached for the bottle of shower gel. "Do you have anything that won't make me smell like a damn fruit basket?"

Marigold was lathering shampoo into her hair. She grinned at him, and giggled. "Nope."

Scowling, he squirted a dollop into his hand. When he got a whiff of the stuff, though, he wasn't too upset. It smelled like Marigold. He could definitely tolerate that.

MARIGOLD HAD a new appreciation for Logan. She'd felt the muscles beneath the clothing, but she hadn't imagined, for some reason, that he would be this muscular. And that was her mistake. Maybe, because she knew he'd been burned, she'd expected him to look weak or something, but he really didn't. The scars wound around his right side, but it wasn't a sheet of scars. It was very patchwork, with some smooth skin interspersed with the damaged. She could only assume it was like that because of the way he was burnt.

He hadn't moved like a man in pain this morning. "I'm glad I didn't wear you out or hurt you too much last night."

"Me too. Although I don't think this morning could have gone any other way. I don't think any amount of pain would have kept me from having you."

Warmth flushed through her, and it wasn't because of the hot water. It was suddenly very hard to breathe. She had promised him that there would be no commitment, but she'd known as soon as she'd uttered the words that she was lying, at the very least to herself. As soon as he'd walked in the door she'd felt something, some connection to him. And it was only getting stronger.

Logan gripped her arm and turned her back to him, pulling her flush against him. Then he began to rinse her hair. Marigold tipped her head back, loving the feel of his fingers against her scalp. "That's really nice," she murmured.

And when he was done with her hair, she turned him to wash his back and down his flanks. Then she turned him and lathered his chest. He watched her, his blue-green eyes narrowed as if he was trying to understand her. Then she went lower, lathering his cock and balls, and an entirely different light entered his eyes. He began to harden, and a smile eased across his lips, but Marigold turned away. "Later. You promised me lunch."

And just that quickly the mood shifted. Logan's smile faded and he leaned in to rinse again. "You're right. We have things to do."

Within just a little while they got out of the shower and dressed. "I need to run down and change my clothes, at least. Meet you in the kitchen in about twenty?"

"Sounds good," she told him, pressing a kiss to his lips. Anxiety was already lining his lean face. "Hey, this is just lunch. More than likely you're not even going to see any of your family. And if you do, I don't think they'll recognize you. It's been more than twenty years."

"Yeah, you're probably right," he said distractedly. "Meet you in a few."

And he was heading out the landing and down the stairs to his own apartment.

Marigold took a moment to just sit and think about the night, as well as the morning. Logan was a good guy, she could tell that much, and she really hoped his family lived up to what she thought his expectations of them were. If not, she and the LNF group would be there for him.

El Toro Arvada was a beautiful, well-kept restaurant on the north-west side of Denver. The parking lot was freshly paved and very full for the lunch rush, which was encouraging. Marigold had to park out, almost to the street.

Logan looked around the area, seeing the attention that had obviously been put into caring for this business. The landscaping was immaculate, and the food must be good considering how packed it was. There was a scent wafting from the building that was making his stomach rumble.

"It's a nice looking restaurant," Marigold murmured, turning off the ignition. "The sign says family-owned for forty years."

Yeah, he'd seen that as well. He looked at the windows of the building, seeing people moving around. It was bright and beautiful outside right now, everything buttoned up for the winter, but there were large red umbrellas on the patio, like they'd started getting them out of storage and ready for the summer.

Logan didn't know how to feel at that moment. Anxiety

churned in his gut, tempered only by the fact that Marigold was beside him.

"Mari, thank you for coming with me. I apologize now if I do anything wrong."

She smiled at the shortening of her name and reached out to rest a hand on his forearm. "If you need to go, we'll go. Just say the word."

"I will," he agreed. Pushing the car door open, he planted his crutches and levered himself up out of the car.

Mari led the way up a few steps and she held a big wooden door open for him. Inside, a hostess greeted them with a brilliant smile. "Just two today? Would you like a booth or a table?"

Logan looked through the restaurant. "A booth, please."

"Right this way," the young woman said, and started to lead them through the tables. Logan took the seat that faced the main entrance of the restaurant. There was a hallway behind him, which he didn't like, but he wasn't going to draw attention to himself by moving. He glanced around the space.

El Toro was a typical looking Mexican restaurant, with brightly painted tables and interiors. It wasn't as hokey as some Mexican restaurants he'd seen. There was something classy and almost antique to the place. It was obvious they'd been here a long time.

A young man with dark hair and pretty, dark blue eyes brought them a basket of tortilla chips and a chunky salsa. "What can I get you to drink?"

Mari looked between Logan and the waiter, and he suddenly realized the problem. There was a bit of a resemblance, scars aside. Dark haired, blue eyed, fairly muscular and handsome. Not Hispanic looking necessarily, but there were some aspects there. It was like they had a common Hispanic ancestor from generations ago.

"Margarita. Actually, make it a pitcher, please."

"Will do," the young man said, smiling brightly. "My name is Michael and it will be my pleasure to serve you today."

Mari watched him disappear into the depths of the restaurant, then she glanced back at Logan. She covered his hand with her own, and he knew she was trying to ease some of the tension away. "We're just getting some lunch," she murmured. "No commitment. There may be no one here to talk to anyway."

Yeah, she was probably right.

The young man returned with a pitcher brimming with lime margarita. "Do you know what you'd like to order?"

Logan flipped open his menu. It had been sitting untouched since they'd taken their seats. "I'll do your lunch special with a side of guac. And can we do a queso for the table?"

The waiter nodded. "Absolutely. And for you ma'am?"

"Same. And an ice water, too, please."

The young man collected their menus. "Back in just a few minutes," he promised.

And he was, as promised, bringing her ice water and their queso. "If I forget anything, please wave me down. We're pretty busy right now and things slip through here and there."

"Will do," Logan promised, reaching for his margarita.

"Seems like a nice kid," Marigold murmured, lifting her glass. "Oh, man, this is a good drink."

Though it was a little early in the day, they both enjoyed the margarita. They were halfway through the glass when an older woman brought their food out. Logan looked up at the older woman and froze, knowing that his plans had just gone to hell.

It was her. His grandmother. He knew it in his bones.

The woman was smiling as she set the steaming plates in front of first Marigold, then Logan. "These are very hot," she warned them. "Don't burn yourselves..."

Her voice drifted away as she looked at Logan, and her professional smile faltered. She blinked several times, then seemed to shake herself. She clasped her hands in front of herself and renewed her smile, though it seemed brittle now. "Enjoy!"

He turned his head to watch the woman go, feeling like his life had just changed. Proof of his ancestry was standing across the room, smoothing her graying hair and talking to a younger woman.

"What, Logan? Did you recognize her?"

Nodding, he looked down at the steaming plate, his throat tight. "I think that was my grandmother."

Logan ate the food but didn't really think about it. He was too aware of being under scrutiny.

"So, are you going to talk to them?" Marigold asked softly.

Logan looked up into her green eyes with the tiny shatter of gold, and he was suddenly struck by the fact that she was there with him. She wore her glasses today, and just a touch of makeup, not that she needed it. The woman was beautiful, and healthy and strong. He had no idea why she was interested in tagging along with an injured vet, but he appreciated it nonetheless. No, not appreciated it. He was a little flummoxed by the entire situation. She was a good distraction though. She kept him from feeling the anxiety that was creeping in around his consciousness. Or maybe she just tempered it.

"I think I need to," he said softly.

They were almost done with their meal when the older woman approached them again. Her eyes darted nervously between them, but they lingered on him. "How was your meal?"

"It was wonderful," Logan told her, though he hadn't tasted anything.

"It was nice and spicy," Marigold told the woman. "So many Mexican restaurants don't use enough spice."

The older woman finally turned and looked at her. "Yes, I agree. My husband and I wanted our food to be memorable. It was very important to us when we started the business years ago. The food is as I remember it as a girl cooking with my *abuela*." She looked back at Logan. "I don't mean to seem forward, but do I know you? You seem very familiar to me. And, you look...well," she reached into her pocket and withdrew her phone. She swiped through a few screens, then held it out to him.

Logan took the phone from her and looked down at an old picture, which appeared to have been taken in the seventies. There was a gentleman in the picture that could have been his twin, but he knew it was probably his grandfather.

Logan showed the picture to Marigold, and she nodded her head at him. Eventually, he looked up at the woman. "I think this is my grandfather. My name is Logan Vance."

The woman almost crumpled before their eyes. "Logan? No..."

Logan started to get out of the bench seat, but Michael, their waiter, swept in and grabbed the woman around the waist. "Nan, what's wrong?"

The woman straightened and shook her head. "Get your Papi. Go, Michael."

The young man took off, glancing back over his shoulder once. Several other of the restaurant crew watched them, but Logan's gaze was brought back to his grandmother. "Why don't you pull up a chair?" he asked eventually.

She blinked, as if she was surprised at the suggestion, then nodded, glancing around at the other customers. Grabbing a chair from an adjoining table, she moved it to the end of their table and sat down, wringing her hands in the apron hanging from her waist. "You've grown," she whispered, her eyes filling with tears. She stared him in the eye, though, in a way that he appreciated.

"Well, it's been a few years," he said wryly.

She laughed as well, then began to cry again, softly. "I don't even know where to start. Where have you been all these years? And the other kids? And what happened to you?" She reached out as if to brush her hand over the scars on his face and he drew back. The woman curled her hand away and sat back in the chair.

"When we left here, we made it to Ohio before our car gave up the ghost. We stayed there for a few months, then moved on to Virginia. As for the other kids..." he paused, glancing at Marigold. She gave him an encouraging smile. "Jana passed away several years ago, and the last I'd heard Clint was serving time in county again for a different drug offense."

The woman's tears grew into sobs and Logan stopped, glancing around the restaurant. "Maybe this isn't the best place to do this," he murmured, reaching out to the woman's elbow.

His grandmother bobbed her head, trying to stem the flow of tears. "Please, will you come back to the house? We, I know my husband will want to talk to you as well."

Logan nodded. "We'll come to your house. What's the address?"

Marigold typed the address into her GPS as his grandmother rattled it off, and Logan appreciated her all over again. Reaching into his wallet he dropped a fifty on the table, hoping that would cover the meal and the drinks.

"We don't charge family," the woman said, stuffing the bill back toward him.

Logan refused the money. "Then use it to tip Michael, or something. Please."

She retracted her hand, nodding. "He's going to school, so he'll appreciate that."

Giving him a long, lingering look, her gaze traced quickly over his body. "I, I'll meet you at the house," she said in a rush, and turned away.

Logan climbed to his feet, hating that he had to use crutches in front of them. Defensiveness roared through him, the look on his grandmother's face stuck in his mind. What had she thought, looking at his broken body? Logan went through the restaurant and out the front door, incredibly aware of the several pairs of eyes on him. This may not have been a great idea.

Marigold hurried ahead and unlocked the car. "We suck at surveillance. We were made within ten minutes."

He snorted. Leave it to her to find the humor in the situation.

"They live just a few blocks away."

"Take the long way, would you," he murmured, settling into the passenger seat and wedging his crutches beside him.

"Of course."

They left the lot and she turned left, away from the house located on the map. Marigold didn't say anything as he stared out the window and tried to gather his thoughts. "She seemed nice," he said, glancing at her, asking for her input.

"Very. You can see she's been traumatized. Seeing you was a shock. But a pleasant shock, I think."

"Yeah, I think I got that as well. I hate that I made her cry." He watched out the window for a while, then caught her eye. "Ok, we can head over there. I just needed to breathe for a minute." Reaching out, he rested a hand over hers on the gearshift. "I appreciate you being with me, Mari. This isn't what you signed up for."

She shrugged and tossed him a grin. "No worries, Logan. You might be surprised what I'm up for when it comes to you."

His throat tightened with emotion as he looked at her. Even when the world was screaming around him, she was proving to be a rock.

Within a few minutes they were pulling up in front of a pretty brick ranch house, long and low to the ground. There were several cars parked in the driveway and Logan wondered who would be inside when he went in. The house, amazingly, looked familiar to him.

"I'll be right beside you, okay?" Marigold leaned close, brushing her lips against his, and he took a minute to just enjoy her touch, blocking everything else out. This was an epically important point in his life-- he was about to meet his family-- yet he found himself wondering how soon they could get back to bed. Mari had rocked his world, and he was ready to just curl up with her again.

No, he needed to get this worked out. Kissing her firmly, he ran a finger down her cheek. "Till later," he sighed.

Stepping out of the car, he adjusted his crutches on his forearms and made his way up the walk. The temperature had dropped again, today, and salt had been scattered on the walkway to dissipate the threat of ice.

Logan looked up at the house, feeling nostalgia creep through him. Around the side of the house there used to be a big, yellow aluminum swing set with a merry-go-round. Just one of those little four-seater jobbies. He remembered playing with someone there, another little boy. Not his brother. Clint had been too little at the time. Must have been a cousin or something.

The front door opened, and an older man stood there. Logan recognized him immediately. Tall, with a shock of bright white hair, he had the bearing of a former military man. He also looked like an older version of his own father. This must be Arthur. Logan held out his hand. "Sir."

The older man shook his hand carefully, looking him up and down. The older woman from the restaurant moved to his side, curling an arm around his waist, and together they welcomed him inside.

As soon as he saw the old organ in the corner, he smiled. "I remember playing that. Actually, I remember flipping the colorful switches, and you," he pointed at the woman, "getting after me."

Eugenia nodded, her eyes filling with tears again. "You just flipped them back and forth. You knew to hold a finger on one of the keys and use the other hand to change the instrument voice."

She waved them into the living room and to a pale cream couch. There was a pitcher of iced tea on the coffee table, and several glasses with ice. Once Eugenia had poured them all glasses and they were settled, she looked to her husband.

Arthur had stared at him ever since he'd entered the

house, and Logan supposed he didn't blame him. A lot had happened to him over the past twenty years.

"So, I guess I'm your grandson," Logan said eventually. He'd brought the file with him that John had compiled, but he tucked it beside his leg on the couch. "I didn't realize there was actually anyone left. Dad seemed to intimate that everyone was dead, pretty much."

Eugenia covered her mouth with her hand. "No, he didn't," she gasped.

"Oh, he did," Logan disagreed. "For my entire life."

Arthur's mouth tightened with anger and he looked down at his wife. "I didn't think he could hurt us anymore, but he has." He turned his bright blue gaze, only slightly faded with age, to Logan. "Is he still alive?"

"He is, but not in good health. He's fought addictions for years."

"We made him go to rehab many times, but it never worked," Eugenia said. "He was always breaking out and partying. I got so tired of that word. Partying."

Arthur looked at Logan. "The other two children? Your brother and sister?"

"Jana is dead," he told them softly. "She was killed when her boyfriend who was high at the time plowed them into a tree. She was just moving out of Dad's house after I left. Clint has been into and out of jail for as long as I can remember. Before I left to come here, he was in jail again."

Reaching for a tissue, Eugenia wiped at her eyes. "Jana was such a beautiful girl. Always so full of life. It was hard for her to accept you when you were born, because she was our first grandchild, so everyone doted on her."

"She became my protector when we left," Logan said. "Mom was caring for Clint, so it fell to her to watch over me."

Arthur nodded. "I can see her taking on that role. She took care of her dolls that way as well."

"Do you have a picture of her? Grown, I mean?"

Logan flipped through the Gallery on his phone, finding his favorite picture of them together. It was the day he'd left for basic training, and their last picture together. He handed the phone over. It was a picture of a picture, but it was all he had.

Eugenia cried more, her hands shaking as she held the phone. "We tried to keep you here, but they wouldn't let us. When we refused to bail Chris out of jail, he said he would make us pay. But what were we supposed to do? He had gotten into trouble so many times, and we just couldn't watch him do it to you kids. Sharon was no help."

"Who was Sharon," Marigold asked.

"My mother," Logan murmured.

"She was a spineless twit who catered to your father, no matter what he wanted," Eugenia said, her own spine straight.

"She still is," Logan admitted.

Eugenia shook her head. "That woman was no mother to you kids. She was a broodmare and a maid, never a partner."

Logan agreed with her. "She worked at the restaurant while my father was in the Army?"

Arthur nodded, rubbing his wife's back. "We gave her a job because he always went through his pay so fast. Usually cigarettes and liquor, gambling. He never cared if you kids had enough to eat or not. He always came first. Yes, he was my son, but Christopher seemed to take joy in doing the exact opposite of what he should have done to be a man and take care of his family."

Logan nodded slowly. "It was only yesterday that I

learned of his criminal charges in the Army, and his jail time."

Arthur's jaw clenched. "It was disgraceful. Our family has served in the United States military for generations with an impeccable record. I felt that pushing him into the military would help him grow and experience the world, but he didn't take to it. Didn't take to the discipline. He was the baby of the family, so we'd given in to him a lot. By that time, he had met your mother, and it was only because she encouraged him that he stayed in. She was pregnant with Jana within a few weeks of meeting him, so they needed the benefits. It wasn't enough to keep his damn mouth shut though."

"We would hear stories of him mouthing off to his sergeants, then getting out of trouble somehow. We think he was...well," Eugenia looked at her husband. "They were supposed to be doing drug tests and stuff, but maybe they weren't as good back then. Or maybe they missed him."

So, he skated through service by being a pusher. Considering his charges later, someone had caught and reported him. Logan glanced at Marigold and he could read the same thought in her expression.

"Thank you for sharing that with me," Logan said. "After so many years I'm finally starting to hear the truth. My father still maintains that the Army screwed him over. He always told us that he was bumped out because he had contraband in his pocket."

Eugenia snorted derisively, her eyes flashing. "He always had contraband in his pocket. I swear, I don't know what happened to him to make him behave that way."

"Sometimes addictions can't be controlled," Marigold murmured. "He may have actually been doing the best he could."

"Well, it wasn't enough," Arthur said, jaw clenched. "Our family had a history. We believe in our democracy and have literally bled for the people of this country, many times over in fact. Your uncle James was killed in action, and the rest of your aunts and uncles have all served. Karen is still serving and plans on retiring."

Logan nodded. "I read that."

Eugenia held out a hand, motioning to his legs. "Did you serve?"

"I did," he said, gruffly. "I almost fulfilled my six-year contract when my squad was hit by an IED. I was the only one in the vehicle that survived."

Arthur's eyes reddened and grew damp with emotion, and Eugenia cried a little. Logan appreciated the sentiment more than they could know. No one in his family had acknowledged what he had been through.

Arthur held out his hand. "Your heart pumps with Showalter blood."

Emotion tightened his throat as he shook his grandfather's hand. "Thank you, sir."

The silence stretched for a minute as they gathered their emotions.

"How did you find us?" Arthur asked. "Was it one of the ancestry websites? We weren't sure where to post that we were looking for you."

"No," he glanced at Marigold for a moment. "I flew out here for a couple of reasons. One of them was to try to figure out where my family had come from. But I ran into this lady, and long story short, her husband is an investigator with a firm that helped me find you and put all the pieces together. I had done my own investigating but when Dad changed his name that kind of roadblocked me. I didn't know what the old family name was. John figured it out."

"Well, we need to thank him," Eugenia said, her eyes filling with tears. "We're so very glad to get to know you again, Logan. A piece of my heart is back where it's supposed to be. You're not returning to Virginia in the near future, are you? There's a lot of family that would love to meet you."

Logan felt his eyes widen with the thought. A *lot* of family? For so long it had just been he and his sister against the world. The thought that there were people actually related to him and wanted to meet him was... odd. And the thought of returning to Virginia hadn't even entered his mind. When he'd first planned this trip, he'd thought that Colorado would be his final destination, and that hadn't changed. He had no desire to go back east.

This entire week had been odd. Glancing at Marigold, he found her watching him, a soft smile on her lips. Impulsively, he leaned forward and dropped a kiss to those smiling lips. When he drew back, her smile had morphed into a full grin. "What was that for?"

Unaccountably, his throat tightened with emotion again, of an entirely different sort. "Everything," he murmured, voice raspy. Then he turned to his grandparents. "I would love to meet them."

16

Marigold lost track of all of the family members that came to the house over the next few hours. At one time there had to have been at least thirty people milling through the rooms and laughing with each other. Some brought snacks or beer. Little kids were running around and being cute. It was so heart-warming watching Logan meet each person and lay out in his mind who they were connected to. She never once saw him misspeak a name. It was like he committed them to memory. Military Intelligence training at its best.

One little boy with dark hair and sea-glass blue eyes latched onto Logan and felt the need to tell him his life story. It was so adorable because they could have been father and son, they looked so similar. The child, Austin, was actually Logan's second cousin, and only six. As she looked out over the people she could see, most of them were dark haired and light eyed, just like Logan's grandparents. The line bred true.

An impromptu meal was pulled together and tables and

chairs were pulled out of the garage to fill the dining room and accommodate all of the extra people.

"Bone apple teeth," Austin called out, sending people into laughter. It took her a minute to realize he meant *bon appétit*.

It was a rowdy, wonderful affair, and Marigold wished she'd had this kind of family growing up. Hers had been small to begin with, and there were only a few people left besides her grandmother and a few cousins.

By the time they left later that night, Marigold was exhausted, and she knew Logan had to be as well. As they headed to her cold car, he limped more than normal, and sagged into the seat. It took him a minute to get the seatbelt wrapped around himself.

Marigold cranked the engine and they wove through the neighborhood, headed south toward Denver.

"Thank you," Logan said, his voice low and soft.

"Why do you keep thanking me?" she laughed. "I didn't do anything."

"But you did," he corrected firmly. "Every time I started to second-guess myself you were there to keep me going. And in the end, it paid off. I can't believe what a family I have."

"You are exceptionally lucky," she murmured. "I would love to have a portion of the amount of family you have."

He laughed then. "It's so crazy. Six hours ago, I had no one I wanted to claim."

Marigold nodded, glancing in the rearview mirror as she changed lanes. "You can only be thankful. And enjoy them while you have them."

He nodded, looking out the side window at the passing lights. "That Austin was something," he murmured, chuckling softly.

Marigold snorted. "That kid thought you hung the moon, and I get it. You look enough like his dad that you could be brothers instead of cousins."

He nodded, looking at her in the darkness. "You noticed that too, huh?"

"That you all look the same? Of course. Only the married spouses looked different and brought some color in. Elliot's wife Brandy had the most amazing hair. It wasn't red. It was like a true auburn. Just beautiful."

"Austin's dad and I played together when we were little. I didn't want to leave," he said softly.

"I can totally understand why. Arthur and Eugenia were getting tired, though. And you were as well."

He heaved a sigh. "Yeah, I know. That was a long day. Thank you for sitting through all that."

She made a face at him in the dark. "You make it sound like I was sitting through opera or something. It really wasn't that bad. I loved watching you meet everyone. I got a few pictures, too."

"Did you really? I didn't even notice. Thank you, again, Mari."

"No problem."

When they got back to Marshall house, Nancy was puttering in the kitchen. She stopped what she was doing and wiped her hands on a dishtowel when they came in. "What have you young people been up to today," she asked, grinning.

Logan sat at the kitchen table, looking tired but extremely satisfied. "Grandma Nancy, I met my real grandmother today. Her name is Eugenia and she's been missing me for a long time. I also met my grandfather Arthur."

Nancy's eyes went wide as she sank down into the chair opposite Logan. "Oh, you found your family," she breathed. "What a blessing that is! We need wine to celebrate!"

They laughed and all took glasses as she handed them out. Marigold grinned at Logan, appreciating that he hadn't shut Nancy down. Marigold had a feeling that this was the entire reason why the woman stayed up, to take part at least peripherally in their lives.

"So, tell me about them," Grandma said as they sipped.

Logan related the details of his family. Nancy hadn't known about Logan's father stealing the family away. When he told her about it, she reached out and covered his hand with her own.

Marigold watched Logan's expression. It had been so expressive throughout the day, though she knew he'd tried to control it. When they'd first gone to the restaurant, it had been tight with anxiety, then tense as he'd talked to his grandparents. Eventually it had eased into acceptance, and maybe even joy as he'd dealt with his new family members as they rolled in, all of which seemed to be sane, intelligent people willing to accept him exactly the way he was. Every time he met someone new, there had been a guardedness, but then relief as they all took in his scars and welcomed him as a hero.

"I'm not a hero," he'd said more than once, but to a family that valued service to their country the way the Showalters did, they'd brushed his words aside and appreciated him for the man he was.

Marigold had been brought to tears several times as she'd watched the interaction between the family. Two of his uncles had been there as well, and they'd fallen into military speak so easily, because they'd all served in the Army. It had been truly a special thing to watch, and she didn't think Logan felt the full repercussions yet. His life had changed today, and she hoped he saw the value of what had happened as much as she did.

They sat and talked with Nancy for almost an hour before they all headed for bed. Marigold thought that maybe Logan would need a night alone to digest what had happened, but when she started to make her excuses, he waved her away. "Mind if I stay with you tonight?"

"Not at all," she said softly, her heart warming.

"Let me grab a few things and I'll follow you up."

So, she stood there watching him move around his space. He grabbed a change of clothes and his toothbrush, then what looked to be a tablet. Rather than see him struggle she took the items from him and carried them up the stairs as he locked his door. Once inside her room she set the items on the dresser by the bed.

Butterflies tangled in her stomach. They'd slept together and played together, but it was still new enough that she wasn't sure what to expect. "I'm going to go clean up a little and use the bathroom. Are you hungry? Help yourself to anything in the fridge."

He didn't especially seem to be listening, so she turned and went in to do what she needed to. When she returned, he was sitting on the blue jean couch flipping through pages on his tablet. When she sank down near him, he looked up with a tired smile. The ball cap was gone, and his dark curls rested on his forehead. "I'm still buzzing," he admitted. "Actually, I think you could blow me over, I'm so tired, but my mind won't stop."

Marigold grinned. "I know. You have reason to be excited. You have an amazing family."

"It seems that way, doesn't it?"

She nodded, reaching out to run her hand down his thigh. He still wore his jeans and boots. Would he mind if she started undressing him?

"I want to talk to Rob and Larry again," he said, staring off into the distance.

Those were two of his uncles. They were older than his father and full of stories about being kids. Larry had actually been stationed on Fort Benning, where Logan had been most of his career. They'd shared stories and had even known a few of the same people, mostly higher- ranking officials on the base. "One of the guys that used to be his sergeant is set to command the fort in the next couple of years."

"That's very cool," she said, nodding. "I wish I had family like that. My dad was an only child. I knew his parents a little, but not as much as my mother's. They passed years ago."

Logan winced and shifted his shoulders toward her. "I'm sorry, Mari. I'm going on about all this and I shouldn't be."

Marigold scowled. "Why the fuck would you say that? You have brand new family that is going to love the hell out of you and they already accept who you are. That's such exciting news. You should be shouting it from the rooftops. At the very least you should let John and Shannon know, and you should bask in that love. No apologies, seriously."

He nodded once, accepting her point.

"Besides," she continued. "You had a lot rougher childhood than I did. You deserve this time in your life. Period."

Reaching out, he looped some of her hair around his finger. "I never expected them to be so...like me, I guess. And I definitely didn't expect there to be so many of them. Shit."

She laughed and pulled her hair from his hand. She shifted, going to her knees in front of him. Logan's eyes narrowed on her with interest, until he realized she was just untying his boots. "You're a tease," he told her, smiling softly.

Marigold shook her head as she tugged first one boot off, then the second. "Nope. It's only a tease if you don't follow through with it," she laughed, running her hands up his jeans-clad thighs.

"You have more of those condoms?" he asked her.

"I do."

Going between his thighs, she leaned up enough to walk her fingers up the center of his chest. "You have the energy? I'm okay waiting until morning."

Logan shook his head. "Not gonna happen. You've been a beautiful distraction all day today, and I can finally focus on you the way I need to. Go do what you need to do in the bathroom, and I'll meet you in the bed."

Marigold didn't need to be told twice. Pushing to her feet, she headed into the bathroom. Brushing her teeth while she brushed her hair out, she tried to be quick, arousal humming in her blood. Logan only had to look at her and her body began to ready for him.

Stepping out of the bathroom, she jerked to a halt in the doorway. Logan was stretched out on the bed on his side, scarred, ripped abs taut as he swung her brilliant pink dildo in his hand. He was grinning as he pressed the buttons, putting her little machine through its paces.

Marigold's cheeks flamed with heat, but the embarrassment was totally worth Logan's broad grin. Had she ever seen him smile like that before? "What? Never seen a pink dildo before?"

Logan laughed. "Can't say that I have actually. Does pink work better than every other color?"

She giggled as she went to her knees on the bed beside him. "I don't know. Works fine for me."

Sitting up, he motioned to the mattress. "Lay down."

A shiver rolled through her at the command in his voice and she moved to comply, laying flat before him. Marigold would have liked to blame the cool air of the apartment for her puckered nipples and the goose-bumps running down her body, but she knew it was the look in his eyes. There was intent, there, and a confidence she hadn't seen in him before. The biggest thing she saw, though, was promise. As tired as he was, he was determined to give her pleasure.

LOGAN LOOKED at the bounty before him and he didn't know where to start. Marigold lay completely naked, blinking up at him languorously. There was a soft smile on her lips, and her nipples, the same delicate color, were puckered, as if awaiting his touch.

The dildo was off, but he knew which button to push to start the gentle buzzing. It was about six inches long and curved slightly, he assumed to reach her G-spot. "Do you use this a lot?"

Her smile spread. "Only when I've been really disappointed with a date."

"So, how often is that," he growled.

"Most of the time," she grinned, shifting her hips.

"I'll make you a promise," he said, voice low. "As long as you're with me, you'll never have to use this. Unless I'm using it on you," he grinned.

She grinned back, her arms lifting up above her head as she arched for him. Turning the vibrator on to the lowest setting, he touched it to the gentle swell of her belly. The skin twitched and she wiggled away, gasping. He followed her though, not letting her shift too far away. "Hold still," he warned.

Marigold went still, until he brushed the head of the dildo around her right nipple. He avoided the tip, but worked all the way around her plump flesh. She moved to try to make him touch her nipple, but he pulled away to focus on another part of her body. He'd seen the way she'd reacted to nipple pressure, and he didn't want her to come too soon. This was too much fun.

Shifting, he touched the arch of her right foot with the head of the dildo, chuckling when she gasped and jerked. Running the machine up her calf, he tried to anticipate which way she would shift as he moved higher, and he followed her. Circling to the front of her thigh he ran it up the length, then danced lightly across her bare mons and down the other thigh. By the time she gasped with shock at the intimate touch in her pubic area, he was already gone.

"Oh, Logan..."

That breathiness in her voice would be his undoing. It became Logan's sole focus, to make her hiss and sigh and moan as he ran the dildo over her skin. When he touched it to her nipples, she arched like she was being snapped by a live wire. Her legs shifted restlessly and he could see the shine of moisture on her thighs. Her legs spread, wanton, as she begged him without words to delve into that wetness and satisfy her.

Mari was completely waxed here, and he'd never seen such a pretty pussy. Her lips were swollen, begging for any kind of touch, and as he neared her center her hips rocked toward him. "Stop teasing, please," she begged.

It was so much fun, though.

Then she reached down to touch herself. "No," he told her, pushing her arms above her head again.

Then she began to play dirty. Rather than reaching for her own body, she reached for him. Logan only wore his athletic shorts, and he'd been hard ever since he'd found the dildo in her nightstand drawer. As he just barely brushed the head of the dildo along the seam of her wet lips, she wrapped her hand around his aching cock.

Logan went still, need roaring through him, then he very carefully drew her hand away from his body. Very deliberately he put her hand on her own breast, and she began to tweak her nipples. Her knees fell open and he glided the head of the dildo through her wetness. He needed to satisfy her, because he didn't think he was going to last much longer. Just looking at her writhing on the bed in front of him was almost enough to get him off. If he focused, he was sure he could.

As he parked the head of the dildo at the entrance to her body, he pressed the button to make it vibrate faster, pushing it forward. The slick silicone slid oh, so easily into her body. Marigold lifted her legs, opening herself up for him, and he manipulated the dildo into, then out of her body. Moving faster, he mimicked the way he wanted to plunge his own body into her. With his second hand, he found her clit with his thumb and began to circle.

That was all it took for her to scream out and arch, her body lost to sensation as she orgasmed. Logan kept the dildo moving, until she twisted away from the touch. "Stop, please," she begged.

Flicking the power off, he set the machine aside. Mari's body was flushed with pleasure, her nipples dark with blood flow. Her body quaked with delicious aftershocks. It took her a minute to even rouse enough to look at him, her eyes glazed with pleasure.

That precious, unguarded look was almost satisfaction enough for him. If she had rolled over and gone to sleep, he would have probably done the same. Instead, she cupped his neck and pulled him down onto her, kissing her way along his jaw and to his mouth. Logan got lost in her kiss, and the feel of her body opening to him. Mari's thighs widened for his hips, and she arched up into him, searching. Shifting, Logan pushed his shorts away. His cock was hard as a rock, and he slid home easily, only remembering at the last minute to grab a condom. Mari waited for him to rejoin her, thighs wide to accommodate him as he resettled between her thighs. She shuddered and huffed out a breath against his neck. "Oh, Logan," she panted. "I didn't think I had another one in me after that, but I might surprise myself."

Logan moved carefully, but she didn't seem to need that, the wetness from her release almost pulling him in. He rocked forward, pushing his hips as tight to her as he could, before withdrawing, then gliding deep again. Mari huffed out a breath each time he rocked into her, then began to moan and twist beneath him. Reaching down, he gripped her hips in his hands, trying to get them the tiniest bit closer as his release slammed into him.

Mari cried out with him, their bodies moving together like they'd always been lovers. Logan lost track of everything as the fire consumed him and flung him from the edge of a glorious cliff. With a final focus, he made sure Mari went with him, and they tumbled together.

It took them several long minutes to recover their breath and control of their bodies. Logan forced himself to roll away and do a slow walk to the bathroom to dispose of the condom. When he returned, Mari was on her side, watching as he neared her. And even though he'd just had her, he knew he could go again in a little while.

Marigold flung the sheets back for him to climb in, stayed long enough to give him a kiss, then slipped out of the bed. "I'll be back. I need a shower," she laughed.

Logan watched her pretty ass disappear into the bathroom, then let himself sink into the mattress. He stared at the ceiling, remembering the pleasure. He felt something hard beneath his hip. Oh, yeah, the dildo. He set it on the nightstand with a grin. They would have to do that again.

Marigold was seriously messing with his no commitment mandate. Hell, it had pretty much gone out the proverbial window. She was winding him around her little finger. And he didn't think he minded.

Two weeks ago he'd been almost ready to put a bullet in his brain, but the thought left him cold, now. So many things had changed. He had family now, quite an extensive one, and the beginnings of a relationship that he hadn't expected. There was a group of men nearby that had been through the exact same things he had, so they *knew* what he was dealing with, and they didn't hesitate to offer their support.

It was a paradox, though, because as happy as he was, his guilt had also increased. Miller would never be with his family again or love a woman again. Logan didn't understand why he'd been the one given the chance to live on.

Early next week, he needed to go see Miller's mom. She deserved it and he'd put if off long enough. If he could get some kind of resolution with Lisa and Ashley, he would feel like he could move on, maybe. There was no way he would ever completely move on, but maybe he could start to take the steps. Maybe he wouldn't feel guilty living life if he could settle Miller's loss in his mind.

John Palmer deserved a huge thanks, as well. Feeling motivated, he reached for his cell phone and typed out a message. Then he turned on his side to wait for Mari to come back to bed.

17

When John rolled into the kitchen with a broad, shit-eating grin on his face, Shannon couldn't help but be leery. "What'd you do?"

John stopped his chair beside her, looking affronted. "Why would you think I did anything bad? Maybe I did something good? Maybe I'm helping my community."

Shannon gave him a look and handed him a dripping dish. Snatching the dishtowel from the cupboard rack, he started to dry it. "I didn't do anything bad. Really. I might have sent in a few recruiter cards. With a few names I knew."

Turning, she pinned him with a look. "What do you mean, recruiter cards?"

"You know those postcards that you get at the library and stuff. 'If you would like information on Joining the US Air Force, drop this card in any mailbox'."

He grinned, looking so satisfied she had to laugh at him. "And whose names did you give them?"

"Oh, just Chad and Zeke. Maybe Duncan. I thought Flynn might be interested too. Diego and Grif I combined into one name because I ran out of cards, but they'll get a nice big information packet at the Vail office."

Snorting, she went back to washing dishes. "You're incorrigible."

"Hey, you have to keep things lively, and the guys connected. Gives us something to talk about in our chat group."

That damn chat. Right about nine o'clock it seemed like the LNF men started to get bored, because the chat notifications began to ring. More than once she'd told him to turn down the volume because she was trying to get the boys to settle down.

It was going on ten and the kids were well asleep. She'd wanted to finish the last few dishes from dinner, then she was heading to bed. It seemed like she was jet-lagging, bad. "I'm heading to bed early," she told him firmly. "Can you let the dog out and make sure she has food? Give her one of those treat bones she likes, too."

John rubbed the small of her back. "I can do that. I can do this, too, babe. Go ahead and go to bed. I'm probably still up for a while. I'm working on a trigger replacement for Harper. I told him we'd go shooting Sunday."

Shannon nodded. The far side of the garage had been converted to a small gunsmithing area, John's version of a man-cave. They'd mounted a big heater in the corner of the space so that he didn't freeze, and he was modifying the area as he went along. With a fridge and TV out there, he could stay for hours and not even notice the time passing. There was also a monitor so that he could hear the kids if they roused.

"Don't work too late," she cautioned him.

"It's Friday night. I'm allowed to play a little later," he laughed.

John would go out there and even though he worked with most of the idiots he chatted with, they would be snickering like school boys over memes and videos into the wee hours, sometimes. Shannon never said anything about it because she knew they loved the connectedness of it.

Leaning in, she dropped a kiss to his lips. "I love you, sexy."

"I love you, too, babe," he said, cupping her face.

His phone dinged with an incoming message as she drew back.

"Logan says he'd like some time to talk to me this weekend or Monday," he murmured, looking at the screen. "Hope everything's okay."

"If it wasn't, he would probably tell you."

"Yeah, you're probably right. Go to bed."

He swatted her lightly on the behind as she left the kitchen. She barely had the energy to brush her teeth and climb into bed she was so tired. As soon as her head hit the blessed pillow she was lost to sleep.

Six a.m. did indeed come early, but the boys were surprisingly malleable as she fed them breakfast in their pjs, which tickled them, and parked them in their high chairs while she cooked bacon. They were usually dressed by the time she fed them breakfast, but they knew that the weekends were different. They still got up at the same time but they didn't have to rush out the door. Shannon felt refreshed after a full eight hours of sleep, and powered through the early morning, starting what felt like ten tons of laundry. How could such little people produce so much work?

She thought about John's assertion that he would help her out more. Would he watch the kids while she went to town?

When she asked him to babysit after she filled his belly

with good breakfast, he immediately said yes. "I don't have any plans. Sunday, I have to go to the range with Harper to test that trigger pull. Why don't you see if Lora and Willow can do lunch or something?"

Shannon was shocked and appreciative. "I'll text them and see. I love you, babe. Thank you."

He shook his dark head. "Don't thank me for watching my own kids. You do too much and it needs to be more even. Now," he said warningly, "throw another baby into the mix and things might change."

Shannon laughed, horrified at the thought. "No other baby right now. I'm going to go hop in the shower."

Another baby, she snorted, as she kissed her boys on the head and headed for the bathroom. They would be crazy to have another kid right now.

Shannon hurried through a shower and got dressed, then checked her phone. Willow was on-call, so a no-go. No response from Lora. Hm. Maybe she should just run over there and steal her away. She was probably locked in her office eyeball deep in some report that she absolutely needed to know by Monday. With a final kiss to John and her boys she hopped in her truck and headed the few blocks to Lora's house.

Mercy opened the door, which surprised Shannon. "Hello, sweetheart. Where's your mom?"

Mercy blinked her big green eyes up at her. "She's in her office talking to Dad. That's why I opened the door. I don't think they're..." she frowned, shaking her blond head. "I don't know. They keep telling me everything is okay, but something's not right."

Shannon frowned and leaned down to hug the girl. "If they say everything is okay, it probably is."

"Hey, Shannon. Sorry, didn't hear the door," Chad said,

walking up and resting a hand on Mercy's shoulder. Bare-foot and rumpled, Chad looked like he'd slept in his clothes. He wore his blade prosthetic rather than the one fitted to his cowboy boots, but he moved like he didn't even notice the strange looking thing. He probably didn't.

"If this is a bad time I can come back. John offered to watch the boys while I grabbed lunch and groceries, and I thought Lora might want to go with me."

Chad smiled and nodded, but she didn't feel like he was okay. Reaching out she rested a hand on his forearm, conscious of worried, eight-year old eyes tracking them. "Are you okay?"

The smile faded and he sighed. "I'm fine. Maybe some lunch talk would be good for Lora. She's in her office." He made a motion down the hallway, and with a final smile at them both, she headed in that direction.

Lora sat in her big office chair, turned away from the desk and looking through the big bay window over the back yard. The house was beautiful, with a wide panorama view of the golf course beyond. It was late Spring, and the fair-ways were already an artificial neon green, too bright to be natural. Shannon was so excited when they'd moved in, because it had plenty of room to expand their family later and was within a few blocks of her own house.

"Hey, woman," she said breezily as she walked in.

Lora turned in surprise, forcing a smile as she crossed the room to meet Shannon. They hugged and when Lora would have drawn back, Shannon held onto her arms. "What's going on?"

Lora's face was blotchy with restrained tears. She shook her head as her eyes welled. "Nothing."

"This doesn't look like nothing," Shannon said, worried.

Lora drew a deep breath. "Just a difference of opinion."

And she stopped there. Shannon was worried for her friend, but she knew certain things were too sensitive to talk about. "Okay. Just know that I'm here for you if you need me."

Nodding, she hugged Shannon again. "I know. Thank you. What are you doing here?"

"Well," Shannon said slowly, drawing back a little. "John has the kids and told me to take time for lunch before I got my groceries. I thought you might like to get out as well."

Lora glanced back at her desk. "I would but I'm having some issues at work. Can we take a raincheck?"

Shannon narrowed her eyes at her friend. "No, we can't. I already have about three of your rainchecks in my pocket I'm still waiting on."

Shannon was shocked when Lora's eyes filled with tears again. Crossing her arms beneath her breasts Lora turned away from Shannon. "Oh, honey, don't worry about it. I was just teasing you. If you're busy it's no big deal."

Crossing the room to the far window, Lora looked out over the golf green. Afraid of the tears she thought she'd see, Shannon joined her, but Lora was clear-eyed.

"Chad has been after me about my work hours," she murmured.

"Well," Shannon said slowly. "I think he has reason to," she told her friend honestly. "You work way too much. You do realize this is Saturday, right? Normally a day to relax and hang with family or friends. Get some chores done. Not go over...whatever it is you think you need to go over."

"I know it's Saturday," Lora said softly, looking down at her hands. "It's the only day my phone doesn't ring off the hook. Which gives me a chance to get a little ahead." Forest green eyes so like Mercy's lifted to face her. "You have no idea how competitive it is in business. They know I'm not built for this and you would not believe the attacks my company has gone through over the past few months. I have to stay on top of the game."

Shannon sighed. Lora had changed so much in the past couple of years, but she felt like the woman had exchanged one neurotic behavior for another. "I understand that, but I want to remind you of something. You have a worried little girl out there and I know you're building this company for her, but she doesn't understand why she can't just have her mother."

The tears really did come then, and Shannon felt like shit in provoking them, but she held her friend as she cried. And when Lora begged off lunch to go make cookies with her daughter, Shannon was okay with getting out of their hair to go grocery shopping on her own.

When she told John about the incident later, he'd gotten an odd look on his face. Wyatt sat on his lap playing with his keyring.

"What do you know?" she asked him, seeing the knowledge in his expression.

John cringed. "I can't tell you everything, but I think they're maybe at odds about having a baby. But you didn't hear it from me."

Ah. That would explain the tension she'd walked into. "Damn," she breathed. "Okay. Didn't hear it from you and I won't say anything. If they need help, we'll be here for them."

John gave her a lopsided smile. "That's my girl."

They ordered pizza that night just to be easy and watched a silly kid cartoon before getting the boys ready for bed. This unscheduled, unregimented time was Shannon's favorite, because they all just laughed and played. John was very good at distractions while she did the business part, and she couldn't have asked for a better partner. Obviously, her week away had highlighted to him how much she did and he was trying to make up for that, but she hadn't had any complaints on the amount he'd helped her before.

After reading them a couple of books, the kids zonked out on the couch. They each took one and carried them to the bedroom, tucking them into Caden's bed, which they seemed to both prefer. She wondered when they would want to sleep in separate beds. The need to be together was so sweet...

The next day ran even more quiet. Shannon lazed around in a t-shirt and sleep pants for a scandalously long time, but it earned her a fun romp when the boys took their afternoon nap.

John had undertaken a large part of the laundry, so Shannon threw together a double batch of chocolate chip cookies to take into work the next day. Since the group had grown, she hadn't been able to cook as much on Fridays anymore. Poor Roger left her messages on the fridge, occasionally, requesting her meatballs, but she knew he was just teasing her. Cassandra, his wife, cooked like a mad genius and Shannon knew for a fact that Roger had bulked up since they'd been together.

The boys had to help her bake, of course, so she gave them the beaters to lick while she assembled the rest of the ingredients. Then, when the first cookies were done and slightly cooled, she split a cookie between them. They ended up covered in chocolate, of course, but they were so damn cute she didn't care. They needed to take a bath in a little while anyway, so they might as well have fun.

John rolled in as she was pulling out another tray. He snatched one of the cookies from the cooling rack and stuffed half the thing in his mouth. "So good, babe."

She laughed at the look on his face, because it looked just like the boy's faces had a few minutes before. "Go see Harper. You can have more cookies tonight when you get home."

He looked at the boys in the chair. "You're sure?"

"Of course," she said, rolling her yes. "Go play."

Dropping a kiss to his lips, she shooed him out of the kitchen.

Shannon and the boys had a quiet night. Once her cookies were done she hauled both boys to the tub in their bathroom and gave them a bubble bath. Carmella wandered along behind, just keeping an eye on things. Once out of the tub she bundled both boys into their room and got them dressed for bed. Then, sitting in the chair with a boy in each arm, she read them a book.

Shannon loved this time of the night, and she loved that both boys still seemed to love to sit with her and read. At some point in the not-too-far future she would have to put them in bed to read, but for the most part she managed.

Caden fell asleep first, curling up against her neck. Wyatt loved seeing the pictures in the book, so he hung on a little longer, but eventually, even he gave in. Shannon tried not to wake them as she lifted them to the bed, but it was hard juggling both solid little bodies. Once on the mattress, though, they snuggled in together and fell asleep quickly. She'd talked to Willow about this today, and her friend was of the opinion that they would separate on their own eventually.

Once the boys were tucked in, she just leaned into the crib, stroking their hair. Though the pregnancy had been a trial, she would do it all over again. Happily. She hoped Chad and Lora came to some kind of understanding, and she hoped Lora didn't work herself out of love.

That seemed harsh to even think, but she couldn't imagine a job coming between her and John, let alone her kids. She wouldn't let it.

With a final breath to draw in their sweet smell, she left the boys to sleep and headed to her room. Carmella curled up by the closet door on her pillow as Shannon climbed into bed, her lids sagging. She checked her phone for messages, then curled up against the pillow and went to sleep. John would wake her with a kiss when he got home.

JOHN EASED into bed as cautiously as he could without waking Shannon. Damn woman looked like a freaking angel, laying there. Before he settled, he leaned over and brushed a kiss against her lips. She smiled, even in sleep, and sighed as her hands found his chest.

"I love you," she murmured, then fell back to sleep.

"I love you too, baby," he whispered.

It had been fun going to the range with Harper, but the former SEAL had been distracted, worried about a former teammate. John didn't press him for details. He figured if Harper needed to talk he would have opened up, but he didn't. Once they had the rifle sighted in, he made his excuses and headed home.

Of the bunch of them, Harper had the oldest kid. His daughter was fourteen. That was almost driving age, and dating age. God. He couldn't imagine the boys at fourteen. If his childhood was anything to go by, they were going to be hellions. He'd been running the streets and stealing food at that age, because the orphanage hadn't given them shit. Barely enough to live on.

John had vowed long ago that his children would never want for anything like that.

And if Shannon wanted another baby, he was going to damn well give it to her and take care of it as well.

God, seeing her pregnant with his child was such a turn-on. Shannon blossomed when she was pregnant.

The thought of having a little girl for the boys to protect made his heart warm, and he fell asleep smiling.

MONDAY MORNING WAS BACK to business. Shannon got the kids ready for day-care and John puttered around, feeding the dog and getting ready for the day. They always drove to work together, even though she knew he'd sometimes like to get to work earlier.

Like today. When Shannon gave him a pointed look, he glanced at her, then seemed to realize he was being a little more aggressive than normal with traffic. "Sorry. I think I'm a little anxious. Have you talked to Marigold?"

Shannon shook her head. "Not yet this morning. It's pretty early yet."

"Yeah, I guess." John drove to the office a little more calmly after that, which she appreciated. She was anxious to find out how the family meet went as well, but it wasn't worth risking their safety.

Once at work they lost themselves in the business of other things. At eleven o'clock Marigold arrived with Logan in tow. Shannon stared, though she knew she shouldn't. Logan had changed, a lot. When he stepped off the elevator he was actually smiling, a little, and he met her gaze with little to no flinching or hiding. It was such a drastic change from when she'd seen him last. How long ago had it been? A week now? What had happened to bring about this change?

Her gaze shifted to Marigold. "Oh..." she breathed.

There was a liveliness to the woman's face that she hadn't seen before. Her cheeks were flushed and her eyes were bright behind her glasses, and she was grinning at something Logan had said. Their arms brushed as they walked in. Ah... Wow. The connection between the two of them was almost palpable.

"Don't you two look happy," she murmured.

Marigold blushed very prettily, her skin flushing under Shannon's look, but she kept her mouth shut.

"Logan, I'll let John know you're here."

She sent John a message and almost immediately he rolled down the hallway. When he reached Logan, the younger man shifted his crutch and reached out to shake John's hand.

"I just wanted to thank you in person for finding my family," Logan told him. "I met them on Wednesday, and again on Saturday, and they're amazing people. I'm not sure what exactly happened to my dad, but they are so different from him it's almost comical. So, thank you. And thank your brother when you next talk to him."

"I will definitely do that," John said with a laugh. "Aiden will love hearing he helped you reconnect. It's a big thing with us, because of our upbringings. He was given into foster care early like I was, before our mother died."

Logan winced. "I'm sorry."

John shook his head. "Don't be. It made us who we are. All of our experiences shape who we are."

"True," Logan murmured. Turning, he gave Shannon a smile. "And thank you, too, for dragging me along with you.

I wouldn't have had nearly the success out here if you hadn't latched onto me."

Shannon grinned, warmth sweeping through her. "You are very welcome, Logan. I knew when I saw you that you were one of us."

He gave her an odd look. "Maybe."

"Have you thought about the job offer?" John asked, crossing his arms over his chest.

Logan sighed. "I have a little, but not enough. I've kind of had a few other things on my plate."

"Granted. Well, the offer is there whenever you're ready to take it."

"Thanks, John. I have one more situation to settle before I can make any big decisions."

Logan's gaze flicked to Marigold, then away. Shannon didn't think the younger woman had even noticed the look, because she was looking down at the schedule on Shannon's computer screen. It was obvious something was going on between the two of them, but she wasn't sure if they wanted to acknowledge it.

She caught John's gaze and he smiled, giving her a nod. Good. He could see it too.

"Do you need me today, Shannon?" Marigold asked.

"Um," Shannon looked around. "No, there's nothing extremely pressing. Duncan is in a meeting downtown."

"Okay. I might drive Logan out to Boulder. Or," she said, turning to look at him, "I can just loan you the car."

Logan frowned. "I appreciate it, but I haven't driven since I've been injured. Do you mind?"

"Nope," Marigold said immediately.

Shannon smiled at the two of them. Had she and John been that careful with each other? Yeah. Probably.

"Well, maybe we'll see you tomorrow, then?"

Marigold nodded, giving her a firm look. "Yes, ma'am. I know I haven't been here much last week. I'll be in."

The two of them left, Marigold holding the doors open for Logan to get on. Once they were gone, Shannon looked at her husband. They both burst out laughing.

"Whether you meant to or not, babe, I think you made a match," John told her, rolling close.

Shannon leaned over and dropped a kiss on his lips. "I think so too," she snorted. "Not that it took long."

John shrugged. "I don't think it's a length of time, per se. It's whether or not the person makes you feel comfortable in your own skin."

Shannon stared at him. "That's very...perceptive, babe. I love you."

"I love you, too. It also helps if you're comfortable in their skin as well." His dark eyes glinted with humor, and she shook her head.

"You're always trying to get in my skin," she laughed.

"Well, it's beautiful skin. What can I say?"

Shannon cupped his face in her palms. "I love you, you horny bastard."

Grinning, John reached out to stroke her ass. "It's your fault I'm horny..."

Shannon drew back, giving him a teasing look, but he could tell by the shine in her eyes that she hoped something would happen between the two younger people. She was such a damn romantic. Just one of the many things he loved about her. "You know, if you want to have another baby, I'm up for it. Maybe we can hope for a little girl this time."

Her eyes widened in her face, and she paled a little. "Another baby?"

John frowned, curious at her reaction. "Yeah, another baby. Like you said."

She leaned her head forward, staring at him. "I love you, babe. When did I say I wanted another baby?"

"In your email when you told me your flight had been cancelled."

Looking confused, she turned to her computer and pulled up her email. With a few clicks of the keys, she apparently found what she was looking for. She crossed her arms beneath her breasts as she read. "Damn," she breathed. "I was a little toasty. I don't even remember most of this. And look at this spelling. Holy crap...Oh, there it is..."

She glanced up at him guiltily. "I love you dearly," she said again, "but there's no way we're having another baby right now. At least, not until the boys are a little older. I can't take three kids in diapers at once."

The thought made him ill, as well, and he sagged in relief. "Holy fuck, woman. You freaked me out when you wrote that," he laughed.

Shannon shook her head, looking pained. "Don't worry about it, babe. It was just the drunken ramblings of your tea-totaler wife," she laughed. "Have you been stewing about that all week? We'll have another baby, and I agree, a little girl would be adorable, but I'm not in a rush."

The relief that rolled through him made him feel a little guilty. If she'd wanted it, they would have worked it out, but more time would definitely be better. "I love you, Shannon."

"I love you too, babe," she breathed, leaning forward for his kiss. "Now get back to work."

John huffed and threw her a salute. "Yes, ma'am!"

Spinning the chair around he sped down the hallway, making her giggle.

18

"So, how do you think it'll go?"

Marigold's question rang in his brain, dragging down the mood, and he didn't know how to respond. They'd just had a long lunch at his grandmother's restaurant where they'd laughed and joked for hours. Now, though, they were heading to the Millers, and the tension in his gut was beginning to build.

Lisa was a volatile woman, as was Miller's sister Ashley. "Honestly, I have no idea. Trent was Lisa's only son, so I know she took his death hard."

Logan's gut churned. Even if she welcomed him with open arms, he had to tell her that he was the one that had gotten Miller killed. He hadn't meant to, of course, but the excursion had been propelled by him.

They passed a Boulder city mileage sign, and his gut tightened further. Marigold's phone was hanging from a dock on the windshield, and the red track of the GPS path was lit. Just a few more miles.

"Thank you for bringing me out here. It sounded like Shannon could have used you in the office today."

Marigold shrugged, her shoulder brushing his own in the narrow car. "Maybe. I think she would have told me if she did. She's just a little bit of a control freak."

Logan chuckled. "I think they all are, a bit."

"Agreed," she responded with a laugh. "Tell me about Trent."

Logan blinked, wondering how he could encapsulate six years of friendship into a few sentences. "We'd been together since Basic. Normally you make it through and you never see the guys you graduate with, but he and I, it was like we were in lock step. We competed through most of our class, both of us blowing away the rest of our group, and both ended up being picked up by military intelligence. We were in different jobs, but still worked together almost every day. We hung out together on our days off and that old competition faded away to friendship. We realized we liked hanging out together. He was a lot better man than I was, though."

Marigold opened her mouth to argue, but he held up a hand. "No, he really was. We joked about it all the time. When I came across a piece of information I wanted to check out, he didn't feel the same, but he agreed to go just to appease my damned curiosity. It's what got him killed," he finished, voice tight. "Without getting into too much detail, I believed that there was a stronghold in this one, deserted location that hadn't seen any action in months. I was proven correct when we were attacked."

He glanced at her, his eyes narrowed in remembered pain. "Not the way I wanted to be proven correct."

"Of course not," she murmured, reaching a hand out to rest on his own.

Logan looked down at their hands, torn. Truly, he appreciated her support, but he didn't deserve it. There was a certain amount of guilt he struggled under, and he didn't think he would ever be free of it. Talking to Lisa would help.

They didn't say anything else as they drove to the two-story cabin set in the woods. As soon as they pulled into the drive, Logan started seeing flashbacks in his mind of he and Miller playing around. There were snowmobile trails all through the area, and they had spent hours mapping them out and just playing. Military Intelligence was a brutal business and they relaxed just as hard as they worked.

Then Marigold was pulling into the circle of gravel in front of the familiar cabin and parking. She turned off the noisy diesel engine and turned to face him. "You can do this, Logan. I have faith in you." She leaned across the seat and pressed a kiss to his lips. "I'll be right here waiting for you. Take your time, okay? I have my tablet and stuff so I won't be bored."

Logan stared at her for a long moment, shocked at what had just come out of her mouth. When had anyone supported him that way before? Never. "Thank you, Mari. I don't know how long it will take."

He gave her another kiss before turning to open the door. The hinges creaked a little as he maneuvered the crutches out first, then his legs. Gathering himself he swung away from the car, pushing the car door shut behind him with the tip of the crutch, then he headed for the steps up to the porch. He'd made this same walk several times over the years, but this time was so very different. Trent Miller wasn't bouncing beside him, anxious to show him his family home and share his family.

Anxiety churned, nauseating him, and Logan rethought coming here. Just for a split second. Then his resolve firmed. This needed to happen.

As if in answer to his thoughts, the front door opened

and Lisa Miller stepped out onto the wooden boards. She wore a thick patterned wool sweater, jeans, and socks on her feet, but no shoes. Her dirty blond hair hung over her shoulders, looking longer than the last time he'd seen her. It had been at least a year and a half. Christmas before last they'd come back for two weeks.

"What the fuck are you doing here?"

Logan blinked and jerked to a halt, wondering if he'd heard her correctly. "I'm, I, uh, wanted to talk to you about Trent."

"I don't want to hear anything you have to say, Logan," she said firmly, her face flushing. "I need you to leave."

Shocked, he kind of stood there, searching his mind for options. This had been one of those possibilities, but it had been low on his list. "I just wanted to..."

"I don't care what the fuck you wanted," she yelled, stomping to the edge of the porch. "Did you actually think I'd welcome you here? After you killed my son?"

Logan swayed at the verbal attack. It was unexpected, but probably justified, so he would take it. "I didn't mean to hurt anyone," he told her honestly.

"But you did. You got one of your hunches and you had to go check it out. He had just a couple of months left to go before he got out, same as you, but you got him killed. Trent called me on Messenger just before you left and told me what a wild goose chase he thought it was."

Logan fought back the words to defend himself. It hadn't been a wild goose chase. They'd literally been attacked in the place that he'd assumed insurgents were hiding out. Logan didn't say that though. A mother deserved to be angry that her son had been killed, and he wouldn't take that from her.

"I'm sorry," he told her, his voice and heart sincere. "He was my best friend. You know that. I never would have gone on that op if I knew it was going to get them killed."

Lisa shook her head, tears beginning to roll down her lean, ruddy cheeks. "My baby is gone. Just wiped off the earth like he was never here. The government says they can't give me any more answers. Won't, I'm sure. They have to protect their precious secrets."

Logan forced himself to step forward. "What do you want to know? I'll tell you anything, as long as it doesn't endanger current servicemen."

Lisa gaped at him. "How can I trust anything you say?"

That struck Logan hard, because he'd never been anything but honest with her. Even when it had been uncomfortable. She knew every sordid detail about his family, because he'd been comfortable with her. All of the guilt for leaving Jana and Clint behind, she knew about, and she'd consoled him about, more than his own mother ever would have.

That's what hurt the most. Lisa Miller had been damned near a mother to him, and he'd let her down. "I'm sorry," he said again, his throat tight, not sure what else to do.

"Stop saying that," she screamed.

Behind him, he heard the door of the Beetle open. He had a feeling Marigold had stepped out to check on the situation and make sure he was okay.

"You show up here expecting some kind of validation for what you did," Lisa continued, tears streaming down her cheeks, "some kind of absolution. Well, I'm not going to give it to you. You got my son killed. And now you show up looking completely fine, and with a woman to boot. Something my son will never be able to experience. Did you show up here thinking I would welcome you with open arms? In place of my son? Get off my property, Logan. I don't want to ever see you again."

The woman turned and left the porch, the front door slamming behind her. Logan looked down, searching for bullet holes or something, because it felt like he was bleeding from the inside. There was nothing there, though, of course.

Very slowly he pivoted on one crutch and turned toward the car, walking slowly back to it. He avoided Marigold's eyes, knowing that she would see too much.

"Logan!" a voice cried.

He turned just in time to catch Ashley in his arms. She was sobbing as well, but she burrowed into his chest, muffling the sound. When she didn't feel like she was going to push him away, he wrapped his arms around the girl's shoulders as they shook. It took several long minutes for her to draw back and look at him, her face streaked with tears.

"Don't listen to her. She's been worried about you, too. We knew you were alive, but didn't know where you were or anything."

"I should have contacted you sooner, but I was in the hospital up until a few months ago."

Stepping back, Ashley looked down his body, lingering on the crutches. "We figured that out, eventually. Mom called in a favor with the Army and she got hold of your mom, I guess."

"Oh, hell," Logan sighed.

"She said the woman was useless and no wonder you'd always come home with Trent," the girl reported, with the tact of a teenager. "But she did get that you'd been in the hospital, but your mother didn't know where you'd went when you were released."

Logan snorted. "I lived across the county from them."

Ashley gaped. "Seriously?"

He nodded. "I always planned to come out here, though. I just had some things to do before I could."

All truth. It just wasn't what she wanted to hear, he was sure.

Ashley glanced at Marigold and gave her a slight smile, before she turned back to Logan. "I think Mom will come around, but it will be a while. Can I have your number?"

Nodding, he gave her his number while she entered the digits into her phone. She tapped off a quick text. "Now you have mine, too."

Logan nodded. "I'm sorry, Ashley. Your mom didn't want to hear it, but I'll tell you. If there was anything at all I could do to bring him back, I would. I swear that to you. And if I could have known what was going to happen that day, we never would have gone out."

Tears were rolling down her cheeks again and she bit her lip, nodding, her arms crossed over her belly. "I know, Logan. I know."

With a final look, she turned and ran back up onto the porch and into the house.

Logan sighed, seriously hoping that Ashley would be an ally. He glanced at Marigold, waiting so patiently. "I'm ready."

They didn't say anything as they headed out of Boulder, and he appreciated that. It gave him some time to collect his thoughts.

For some reason, he'd expected Lisa's anger, but she'd always been a practical person. She'd been former military. Logan hadn't expected the irrationality and the loss of control that left her screaming. Looking back, he wasn't sure what he should have done sooner. Maybe come to her first?

Showing up so many months after the incident had to seem disrespectful to their relationship. He could see that now.

There had been glimmers of truth in what she'd said, though. It was his fault that Miller was dead. There was no escaping that detail. Why did he deserve to live after Miller had died?

"You've gotten very quiet over there," Marigold said softly.

Logan watched her shift gears as they slid through traffic. It was seamless, the way she moved, and he remember the feel of a manual transmission. There was a lot of leg work involved, and he doubted he would ever be able to drive one again, just because he wouldn't have the muscle control. He could admire the grace it took to drive smoothly, though.

Logan looked at Marigold's profile. Her black-framed glasses were parked firmly on her nose, and he could see the reflection of the car's headlights coming toward them in the lenses. Her hair was back in a low ponytail, but it lay over her shoulder to the front. He wanted to see it spread out across the pillow again as he slid into her.

Why did he get to have a relationship, though? Why did he get to go on with his life?

They pulled up to a red light and Marigold reached for her phone. That kind of surprised him. She was very cautious about when she used her cell. It looked like she tapped out a message and sent it. Just a few seconds later, the screen lit up with a response. "Everything okay?"

She nodded, not saying anything. Logan watched the dark scenery pass by, content to be silent. Night had arrived and he hadn't even noticed. They'd left LNF hours ago. They drove through a more crowded suburban area with shopping malls and restaurants, then back into the darker night.

A few minutes later, though, they pulled into what appeared to be a nice subdivision. The houses were built very similar, but owners had tried to individualize them with landscaping and different paint themes. He had no idea where they were, though, when she pulled into a driveway. Until he spotted the black truck.

"Is this John's house?"

"John and Shannon's, yes. Come on."

There was a wooden handicapped ramp on the front of the pretty house, and he didn't know what to think about that. John Palmer seemed stronger than to even admit to needing one of those. "Why are we here, Marigold?"

"Because you need to talk to John about things I can't help you with," she said simply, before turning off the car and heading up the ramp.

Gritting his teeth, Logan climbed out of the car as well, legs aching, soul aching. John had more experience with this stuff, so maybe it wouldn't be a bad idea to talk to him.

Petite Shannon answered the door with a little boy on her hip. She grinned at them and stepped back. "Enter at your own risk," she told them, laughing. "This is Caden."

Marigold laughed as she crossed the threshold and Logan stepped in behind her. The Palmers had a beautiful house inside with all hardwood floors, probably easier for John's wheels, though it was cluttered with brightly colored toddler toys at the moment. There was a toddler in a car thing on the floor. Shannon motioned to him. "And that's Wyatt."

The two boys looked very similar with dark hair and pale eyes, but the one in the go-cart thing was definitely bigger. He was probably a lot for Shannon to handle, considering her size. Marigold had knelt down on the floor and was talking to the little man. "Aren't you a bruiser?" she said, wiggling his hand.

Wyatt grinned at her and pounded the tray of the conveyance.

"What is that thing he's in?" Logan asked Shannon.

"That's a walker. Wyatt doesn't really need it, he's pretty steady on his feet, but it does help slow him down a little, and keep him corralled," she laughed. "That's more for my sake."

A blond dog with a lot of hair had also wandered up to them, sniffing their legs. "That's Carmella," Shannon continued, "and there are a couple of cats running around as well, so watch your step."

Logan moved forward cautiously, watching where he put the tips of his crutches.

"Marigold, if you occupy Wyatt for a moment, I'll show Logan where John is."

"Can do," she said with a smile.

She was about to turn away when he grabbed her hand and turned her around. Knowing eyes were on him, he dropped a quick kiss to her surprised mouth. "Back in a bit," he winked.

Marigold seemed a little shocked at the interaction, but she smiled softly at him. "Okay."

Logan's smile faded as he followed Shannon across the big room and into a beautiful kitchen, then through a door and onto a ramp down into a garage. It was a two-car garage, one side taken up by a four-door Jeep, and the rest of the space was taken up by man-cave 'stuff', and something covered with a big tarp. There was a TV on one wall broadcasting a football game, and a couple of neon beer signs. At the other end of the bench was a massive gun safe, the door open. Logan wanted to peer inside, but that would be rude.

John sat at a wooden workbench, the pieces of an M4 scattered on the surface. He wore a pair of glasses, but when they came in he ripped them off his head and tossed them aside.

Shannon chuckled softly and turned to look at Logan. "Would you tell him that he doesn't look old with the glasses on?"

"You don't look old with the glasses on. If anything," he continued, grinning, "the gray hair at your temples makes you look older."

"You fu...fudger! Who asked you?"

They all laughed as Logan went down the ramp into the space. John waved to the fridge at the base of the ramp. "Go ahead and get a beer. And grab me one, too."

Logan did as he was told then moved to the bench, handing one of the beers off to John. There was a stool at one end of the bench he swung around to sit on. Oh, hell. Wouldn't be sitting on it long.

John must have noticed because he pointed at the far wall. "There are regular nylon folding chairs over there. That might feel better."

Logan swapped out the chairs. The new one didn't hurt his legs nearly as bad. "Thanks."

"No problem."

"What are you working on?" Logan already knew because he'd used the weapon as well, but he thought it would be a good conversation opener.

"This is an M4," John said, as if instructing a class. "It fires a 5.56 mm round and is the shortened version of the M16A2..."

"I know that," Logan laughed, interrupting him. "What's the issue?"

John grinned at him. "No issue. I'm just cleaning it.

Harper and I went to the range the other day and I hadn't gotten back to it. It's actually closer to an M4A1."

His interest piqued, Logan leaned closer. "Like Special Forces uses?"

John nodded once, showing him the barrel. "Don't tell the government. I tweaked the trigger and changed this out to a heavier duty version."

Logan grinned. "That's badass..."

"So, how did it go?"

In that five-minute period of time, he had allowed himself to forget what had happened an hour ago. "Did Marigold tell you what we were doing?"

"Nah," John said, continuing to clean the barrel. "You said you had one more situation to deal with. I assumed you were dealing with it today."

Logan sighed, resting the beer on his knee. "Yes, I tried." He told him about the op when he was injured and his team was killed, talking to the family, and Lisa's blow-up. Then about Ashley's conversation.

"And you're struggling with the guilt."

"Basically," Logan admitted. "Everything she said is true. I did get him killed, and I think I was looking for absolution. I may not have recognized it when I went there, but I did when she pointed it out."

"You're never going to find it," John told him softly, letting his hands rest on his lap. "It doesn't come from an exterior source. I'm gonna sound like a fucking shrink for a minute, but it needs to be said. It comes from inside you. It's a process you have to go through to allow yourself to let go of the guilt. I can tell you exactly how many men died under my command, starting with the first grunt in Desert Storm to the last in Iraq."

John frowned and looked down for a moment, an odd

smile twisting his lips. "I'll be damned," he murmured. He shook his head, looking back at Logan. "What you have to remember is you were under orders to find insurgents. That was your entire job. Unfortunately, your job demanded sacrifice. But it's not to be borne only by you. The military has responsibility as well."

"Yeah, I know."

It just didn't make him feel any better right that moment.

And it didn't make him feel any better moving forward with Mari. Hell, when had he even thought there was a *forward*?

"How do you move past it?" he asked. "The guilt."

John sighed. "You just keep moving through life. It's just like the suicidal thoughts. You keep moving through, day by day, and try to keep yourself occupied with other things, other goals. Eventually you'll realize those thoughts don't happen as much anymore, then they never happen."

Logan nodded, trying to sort through his emotions. "I don't feel suicidal like I did before. When I came out here, I was bad, I'll admit that, but since then so much has changed. This week has been life-changing. I have family now, and a relationship I find myself..." he hesitated, searching for the right word, "enjoying. I don't want anything to change."

John reached out a fist expectantly and Logan bumped his knuckles. "That's good to hear. Just so you know, though, you'll still be expected to see our counselor when you hire on."

Logan nodded, not surprised, and not averse to the idea either. And he wasn't surprised John knew he was going to accept the job, either. He would be stupid not to.

"Let me show you some of my other toys," John said

grinning as he swung his wheelchair toward the safe to his right.

19

Marigold's attention was torn between the beautiful boys in front of her and the garage door, where Logan had disappeared almost half an hour ago.

"They'll be back in a little bit," Shannon told her, catching her watching.

"I know," Marigold sighed. "I just worry. That woman was so mad, blaming Logan for everything that happened to her son."

Shannon sat at the table across from her, a big bowl of applesauce in her hand. The boys saw the treat and began clamoring for the first bite. "You have to imagine how that woman feels, though, seeing the only man that survived the bombing. It was shocking for her, I'm sure. Logan didn't call or notify her before he went out?"

Marigold shook her head. "I don't believe so."

"Then it was a total blindside. He maybe could have approached it a little better."

Yes, she was probably right.

Within two minutes the applesauce was gone. It actually

took Shannon longer to clean the boys up with a wet wash-cloth than it had taken them to eat the snack. She lifted both boys out of the high chairs and let them go. Marigold laughed because they looked so silly, their short little legs moving as fast as their tiny tennis shoes would carry them toward the toy area.

Shannon motioned to the couch and they sat, within eyesight of the boys. "So, you and Logan seem to be hitting it off."

Marigold grinned, removing her glasses and rubbing the bridge of her nose. "Yes, we are. I'll be honest, the first time I saw him I felt something click in me, like something engaged. I've never felt anything like it before, Shannon." She replaced her glasses and looked at the woman she was beginning to consider her friend. "I've been in relationships before but never been so invested in the other person's happiness. It hurt my heart when I heard that woman yelling at Logan, and I wanted to go kick her ass." Marigold scrubbed the angry tears from her eyes. "And I'm not that kind of woman. I'm pretty chill with everyone, but I wanted to jump out and protect him."

Shannon nodded in understanding. "I've done that before, but you have to remember that he has to fight his own battles. And it might not be as pretty anymore. Mentally, he's the same and he wants to do everything he used to, but physically he's changed. They're not lesser men, though. Let him figure out how to do it."

"Yeah," she said slowly, "I get that. I worry about his mental health, though, too. My mother..." she hesitated, wondering if she should even bring it up.

"What about your mom?" Shannon asked, her voice incredibly kind.

Tears started in Marigold's eyes, and she couldn't help

but respond to that kindness. As the kids played with their toys, she told Shannon about losing her dad first, then her grandpa and her mom, and her suspicions that her mother had allowed herself to die.

"Oh, dear," Shannon breathed, leaning close to wrap her arms around Marigold. She took the hug and appreciated it for what it was, but then she pulled back. "So, when he says these offhand things about ending it all, I think I'm a little more sensitive."

"Possibly," Shannon agreed, "but wouldn't you rather be too sensitive than not sensitive enough?"

"Yes, of course. I just... he worries me."

"And you need to tell him that. Don't bitch at him, necessarily, just tell him your thoughts. Maybe he doesn't even realize how often he says something like that."

That was possible, she supposed.

And she was thinking about it on the way back to Marshall House a little while later. When they entered the kitchen, it was dark, but Nancy was sitting at the table, sipping from her aluminum cup. "There you kids are," she giggled. "Aren't you cute together."

Marigold grinned and crossed to lean against the edge of the table. "How was bingo, tonight, Grandma?"

"Dreadful," she snapped. "Didn't win a damn thing. I haven't won anything since my W.C. passed on." She peered up at Logan, standing beyond Marigold's shoulder. "W.C. was my lucky piece. Every night before I went to Bingo I would rub his package." She made a circular motion with her open hand. "And I would win!"

Marigold giggled. "Wouldn't that be his money you won, then?"

Grandma waved a hand. "Sometimes I would split it with him, but more often than not he would just tell me to hang onto it. He had his own side deals going to bring in extra money."

Marigold laughed, her gaze connecting to Logan's. He was grinning too and shaking his head.

"W.C. sounds like a very cool guy," he told Nancy.

The sparkle in her eyes dimmed. "He really was. I miss him dearly. I miss all the silly things we did together, and the meals. I even miss the cross words we had," she said softly, reaching for her cup. "But I wouldn't have missed being with him for anything."

Marigold reached out and rested her hand on the older woman's. "Are you okay?"

Grandma nodded. "Just a little tired. I'll head to bed in a little while and read for a bit."

"Sexy books tonight or bible books?" she asked with a giggle, remembering the book shelf in Nancy's bedroom near her bed.

"Oh, definitely the sexy books tonight. It will help me dream of my W.C.," she grinned. "You kids have a good night."

Without saying anything, they headed up the stairs to her apartment. Logan didn't even pause at the door to his room. Once inside her place, they hung their coats and took off their shoes. "Want a cup of tea or hot chocolate?"

Logan shook his head. "I might do a glass of water."

"Gotcha."

They settled onto the couch and when he opened his arm, she leaned against him with a sigh. "What a day," she breathed, recounting everything they'd done in her head.

He snorted, but it sounded exasperated rather than humorous. "Agreed. I'll be honest, today didn't go as well as I'd hoped."

"Yeah, I'm sorry about that, Logan."

"It's not your fault. You have nothing to be sorry about. It was my fuck-up."

She drew back to look at him. "You need to stop taking on all this guilt. It wasn't your fault you got hit with an IED."

"I know," he admitted, "but I should have gone to talk to her sooner."

Marigold shook her head. "It wouldn't have mattered. You're alive and her son is dead. Period. I hate to be so blunt, but she was looking for an outlet. She needed an outlet."

Logan blinked and stared sightlessly out the far window. "Yeah, I know you're right. It's just incredibly hard to let it go."

"I do understand that," she said, reaching for his hands. "But I'm here with you now, and I have no plans to go anywhere."

"Why not?" he asked abruptly, giving her a hard look.

"What?"

"Why are you with me?" he asked her, his blue eyes dark with some emotion. "I'm a seriously fucked up dude. Honestly. My family is a damn daytime soap, my personal life is not much better. I'm permanently disabled and I'm going to need a lifetime of care. Why would you even consider being with me?"

Would he freak out if she told him she loved him? And that he felt like the half of her soul that she hadn't even noticed was missing? "Because you keep life interesting," she said instead, taking the coward's way out.

Logan's expression chilled a little and she thought he seemed a little disappointed. She wondered if she should have just admitted everything to him? It was crazy, because they'd only been together a week, a little less. It just seemed longer. And not in a bad sense. Being with him made her very happy. It made her feel...settled inside, like she'd been waiting for him.

"I like, love," she said carefully, "the direction this is going. I want to pursue it and see where it takes us."

He looked at her for a long moment, his expression guarded, before he nodded. "I do, too. You're very easy to be around," he said quietly, "and I feel like I should fight against it to keep myself safe, but I really don't want to."

Marigold gave him a serious look. "I need you to be straight with me, though."

"About?"

She drew in a breath. "If you're getting thoughts of hurting yourself, I need to know about it. My mother pretended everything was great until she broke, and I never had any indication that she wanted to hurt herself. I know this is a big ask, but you have to try. I can't be blindsided by that again."

Logan nodded once, his gaze steady. "I swear to you that I will. Right now, even with what happened today, I still feel moderately solid. It helped to talk to John, and he gave me some ideas to distract and redirect my thoughts. I also have to have counseling if I hire onto LNF."

Marigold sat back, startled. She wasn't sure if she was more surprised by his openness or the fact that John had given him the guidance. "That's really good," she said eventually. "And completely right. I haven't even been to school yet and it sounds like good advice."

Logan gave her a smile. "You're important to me, Marigold Lee, and I will be here for you."

Tears filled her eyes at the words, and she wondered when she'd gotten so emotionally invested. As soon as he had walked in the door of the office, she thought, and something in her heart had clicked.

Logan pulled her into his arms, tight against his chest. Marigold took the comfort, happily, feeling her worries ease away. She drew the scent of him in, the laundry soap and body wash, and knew that she would recognize his scent anywhere. Already she recognized it on her sheets, and she loved the contentment it brought her. As soon as she drew him in, she knew everything would be okay. He didn't have to be a big, brash alpha male to be her hero.

They settled in to watch trash tv. When they realized they hadn't eaten anything for dinner, she headed downstairs to look for a snack. She found Grandma's flat cookies and made up a tray with a plate of them and two big glasses of milk.

Logan laughed as he set the tray on the coffee table. "I am totally okay with this," he said, reaching for a glass and a cookie.

They had a quiet night, and by the time they went to bed, Logan seemed to have accepted that he may not get resolution when it came to the loss of his teammates. Marigold held him as he told her stories about each of them, and others that he'd lost.

"I would have loved to meet Jana," she whispered into the night.

"I think the two of you would have gotten along very well," he said with a sigh.

"And I think my mother would have loved you, as well," she whispered. Logan drew her in against him, breathing into her hair.

They slept for a while, and she wasn't sure what made her open her eyes, but when she did, she could feel Logan's heat behind her. He gave a hard body twitch, like he'd been hit, or something. Then another. But when she tried to draw away, his arms tightened around her.

"Logan, wake up."

When he didn't release her, she pulled at his hands. "Logan!"

Finally, he let her go, jerking to consciousness. "Mari, are you okay?"

She nodded, sitting up beside him. Leaning over, she flipped on the small table light. "I am. Are you okay? You must have been dreaming or something."

"I was," he admitted, running shaking hands over his face. His eyes were hazy with sleep, but he was blinking back to consciousness. "I was back in the sand and Miller was yelling at me to get my head down. But I was getting shot."

Marigold ran her fingers down the length of his arm to hold his hand. "You're not out there anymore. You're here, with me, in Denver. More specifically, you're in my warm bed," she grinned, rubbing the sleep from her eyes. With a quick glance, she saw it was after two in the morning. Damn, she'd been sleeping really good, with the heat of his body behind her.

Logan tugged on her hand, pulling her back down into his arms. "I don't dream like that very often, but with everything that happened yesterday, I guess it kind of stirred everything up."

They settled back down in the sheets, relaxing into each other. One of his hands settled on her hips, and that was when she noticed how aroused he was.

"Sorry," he murmured, not sounding sorry at all. "You were just backlit by the light and I could see your breasts through the fabric."

She snorted, nudging her hips back into his erection. "Even in the midst of the dream..."

"What can I say? You're a completely different kind of dream, and I recognize how valuable you are."

Aw...

Marigold rotated her hips, gratified when his hand tightened on her. "I want to take you this way."

"Ok," she agreed, losing her breath.

They fumbled beneath the covers, shucking clothes and flinging them away. Logan found a condom in her bedside table and within just a few seconds, he was pulling her tight back against him .

"Oh, damn... I think I like it this way," she breathed, arching back into his rolling thrusts. She gripped the sheets in front of her, trying to get some leverage to push back more. And she hadn't been kidding about the feel of his dick. Though the scarring muffled his pleasure, it enhanced hers.

The only problem with this position was that there was no kissing. It did put her in perfect position for him to grab her breasts. Oh, yes, that was damn good... then his hand crept over her hip to the apex of her thighs. Knowing what he was going to do, Marigold lifted her thigh a little, enough for him to run a finger between her wet, swollen folds to find her clit.

"Oh, Logan," she sighed.

They weren't moving fast or hard, but something about the attention he was paying her was absolutely perfect. Or maybe it was just that they were getting to know each other's bodies better. She knew that if she arched her hips more sharply that he would gasp and plunge deeper, but that he would also tighten his hand on her mons, which was so damn sexy.

The hot, tingling edge of orgasm was building, cranking her body tighter and tighter. Suddenly he pulled his hand away, leaving her gasping and needy. He pushed her over onto her front, one of his long thighs going over her hips. Then he reseated himself inside her. "Oh, fuck," she sighed. "I think I like this better."

Now she had the leverage to push back into his thrusts, and it felt so good. Logan rocked into her, his breath gasping in her ear. One of his hands reached beneath her, searching for that magic spot that would send her over, but she could have told him he didn't need to. The way he was grinding into her was enough, and her orgasm was cresting. "Logan, Logan," she panted. "Yes...."

He must have felt her body tightening, because he began to surge harder. That was all she needed. Marigold cried out, not in control of her own body, as the pleasure rolled over her. It was sublime and went on for what seemed like minutes. And just as she began to blink back to awareness, his pleasure took him. It was perfection. She loved feeling him arch into her so hard, and she loved that he had found pleasure in her.

Logan literally collapsed on top of Marigold, but she would not protest. The feel of him on her, in her, was one of the most... amazing things. Besides, she could take his weight. And he seemed to have completely passed out. If she wasn't afraid of waking him, she would have chuckled.

Letting her eyes drift shut, she breathed steadily. Her body had found its pleasure and it was reminding her that it was the depths of the night.

Logan suddenly drew in a heavy breath and shifted. "Oh, God, am I crushing you? I'm so sorry."

He shifted away, moving to the side of the bed. "I kind of dozed off, because my bed," he turned to grin at her, "you, was really soft and warm. I need to get rid of this condom," he laughed.

Marigold stepped from the bed and circled it to hold her hand out to him. "I think we both need to visit the bathroom."

Surprisingly he took her hand and let her pull him up. Immediately, he dropped a kiss to her lips. "Thank you for being my pillow. And my chair lift."

"Anytime, baby."

They walked to the bathroom and did what they needed to do, then headed back to bed. Logan pulled her up to rest against his chest, and they drifted off to sleep.

When Marigold opened her eyes, it was to find Logan staring at her in the light of dawn. She grinned and stretched, her bones cracking and joints popping. Then she tucked back under the covers, grinning at him. "It's chilly out there," she whispered.

Logan chuckled, popping his brows at her. "I know. Someone stole all the covers."

Marigold lifted up enough to see that she had, indeed, stolen most of the covers. "I'm sorry," she laughed, shifting some of the blankets over.

He shrugged as he pulled them into place. "Just gave me more reason to wrap around you."

It was ridiculous how much she appreciated those whispered words. And it was scary hearing them, because things felt like they were getting serious.

"You're screwing up my life plan," she told him, deciding to be blunt.

"Why do you say that?"

"Because you have. I planned on working my ass off for a while and stashing the money, going to school, getting my degree.... nowhere in there was start a relationship."

"Same," he agreed. "Starting a relationship was the furthest thing from my mind when I came out here. And I'll be honest. I wasn't in a good place when Shannon spotted me and dragged me along to LNF."

"Were you really thinking about suicide?" she whispered, afraid to know the answer. "Or are you still?"

Logan blinked and turned onto his back, as if looking at her were too hard. Instead, he stared up at her bland ceiling. It took him a few seconds to get his words together. "Yes, and kind of." He flicked a glance at her, his blue eyes crystalline in the light of the morning, then back to the ceiling. "I never considered myself to be the type of person to even consider suicide. I feel like I'm level-headed and methodical, deliberate. In spite of my father's issues, I didn't feel like I was deficient in any way."

"Agreed," she said when he paused.

"But when the world keeps telling you you don't deserve shit, and continues to take away every glimmer of happiness and, and... groundedness, you start to listen. The world was telling me I didn't need family, because it took away the only person I really needed, my sister. Then it told me I didn't deserve friends, or the Army, because it took them away. Mobility? Meh, who needs it? I'm tired of fighting against the world. So, yeah, when I came out here, I had a job to do. I had a plan. I had spoken with my other teammates families and Miller's family was the last. I was going to cruise by the old family home if I could find it, which I realize now that I never would have. But once I was done doing those two things, I thought I would be able to exit stage left." He shrugged on the mattress. "No one would even know I'd done it. I had no family, no significant friends."

Marigold tried to keep the tears in, but there was no way she could. The utter loneliness... She'd never been in that place herself, so she couldn't say exactly what she'd do in his place. Logan continued to stare up at the ceiling, clear-eyed.

There were no tears or emotion, just flat acceptance. It was chilling to see, because she knew he had the determination to do it. And she wondered if her mother had felt the same way.

"You have to realize things have changed, though," she said, unable to stay quiet.

Slowly, finally, he turned his head to look at her, and he blinked. "Yes, I'm beginning to. And in turn, I'm not feeling as... directionless. If that makes sense. Before, I didn't feel a need to stay here, but a lot of things have changed, and I don't want to go anywhere."

She swiped her tears away, nodding. "That makes me happy, because you are so worth having in the world. And I'm not just saying that because you're a great lay."

He barked out a laugh and rolled toward her, going up on one elbow to look down at her. "Thank you, Marigold Lee. you've made me laugh more in the past week than I have in the past year, and I really appreciate that."

She accepted his slow kiss, loving the tingle that went through her every time he touched her. Even when it wasn't building up to sex, he took his time, and she appreciated that. When he drew back, she gave him a serious look. "I will make you laugh as much as I possibly can if it means you will stay with us."

Eyes somber, he nodded. "I'm going to hold you to that, because I know these thoughts are something I can't just wish away. It's going to take work, and goals. Like John said. And distractions. Working toward something."

"I have faith in you," she told him softly, very aware that her heart was on the line. "And I will stand by you as long as you want me to. No commitment stated, inferred or requested, though."

He smiled a little crookedly, recognizing the words.

Then he looked at the bed rather pointedly. "I think we've kind of moved beyond that, now."

"Yes," she agreed softly.

"Plus, I'm going to take the LNF job."

She blinked, then grinned. "Congratulations! That's definitely commitment."

"Yes," he sighed. "I don't know exactly what I'll do there, but I think I could be an asset to the group."

"Oh, I do too! Have you told John and Shannon?"

He shook his head against the pillow. "I thought you should know first."

Marigold blinked, not sure exactly how to feel. Did the fact that he was telling her first mean that she had some significance to him? Or was he just voicing his thoughts to the only person in the room?

She must have seemed confused, because his face shut down and he seemed to retreat. "I apologize. I thought you'd want to know."

Marigold sat up, in spite of the cold room. "I do want to know, but I guess I'm kind of at a loss. Why do you care what I think? I mean, physically we get along like gangbusters, but I thought you wanted to avoid anything emotional?"

"Yeah, fuck that," Logan said, sitting up and leaning toward her. "I know that's what I said before, but I don't think it's what I necessarily meant. If I had reliable people to commit to, I wouldn't have an issue. My family failed me, my ex failed me."

Marigold blinked. "What are you saying, Logan?" Her heart thudded. Emotions chased across his face. Anticipation built inside her as she watched him choose his words.

Finally, he looked at her, his brilliant eyes clear, and she had to admire the courage she could see building in his expression. "I'm waking up, literally and figuratively, and I love having you beside me, Marigold Lee. If you don't have anything else going on, maybe you wouldn't mind spending some time with me to see where this goes."

Emotion tightened her throat, and she nodded. It was what she'd wanted when he first walked into the office. She hadn't understood what she'd felt at the time, but she did now. When he leaned in for a kiss, she met him halfway. Slowly and leisurely, he worshipped her mouth, reaching out to cup her jaw and hold her to him. Marigold loved it when he took her in hand, reminding her that even damaged, he was still very much a man.

LOGAN LOVED the feel of Marigold in his arms. She was strong and solid, and completely competent. Her mind challenged him and her humor nudged him out of the hole he'd been in for so long. He was the happiest he'd been in a year.

That was a lot to put on another person, though, and Logan was very aware of that fact. When he would have told her that he wanted to live with her and wake up with her every morning, he clamped his jaw shut. It wasn't fair to make her his savior, even if he did feel that way.

"Can I cook you some breakfast?"

Her dark brows arched in surprise. "Can you cook?"

"I used to be able to," he admitted. "I would cook for the guys in the tent all the time. Just quick and easy stuff, but it was better than the MREs the Army handed out."

"I would love for you to cook for me then. While you do that, I'll hop in the shower."

Good! No witness for what could be a serious mistake in judgement. "You do that."

With a bemused smile, Marigold gave him a kiss and

shuffled out of bed to the bathroom, the cheeks of her ass jiggling deliciously. Within just a few seconds he heard the shower start.

"Better get my ass in gear," he muttered, bracing himself for the pain of moving.

She had eggs and ham in her fridge, and some really sharp cheddar. There was a bag of onions and green peppers in the freezer, and some jalepeño. Oh, that would be a good omelet.

And it turned out pretty well. It was a little darker brown than he would prefer, but when Marigold sat down at the little kitchenette table, her eyes widened appreciatively. "This looks damn good, Logan. I could get used to this."

As he sat down at the table across from her, he decided he could as well.

"What's on your agenda for the day?"

That made him pause, fork halfway to his lips. "Well, I guess I'd better contact Palmer and let him know I want the job and move on from there."

"There's more work than you would expect there," she told him, tucking her dark hair behind her ears. "And I know Shannon loves to be the boss of everything, but she has more work than she can handle. I'll be going in today."

"We both will," Logan told her.

What an odd change of fortune. He and his girlfriend? Lover? would be heading to work together.

Huh... The thought didn't scare him as much as it should have.

20

S hannon bounced from one emergency to the next, and it just didn't seem to let up. It was ridiculous for a Tuesday.

Flynn had a caller on the line from out of country that he'd been trying to get ahold of for weeks. Putting the man on hold Shannon did her best to find Flynn, but he had apparently decided not to answer his phone today. Instead she got Willow on their personal text chat, and she tracked the man down. The two lines were now connected and she hoped Flynn was getting the information he needed.

She moved onto the next issue. Harper had a significant medical bill that insurance was refusing to pay. After being on hold for almost an hour, Shannon managed to get it recategorized so that it would be paid, in full, the way it should have been in the first place.

Rachel had an issue with shorted overtime that she'd forgotten to get approved two weeks ago. The cleaning service responsible for doing the offices had a flu outbreak and they would have to reschedule for next week, assuming everyone was healthy enough to come back. Elizabeth

Wilkes was waiting on the original report Jordyn had done when they'd retrieved the men from the jungle. Shannon just hadn't had a chance to send it.

On top of everything, she was feeling off. In the back of her mind she was praying that she hadn't picked up some kind of convention bug, because that would screw her whole schedule.

When Marigold rolled in later that morning, she was very happy to hand a few things off to the younger woman to take care of.

"Absolutely," Marigold told her, grinning. "Why don't you go get a cup of coffee? When you come back, we'll talk."

Shannon was curious. Logan had gone back to talk to John, and she had a feeling she knew what about. It would be a great time to teach Marigold the new-hire system.

She looked at the coffee maker in the break room. It did not appeal to her. Instead, she ran a cup of water through the microwave and dropped a tea bag in. If she was getting sick, she would need to hydrate.

Man, the boys were beasts when they didn't feel good. And John was even worse, she thought with a snort.

She returned to the reception area and sank into her chair, her legs weak. What the hell...

Marigold gave her a look. "Are you okay? You seem pale."

"Yeah, I'm okay, just...tired, I guess."

If she put into the ether that she was feeling sick, it would manifest that she was sick. Deny, deny, deny...

Shannon knew as soon as he walked out that Logan was their next investigator. John rolled out behind him, grinning. Circling the desk, she wrapped Logan in a hug. "Welcome to the group."

His lips twisted into a smile. "Thank you. I really do appreciate it."

Marigold was smiling as well, but it was obvious she had already known what Logan was going to tell John. Shannon sighed, saying a little prayer that their relationship would survive. It wouldn't be any fun at work if two people were at odds after a breakup.

Shannon walked Marigold through the metric ton of paperwork that needed to be completed for a new hire. There was no way she would remember it all next time, but at least she would have a grasp on it. Then Shannon printed everything out for Logan to sign. John witnessed everything. Duncan came out of his office as Logan was finishing up, and shook his hand.

"Welcome to the group. We'll try not to work you too hard at first." Duncan grinned, obviously playing.

"I don't mind hard work, sir. I'm curious what I'll be doing for you, though."

Duncan glanced at John, then back at Logan. "We'll probably start you off watching surveillance tapes or going over case files. Believe me, we'll find what you're good at."

Logan nodded, bracing against his crutches. "I have no doubt, and the Army will be more than happy to help out the Marines."

A dark glitter lit Duncan's eyes, and he barked out with laughter. "Oh, buddy, you're going to fit in just right," he laughed.

JOHN GRINNED when Shannon stopped at his office a little while later.

"Another chick to mother over."

Shannon laughed and sank down in the chair across from him. Then the color in her face faded, and she blinked in surprise. John wheeled around the desk to grip her hand. "Are you okay?"

She nodded, waving her free hand. "I've been feeling a little off, and I wonder if I haven't picked up the conference crud or something. Or some germ from the planes."

"That would explain why you've been so tired," he said, worried.

Shannon nodded. "Yes. I might have Marigold drive me home. Can you pick up the kids on the way home?"

"Absolutely. Why don't you let me take you home?"

"Because Logan is going to be done with his paperwork in a bit and you need to find him something to do."

Yeah, she was probably right. He could use another set of eyes on the McClain case anyway. "Are you sure babe?"

Shannon leaned in and started to kiss him, but veered away to land on his cheek. "Just in case, I don't want to infect you."

John grinned and wiggled his brows. "We've been a lot closer than a kiss recently, and I feel fine."

She gave him a smile. "I know, but I'd rather be safe than sorry."

"Okay, babe. I'll hold down the fort. And I'll bring the minions home with me. Text me if you need anything else."

SHANNON STARED down at the stick cradled in her hands, nausea making her stomach boil.

Even though it wasn't the first pee of the day, the hormone coursing through her body was strong enough to register. She was pregnant. What the fucking hell... After the mixup with the email and John thinking she wanted another baby and stressing about it, fate deemed that she needed another baby. Snorting, she set the test to the side, cradling her head in her hands. Carmella nudged at her with her wet nose, and Shannon opened her arms to the dog, ruffling her ears. "Just what you want too, huh, another creature taking attention away from you."

Carmella flopped on the floor in front of her. Shannon sat on the floor near the bed. Marigold had been more than happy to drive her home, and happy as well to stop at the drugstore for 'medicine'. As soon as John had mentioned mothering chicks, the fear that she was pregnant had refused to leave her mind. And the symptoms lined up, but she'd bought a pregnancy test to confirm. Actually, she'd bought two, one for mid-afternoon pee and one for morning pee just to confirm.

She didn't think she needed to run the morning test, though. It was obvious she was pregnant. The only thing she needed to do was count back a few days to the conception.

When she'd gotten pregnant with the boys, her body had begun to change immediately. She'd known within days that she was going to be a mother. And it was the same this time. It had to have been the welcome-home sex last week.

John was going to kill her.

Shit. Chad and Lora were going to feel even more under the gun. Maybe they should keep the pregnancy under wraps. Shannon was still deciding what to do when John pulled into the driveway a few hours later.

As soon as he rolled inside, there was a melee with the kids, but his dark eyes scanned her.

"I'm okay," she promised.

"Why don't you go back to bed?"

She shook her head. "I want to see my boys."

After an easy dinner, they played and laughed with the kids until they put them to bed. Shannon was very aware of John watching her, probably for signs of sickness she could be transmitting to the kids.

"Come on, Sex-on-wheels, we need to talk."

John followed her into the bedroom. When she turned to talk, he was grinning at her. "You're pregnant, aren't you?"

Shannon laughed. "How did you know?"

John shook his head, rolling close. Reaching out a hand, he tugged her to settle across his lap. Shannon wrapped her arms around his broad shoulders and leaned into his chest. "You got pretty sick with the boys at first, then it petered off. Remember?"

She nodded against him. "I really did think I'd picked up a bug, at first. It seemed plausible, just coming in from the convention and stuff. But I had Marigold stop by the drugstore and I picked up a couple of tests. It confirmed that I'm very definitely pregnant. That plus sign popped up almost immediately."

John chuckled, the sound so precious beneath her ear. "I have good swimmers, huh?"

"Very," she agreed. "What are the chances we talk about this and decide against it and it happens? We jinxed ourselves."

"Apparently," he sighed, and there was a somber note in the sound.

"Chad and Lora," she said, guessing what he was thinking about.

"Yeah," he said. "Maybe we can keep this under wraps for just a bit?"

She leaned up to look in his eyes. "I had kind of decided that as well. She's not in a good place right now."

"It's not our place to interfere, but we can try not to hurt them unnecessarily."

"Agreed. So it will be our little secret for now."

"Yes," he said, leaning in for a kiss.

Shannon loved John with her entire being, and she loved that they shared one mind and one heart. Chad and Lora were their friends, and they wouldn't hurt them for anything.

"So, let's curl up in bed and dream about what this baby will be."

Shannon laughed and slid off his lap. "Sounds perfect to me."

EPILOGUE

ne Month Later

L ogan kept waiting for the pain, but it never came. Well, there was everyday, bone-creaking pain, of course, but it wasn't the soul-eating emotional kind that made him want to eat a bullet.

He still worried about Lisa and Ashley. The fact that Lisa had looked for him at Walter Reed gave him hope that at some point she might be able to talk to him. Ashley had texted him a few times, just silly memes and things to make him chuckle. He'd sent her one serious picture of his team posed in front of the barracks about a month before the bombing. It was a good pic because everyone was actually smiling and looking at the camera, and Trent looked like he always did, happy and open, his arm slung around Logan's shoulders. Ashley had responded with a heart and a crying icon, as well as a thank you.

Logan was okay with waiting for Lisa to contact him. He knew she would eventually. Until then, he'd keep his head down and focused.

The job that John had given him was as in-depth and nuanced as anything he'd ever worked on before, and as soon as he was done with it there was more work waiting. They hadn't been lying when they'd said they had as much work as they wanted. More times than he could count, he'd gone out to the reception area and Shannon or Marigold was guiding a weeping woman through the door to Duncan's office, or a worried couple, or angry men, all looking for an answer to their problems. They didn't take all of the cases simply because they didn't have the manpower. Somehow, Duncan weeded through the cases that needed them the most.

Logan had worked with Marines before and hadn't been impressed. Duncan Wilde and the group that he'd created put them all to shame.

Logan looked around his office. It wasn't his exclusively, but he shared it with two graveyard shift guys, and they weren't here right now, obviously. Marigold had bought him a plant to go on the corner of his desk. It had broad green leaves and trailing arms, but she promised that it was very hardy. He enjoyed looking at the plant, and watering it, and he couldn't decide why for a long time. Then it occurred to him. It was something he needed to take care of. And it was something else to anchor him into the world. That plant on this desk meant commitment and people depending upon him.

Then his grandparents had gotten him an *Investigator Logan Vance* brass nameplate for his desk. It would be a while before he was certified to be an investigator in the state of Colorado, but he appreciated their enthusiasm for his job.

The Showalters had become a very important part of his life. They had lunch at least once a week, and he and Marigold had been to the house twice, once for a birthday party for two of the great-grand children with close birthdays and a second time because Karen, his active duty aunt, came home for a visit. It was a little crazy, but she looked familiar to Logan, and they realized they had been on several of the same forts at the same time, so there was a very real possibility that they had seen each other before. The thought that he had been so close to legitimate family and hadn't known it bedeviled him. She was a fascinating woman and viewed her time in the service very differently than he had. Karen had been in combat and had led men into danger many times, and had lost men as well, but viewed the losses with pride.

"Those men served exactly as they meant to serve, and they all knew that their lives could be snuffed out in combat. There's no need for you to feel guilty for their loss. You were doing your job, as were they. No regrets."

Yeah, that was the sticking point, though. He had regrets. Thanks to the LNF job he was now working with a counselor and getting all those regrets out in the open. It was painful and harrowing, but somehow cleansing, as well. And he knew it would be a process.

Logan glanced out the window. Spring was coming to Colorado, and he was the happiest he'd been in a very long time.

"Hey, babe. Here's that info you needed on the McClain wrap-up."

Logan looked up at Marigold. The woman wore a pair of black pants, short heels and a red blouse that went really well with her dark hair. It was curled slightly and hung over one shoulder. Those squarish black glasses were high on her nose, and she looked damn cute. And damn intelligent. Yes, he was in the slot for investigator, but she could totally do the job herself.

Marigold seemed content to help Shannon for now. In the fall she would start her undergrad psychiatry classes and things would change.

"I'm going to miss you when you start classes," Logan told her, already worried about the loss.

Marigold made a face. "I know. I'm going to miss everyone here and I'm going to have a serious case of FOMO."

Logan snorted, shaking his head. "I don't think you'll miss anything too big. If you do, we'll whisper about it in bed."

Giggling, she came further into the office to lean on his desk. "In *my* room. I didn't realize how much Grandma could hear from your room until she asked me about one of the cases. She was hoping for something juicy, I think."

"I think she has 'fear of missing out'. Although if you tell her that she'll think it's a disease or something."

For a moment, he thought about offering to find a more private place together, which shocked him. He'd lived with his ex, but this felt very different. Occasionally, they hung at his place, but hers was more homey and settled. They both preferred it.

Logan shook his head, getting back to the conversation. "That woman... I have a feeling she ran circles around her husband."

"Or maybe he'd just been with her long enough to know how to keep her busy."

"They did have a bunch of kids," he suggested.

Marigold grinned. "That's her fault for rubbing his junk when she went to Bingo. And that's probably one of the tamer things she can tell us."

They both laughed, and she leaned down to drop a quick kiss to his lips. When she would have drawn away, he caught her hand, looking into her eyes. She seemed to sense his introspection, because she paused and cocked her head. "What's up, babe?"

For a moment, he couldn't say anything, just held her stare, the emotion almost smothering him. Yes, he'd been engaged before, but he didn't remember feeling anything like this with his former fiancée. Amber had been fine to talk to, but he didn't remember the rush of emotion that seeing Marigold brought. His entire life before his Alive day —the day he survived the bombing—was a bit of a haze. The past month had brought a clarity he hadn't had in his life ever before, and this woman was a very big part of it.

"I love you," he told her abruptly.

Her eyes widened, then filled with luminous, glittering tears. "Seriously? You do this now, at work when I have makeup on?"

Logan shrugged, pushing to his feet. He needed to be upright to do this. Reaching out, he cupped her face in his hands, swiping the tears away with his thumbs. "It just seemed like the right time. And you will look beautiful, makeup or not. I prefer not, actually."

She laughed a little. "Well, of course you do. That usually means we're in bed if I have no makeup on."

"Yeah," he grinned, shrugging. Then, seeing the vulnerable expression in her eyes, he kissed her, noticing that she hadn't said it back. But she would.

Logan licked and teased at her mouth, his tongue tangling with hers. They'd been together long enough that he knew what she loved, and he did his best to give it to her every time. When he drew back, her irises were blown wide around the pupil, showing him how aroused she was.

"It's okay if you're not in the same place I am. I've just had a lot of change this month, and a large part of it wouldn't have happened without you. I was engaged before, but I feel like that was a near miss. I'm glad she didn't have the stomach to stay with me, because now I have you."

"Logan," she said softly. "I'm sorry she hurt you but I'm glad she didn't stay as well. I would have hated to have gotten blood on the sheets fighting her for you."

He gave her a sardonic look. "I think you would have been okay with that actually."

She grinned, tipping her head. "Okay, yeah, maybe. When you told me what she did I wanted to hang her up by her tits."

Logan pulled back to look down at her. "You know, I think Grandma Marshall might be a bad influence on you."

Giggling, she pulled him in for another kiss. "Oh, I don't know. She told me three weeks ago that we would fall in love."

His heart stilled. "And did *we*?"

She gave him an affronted face. "Well, yeah. You're not the only one in love, stupid. I have you beat. I knew when you walked in the door of the office that we were going to be together. Something inside me clicked when I saw you. I think my heart stopped, then restarted. Maybe that's what it was. And I wanted to tell you sooner, but I didn't want to hold you if you didn't want to be held. Know what I mean?"

He nodded. "I definitely want to be held. I didn't at first, I'll give you that, but I definitely do now."

Grinning, she wrapped her arms around his shoulders. "I love you, Logan William Vance."

"I love you too, Marigold..." he hesitated. "What is your middle name?"

She grinned at him and shook her head. "I don't think I know you well enough to tell you my middle name."

"What?" He pulled back, looking down into her beautiful eyes. "Seriously?"

Laughing, she gave him a sharp nod. "Maybe if you agree to the tattoo, I'll tell you..."

Logan laughed so hard tears came to his eyes. "I'm not getting 'gone to market' on my foot."

"I think it would look fabulous," she said, expression pert.

He fucking loved the hell out of her, and if it would make her happy, he would probably do it. "Kiss me woman."

She did as she was told, happily. And when he let her up for air, knowing she was susceptible, he told her, "Let's move in together."

"Okay. Right now? I think we need to go home and move you in immediately."

"We can do it tonight," he chuckled. "And I'll make it worth your wait."

"You'd better," she warned, drawing back when his phone rang. He didn't want to be interrupted, but it was Shannon. He picked up the receiver. "Yes, ma'am."

"You have a woman on line three by the name of Rebecca. Are you in?"

"Yes," Logan said quickly. He'd been trying to get a hold of this woman for a week. He gave Marigold an apologetic look, but she was already waving as she left, blowing him a kiss. Logan's throat was tight with emotion as he answered the call.

MARIGOLD DAMN near skipped down the hallway, but that would be difficult in heels. Her insides felt effervescent. As soon as she got to her desk, Shannon looked up and grinned. "Something has changed...You're floating."

Marigold glanced around, but they were alone. John's door was shut and Duncan was out of the office. And it was late enough on a Friday that most everyone else was gone. "Logan just told me he loved me," she whispered, tears filling her eyes.

"Oh, Marigold," Shannon whispered, drawing her into a hug. "Congratulations. That's huge for him."

Marigold nodded. "I know. I've loved him for weeks, now."

"I know you have," Shannon murmured, straightening some of Marigold's hair. "But you waited for him to tell you, and that was exactly the right thing to do."

She nodded, wiping away tears. "He asked me to move in with him."

Shannon laughed. "Well, you pretty much were, already."

"Yeah..."

She hoped he didn't mean he wanted to leave Nancy's house. That would kind of break her heart. No, she knew he loved being there as much as she did.

Tears flooded her eyes again as she thought about how much he had changed recently. Coming to Colorado had been the best thing for him, she had no doubt. And the series of little incidents that added up to him being in her line of sight that day... she would be forever thankful to Shannon for latching onto him.

"What's with all the waterworks?" John said, rolling into the reception area.

Marigold wiped her face and turned away.

"Logan and Marigold are officially together and in love," Shannon told him softly.

John snorted. "Not like we didn't see that coming a mile away."

"John," Shannon hissed.

Marigold was surprised when John rolled into her line of sight and reached for her hand. Shocked, she let him take it.

"Your dad would have been so happy for you to be with a man like Logan."

Marigold blinked, wondering if he was assuming her dad would have liked him, or...

"Derek talked about what he wanted for his child, and he always said he wanted a man to love her as much as he did your mother."

Marigold gasped at the mention of her father's name and dropped into her chair. "What?" Tears flooded her eyes and rolled down her cheeks, unnoticed.

John gave her a gentle smile. "It took me a while, but I remember you now. I should have known when I saw that damn Beetle. He went on and on about that car. But the only picture I'd seen of it was smudged and water-stained, and you couldn't have been more than three or four when I came to the house. But Derek was so incredibly proud to have a daughter."

Marigold wept, though she tried to hold it in. When she'd come here looking for John, some part of her had hoped that he would remember, but he never said anything. "You remember my dad..."

He nodded. "I do. He was a fantastic guy. A true, honorable Marine, and I was privileged to serve with him. He talked about his baby girl all the time, and his beautiful wife. I remember him talking about being worried about who she was going to date and hanging onto the car so that he could teach her to drive a stick..."

Shannon handed Marigold a pile of Kleenex to wipe the fresh tears from her face. Her makeup was fucked. "My Grandpa taught me," she said when she'd gotten some control over herself.

"Well, if it counts for anything, I approve of you being with Logan, and I know Derek would have loved him, even though he's Army."

Marigold snorted, shaking her head, full of so much emotion... "Thank you, John."

"Maybe, if you, uh, get married," he shifted in his chair, looking uncomfortable. "Maybe you'd let me walk you down the aisle."

The damn tears were back, more than ever. She nodded, mopping her face, and leaned over to let him hug her. John Palmer didn't deal with emotion very well and he was still a dick, but he gave great hugs. "It'll be good practice for when you walk your own little girl down the aisle," she mumbled.

John and Shannon shared a sharp look, and Marigold laughed. "Do you really think I didn't notice the nausea and the tiredness? And all the little shared looks?"

Shannon grinned. "We're trying to keep it under wraps for a while. And we don't know that it's a girl."

"What's a girl?" Logan asked, walking into the reception area.

"John and Shannon's secret baby," Marigold told him before they could tell her not to.

Logan was more concerned with her tears. He crossed the floor and cupped her face in his hands, setting his crutches to the side as he leaned on her desk. "What's wrong?"

"John remembered my dad."

Knowing it was too girly but unable to help herself, she let Logan hold her as she wept some more. The emotions flowing through her had no beginning and no end, they just kept bouncing between one another. Sorrow, pride, love, joy, appreciation, loss, surprise. Everything was there, and Logan's arms gave her a place to deal with them all.

"I love you, Logan," she whispered.

"I love you too, baby," he murmured, pressing a kiss to the top of her head.

TAKE A MINUTE TO FOLLOW JM!

✔ My Facebook LIKE Page-
    ✔Follow me on Twitter-- @authorjmmadden
    ✔Sign up for my Newsletter if you haven't already. You get 4 free books!
    ✔Follow me on Instagram--
    OR you can email me at authorjmmadden@gmail.com

ALSO-
    If you love the book, **PLEASE** leave a review! We really do notice a difference when readers support us!
    Thank you so much!
    JM

ALSO BY JM MADDEN

If you would like to read about the 'combat modified' veterans of the **Lost and Found Investigative Service,** sign up for my Newsletter and check out these books:

The Embattled Road

Duncan, John and Chad

Embattled Hearts-Book 1

John and Shannon

Embattled Minds-Book 2

Zeke and Ember

Embattled Home-Book 3

Chad and Lora

Embattled SEAL- Book 4

Harper and Cat

Embattled Ever After- Book 5

Duncan and Alex

Her Forever Hero- Grif

Grif and Kendall

SEAL's Lost Dream-Flynn

Flynn and Willow

SEAL's Christmas Dream

Flynn and Willow

Unbreakable SEAL-

Max and Lacey

Embattled Christmas

Reclaiming The Seal

Gabe and Julie

Loving Lilly

Diego and Lilly

Her Secret Wish

Rachel and Dean

Wish Upon a SEAL

Drake and Izzy

Mistletoe Mischief

Cass and Roger

Lost and Found Pieces

Lost and Found Pieces 2

There are two Lost and Found Spinoff series, the Lowells and the Dogs of War, which heads in a bit of a paranormal direction.

The Lowells of Honeywell, Texas Box Set

Forget Me Not

Untying his Not

Naughty by Nature

Trying the Knot

The Dogs of War

Genesis

Chaos

Destruction

Retribution

Catalyst

If you love dogs and would like to read about a concierge service helping military personnel out of difficult spots, check out:

Healing Home

Wicked Healing

Healing Hope (Coming Soon!)

If you would like to read a Navy SEAL book with more mature characters, check out

SEAL Hard

Flat Line

Other books by J.M. Madden

A Touch of Fae

Second Time Around

A Needful Heart

Wet Dream

Love on the Line

The Billionaire's Secret Obsession

www.ingramcontent.com/pod-product-compliance
Lightning Source LLC
Chambersburg PA
CBHW071127200626
46817CB00018B/2380